Urban Dragon

Volume 1

by

JW Troemner

For Andrew, who gave me hope,

for Tane, who gave Arkay her chair,

and for the woman with knitting needles on the edge of the

circle

Table of Contents

Book 1:

Mark of the Dragon

Rosario

There are certain problems you kind of expect when you first start living on the streets. It's typical stuff— where am I gonna sleep, what am I gonna eat, how am I gonna keep clean, who the hell has public bathrooms anymore?

When my parents first kicked me out, I was naive. When I pictured violence, I saw it coming from Jack the Ripper wannabees and Ted Bundy lookalikes. Don't get me wrong, there are some sick fucks out there, but they're few and far between. Most of the harassment I dealt with came from regular guys who drank too much after work and thought it'd be hilarious to mess with the first person they found sleeping under a bridge. To people like that, a plus-sized Latina made as good a target as any.

Take this guy, for example: he probably thought himself all stealthy and shit as he grabbed the duffel bag of laundry I'd been using as a pillow. Maybe he meant to empty it onto the road and watch me scramble to collect my clothes before they got ruined by traffic, or maybe he thought he'd throw it away. Hell, maybe he wanted to take it home as a trophy or something. All of the above happened to me at one point or another over the years.

Then I found Arkay.

She didn't look like much: short, skinny, and baby-faced. She could pass for a teenager if you put her in the right clothes. Maybe even younger, with the way she nestled into my side, the shape of her body obscured by a thick winter coat.

She tensed as stale beer breath wafted over us.

His hand closed around the strap of the makeshift pillow, and in the same instant, her hand closed around his throat. He made a surprised, sputtering sound, but the words never made it to his mouth.

"You really don't want to do that," Arkay said, sliding upright without relaxing her hold. "My friend here has had a very long day, and she needs her sleep. You wouldn't want to wake her."

The stranger grabbed at her hand, but she didn't let go. He tried to pull away, but only managed to step on my hair. I let out a hiss of pain.

"What did I *just* say?" With a twist of her wrist, she forced him backward and away from my head. The poor drunk's eyes bugged, wide and bloodshot. "That was very rude of you. I expect you to make it up to her." Slender fingers curled, and her nails dug into his trachea. "We accept cash."

"That wasn't necessary," I told Arkay once the stranger fled.

"No, but it beats the hell out of panhandling."

I couldn't argue. Less than five minutes of Arkay's snarling, and the guy had thrown us more than I'd been able to scrounge up all day, most of it in the form of crumpled twenties. Still, somebody had to have the moral high ground here. "You could have really hurt him, though."

"Come on, Rosario. He didn't even bleed." She dug a can of blue spray paint out of her backpack and gave it a vigorous shake. "I think I taught him a valuable lesson about respect and personal dignity."

I sighed, and it turned into a cough as a sharp chemical smell filled the air.

"I mean it," she said. "Now he'll think twice before he does it to anyone else. That's one less douchenozzle out bothering people who can't defend themselves. I say that's a point for the good guys."

She stepped back, admiring her work. It wasn't the most intricate tag: just a stylized 'RK', made of sharp edges and straight lines. Arkay thought it looked like lightning and teeth; I thought it looked like neither of us actually knew the first thing about graphic design. Dozens of tags just like it littered this side of town, and each one marked another 'point for the good guys'. In reality, they served the same purpose as any other gang sign: a stake on our turf, and a warning to anyone who might want to mess with us.

I found Arkay years ago, on the underside of the Washington Street Bridge over the White River. At the time she was sick to dying, fed on poisoned fish and polluted water. I was the one who taught her how to subsist on hamburgers and fried chicken, how to pass for human long enough to get them, how to stay out of the kind of trouble that might get somebody killed—though I was admittedly still working on that last part. In return, Arkay kept me safe. Safer than I'd ever been on the streets without her, anyway. Maybe even safer than I'd been when I was living with my parents. I never had to worry that she might turn on me or suddenly decide to throw me out on my own. She didn't just need me, she cared about me. She'd kill for me if I let her.

Which, admittedly, came with its own set of problems. But at least those I could handle.

I stretched out my stiff joints and got to work rolling up our blanket. There was no point staying. Even if the odor of the spray paint didn't keep us awake all night, the man we'd just robbed might still call the police to this corner, and we needed to not be here if that happened. Besides, the promise of a fight would leave Arkay wired for at least another few hours. If I had to stay awake, at least I could do it someplace that served coffee.

A ten-minute shamble brought us to Stella's, a homey little diner at the edge of what reasonably counted as downtown. I grabbed our usual booth while Arkay ducked into the bathroom.

Cheap fluorescent lights washed the color out of the air, leaving everything inside papery and pale, like an old photograph. The sharp smell of lemon cleaner cut through the clinging odor of frying grease. The table in front of me was chipped, and our tag peeked out at me on the exposed particle board, alongside half a dozen other sets of initials.

"Just coffee tonight, hon?" asked the waitress, a squat woman with crooked teeth that seemed blindingly white against her mocha lipstick.

"Actually, can I get a burger?" I asked. "And a fish sandwich for Kay. And give her decaf."

She didn't give more than an acknowledging nod, even when Arkay came back out with a few flecks of blue on her cheek. That was the nice thing about Stella's. Nobody asked awkward questions. That quality attracted a lot of people to the diner, really. A red-eyed white girl in a college hoodie poked listlessly at her chicken fingers; a man from the nearby homeless camp slouched at the bar, nursing a coffee; a gorgeous dark-skinned woman in a button-down shirt tapped her nails against the surface of her table. She caught my interest, and not just because she kept biting her full lower lip and scowling at the door like she'd been stood up for a date. The kind of women who wore office chic didn't usually come to a place like Stella's, especially not at two in the morning. This was the kind of place people went to avoid being seen.

So, naturally, I looked.

"I don't see a ring on her finger," Arkay pointed out as our food arrived. "You gonna ask for her number?" I shot her a dirty look, and she flicked a waffle fry at my face. "If you don't, I will."

Okay, so yes, I really wanted to. "Leave her alone," I said. "She's waiting for someone."

"Looks to me like they're not coming." She didn't push it much further, but she didn't need to. Nobody had joined the woman by the time I finished my burger, and she only took her eyes off the door to look at her phone.

As I stood up to pay, I resolved to actually talk to her. After all, the worst she could do was say no, right?

But as I handed the waitress a crumpled twenty, a draft of cold November air blew through the room. The door swung shut behind a balding man in a rumpled suit. He swept the room with his gaze, picking at his nails, which were already inflamed and bloody. Even though the diner was practically dead, it took him a second pass before he made a beeline for the woman we'd been watching.

"Yeah, I'm pretty sure she would've been better off with you." Arkay didn't bother lowering her voice— tact wasn't exactly her strong suit— but the subjects of her comment didn't seem to notice. The two of them had started arguing in hissed murmurs.

"Is Driscoll here yet?"

"How the hell should I know?" the woman asked. "You're the one who hired this guy. Those two are the only ones who've come in since I sat down." She waved a flippant hand at us, and the newcomer turned to stare at us with bloodshot eyes.

Caught eavesdropping. Classy.

I ushered Arkay to the door. "Come on, let's go."

"Wait." The man stepped closer, squinting at us against the fluorescents. "Don't I know you?"

I flashed an apologetic smile. "Just one of those faces. Kay, let's go." The man spoke up again, but whatever he said was lost as we stepped outside.

Arkay hugged her thin frame, bracing against the sudden cold. The wind ruffled her spiky black hair, but her attention was on me. "You alright, Rosa?"

"Fine." I wrapped the coat tighter around myself and zipped it to my chin. "That guy gave me the creeps, is all."

"All the more reason to bail the poor lady out," she said. "There's still time to swoop in and be all charming and heroic, you know." She flashed a wry grin. My answering smile was probably as weak as it felt, because her expression turned serious. "You know I wouldn't have let him lay a hand on you, right? I don't care what he was on."

"I know." All the more reason to get the hell out of there. The staff at Stella's had put up with a lot from us over the past couple of years, but they wouldn't be so tolerant if we started a brawl in the middle of the dining area. It wouldn't be the first place that kicked us out. "Let's just find a place to bunk down for the night, okay? I'm tired."

It wasn't even a lie. Despite all that caffeine, my eyelids still dragged. The worst of Arkay's jitters had subsided, and hopefully she could get the last of the adrenaline out of her system by the time we found a place to sleep. We couldn't go back to the bridge we'd been using, but this side of town had plenty of empty storefronts we could huddle under.

The area used to be a pocket of blue collar pride, but it started going downhill even before the economy tanked. A depressing number of the people living here gave up, beaten down by circumstances, yet scattered among them were signs of a community clinging stubbornly to hope. Foreclosures sagged on every cross street, side-by-side with fixer-uppers with Lisa Frank paint jobs. Cracked, empty parking lots stretched out between struggling small businesses and the hollowed-out buildings that had already surrendered the fight.

Even though we weren't far from downtown, the street was nearly empty, which made it hard to ignore the white van slowing down to idle beside us as we walked.

I kept my eyes fixed straight ahead, but Arkay watched with interest as the passenger window rolled down.

"Hey there," said the driver, a middle-aged white guy with a crooked nose and a faint Chicago accent. "Now where's a pair of pretty girls like you going at this hour?"

Girls? Seriously?

Arkay might have looked like a kid, but I was twenty-five, thank you very much. Hell, I'd been mistaken for her *mother.*

"What is with people tonight?" I muttered.

"Full moon's this week," Arkay mused. "Maybe people are getting their crazy on early."

"Awful cold out here for a walk," the man said. "Can I give you ladies a ride?" He grinned wide, a gesture that was probably meant to look disarming, but mostly looked skeevy.

I forced a polite smile of my own. "No, thank you."

"C'mon," he said. "Won't be any trouble at all."

"We're fine," I said. "We like walking."

"What, trying to get your cardio in?" He laughed. "No need for that, hon. I like girls with a bit of meat on 'em."

Notice how I didn't ask your opinion? My smile took on an edge. "You know, we're almost home. Thanks anyway."

I grabbed Arkay's hand and made a sharp turn, cutting across a moonlit parking lot toward the next cross street.

10

It probably would have worked better if I'd picked an obstacle that wasn't paved.

The van's tires squealed as it picked up speed, lurching over the curb and onto the blacktop in front of us.

"Come on, don't be like that." The driver's jaw tightened. "I was trying to be nice." There was nothing nice about his tone.

"And we really appreciate it," I said hastily. "But it's late, and we really need to go."

"You heard him, Rosa." Arkay squeezed my hand. "Don't be rude."

I eyed the van again. The damn thing practically had 'free candy' scrawled across the side. "I said no, Kay."

"Hey, it's cool," the driver said, his anger abated for a moment. "If you ain't interested, you don't have to come. Your friend here knows where it's at."

"You hear that?" She grinned, all teeth. "I know where it's at." She turned to the driver, bouncing on her heels. "Actually we're heading to the Skyline Motel. It's just down that way. You know it?"

"Can't say I do," he said. "But I bet you give *great* directions." Judging by the look on his face, he wasn't thinking about transit.

Arkay opened the passenger door and took one step inside. "You coming, Rosario?"

This whole idea was all kinds of bad, but no way would I let Arkay get into some creeper's molest-o-van on her own.

"What was that you were saying about the moon?" I asked, and I pulled open the sliding side door. The van reeked of stale fries and cigarettes, and even though it was mostly clear of trash, a layer of grime had settled over most of the surfaces inside.

"So I haven't seen you around before," Arkay chirped once the van started moving. "What brings you to this side of town?"

"Got some business in Indy," he said. "Delivering a package. For a client," he added, with the smug pride of a man who didn't get to say that word very often.

"*Ooh.*" Arkay oozed awe. "That sounds fancy. What is it?"

The man grinned even wider. "Sorry, babe. Can't tell. Courier-client privilege, you know."

"Oh. Right. I know all about that." Arkay flashed a coy smile, like she could totally keep a secret.

"But, ya know, I've got another package." The courier laid a hand on her thigh. "If you wanna see it."

I debated whether throwing up would make the van smell any better. Could this guy actually hear himself talking?

"I don't think we have any time for that," Arkay said. "The motel is just on the corner over there."

"I think we can make time." He made a wide right turn, pulling the car into a lot behind the husk of an old car wash. "I don't have to meet my client for another hour."

"Yeah, but we're really tired," she said. "Thanks for the ride and all, but we really need to go."

"Sure thing," he said. "Just wanna have some fun first."

I tried the sliding door, but it wouldn't budge. Apparently *someone* had engaged the child lock.

Arkay's mask dropped, and her expression turned sharp. If he'd been looking at her eyes, the courier might have noticed. "That's not what you said when you picked us up."

12

"It was understood," he said.

"That's funny," I said dryly. "It's not what I understood when I got in here."

"If there's been a misunderstanding, you can just drop us off right here," Arkay said.

"Come on, baby, don't be like that. Pay me back for gas, at least." He slid his hand further up her leg and gave a squeeze.

Not a very smart move.

Arkay wrapped one hand tenderly around his bicep, laid the other on his forearm.

Then she inverted his elbow.

He screamed, not the kind of long, one-note screams you hear in movies, but something worse. It tore through his vocal cords, deafening even when it broke down into a whimper.

"Oh, I'm sorry," Arkay said, pulling off her seatbelt and squeezing between the steering wheel and his lap. "Did you not like me touching you like that? We're just having all sorts of misunderstandings today, aren't we?"

He whimpered, flattening himself against the seat, and I cringed in sympathy. Pain was never fun to listen to, even when it happened to a slimeball.

While Arkay dug through his pockets, I wedged my way into the now-empty passenger seat. She tossed a wallet into my hands as I climbed out onto the broken pavement. I leafed through its contents, pocketing the cash and credit cards before tossing the rest into the back seat. Sure, getting robbed sucked, but I wasn't about to steal his driver's license and loyalty cards. That would be petty.

The courier tried to shove Arkay away with his good arm. "You— you little whore."

"Ha! Like you could afford me." Arkay planted a chaste kiss on his forehead, and the courier's whole body shuddered like he'd been stabbed with a cattle prod. When she pulled back, a spark danced off her lips. While he twitched, she kicked open the door and rolled off his hips with a graceful flourish.

"Hey, Rosa, he's got the new iPhone! What do you wanna bet he's got Netflix?"

She started around the front of the car toward me, but she didn't get far before I heard a sharp, metallic click.

The courier tumbled out of the car, still twitching. A handgun shook in his good hand. His finger wrapped around the trigger.

"F-fuck," he grated through clenched teeth, pointing the barrel at Arkay. His face had turned an alarming shade of green. "Nobody told me you were one of them freaks."

She took a step back, but her eyes flickered in my direction. "Hasn't there been enough name-calling for one day?"

He bared his teeth. "I ain't about to be robbed by some— some *thing*. On your knees, bitch."

"Apparently not," she muttered.

Arkay was impossible to ignore on the best days, but she'd seriously pissed this guy off. The courier seemed to have completely forgotten I was there. I crept back into the car slowly, silently, so I wouldn't draw his attention back to me.

"I said get on your knees," he repeated, and I froze. No, he was still turned away.

"Or what?" she asked. "You're gonna shoot me?"

14

He snarled. "Or I'll start with your kneecaps."

"Not really the most eloquent argument ever," she said. "But I'll give you points for being concise."

The keys were still in the ignition. The keychain tapped against my knees as I slid into the driver's seat.

"You know what?" the courier asked. "I think I've had about enough of your—"

I twisted the keys, throwing the van into gear as the engine roared to life. My foot slammed down on the gas pedal, and the van smashed into its owner.

Arkay leaped out of the way, snatching the gun as it fell out of his hands.

"Could you say that again?" she asked cheerfully, leveling the barrel at what I assumed was his head. "I don't think I caught that last part."

A strangled groan seeped from somewhere past the front bumper. I put the van back in park and hurried out to get a better look. My stomach twisted. I'd only wanted to stop him from shooting Arkay. I didn't want to hurt him.

Apparently Arkay had no problem reading my expression. "Don't worry, he'll live." She grabbed him by the ankles and dragged him across the pavement, well away from the van's wheels. He moaned as the concrete scraped across his skin, but made no move to get up.

"Better than that," she continued, seizing the collar of his shirt and ripping it open. "You're going to go home with an education. Won't that be nice?" She grinned, showing off more teeth than rightfully belonged in a human mouth. "See, back in Ancient Greece, there was this rule. *Xenia.* When someone comes in your home, or gets in your car, you have to be nice to them. Take care of them. And you wouldn't *ever* do anything untoward to them. Ever."

She traced one fingernail down his chest— only what had once been a fingernail was now a vicious, curved claw. The pale skin of his chest split underneath the pressure, and blood bloomed in the moonlight.

"People used to think that gods would punish you if you violated *xenia*. That they'd do all sorts of nasty things to you. What people keep forgetting is that the gods aren't the ones you have to be afraid of."

She spoke slowly, her voice so low it was almost a purr as she carved line after line into his flesh. Tears leaked from the courier's eyes, but he didn't move. Maybe he couldn't. Maybe he just didn't dare.

"See, I'm the one you should be worrying about."

She dipped one clawed finger into the fresh wound and brought it to her lips, flicking out an inhumanly long tongue to taste it.

"I'm much more creative."

She rose, leaving her symbol branded into his chest.

The courier didn't have the chance to get up again before we were inside the van and peeling out of the parking lot, down one street and up another, into the labyrinth of residential areas and foreclosed houses.

Arkay settled comfortably into the passenger seat, digging through the glove compartment for its obligatory stash of fast food napkins to clean the blood off her hands.

My own fingers were bloodless, white and tense on the steering wheel.

"Seat belt," I grumbled, and Arkay obeyed with a dramatic flourish.

"What's got you all sour puss?"

"'Sour puss' is a noun, not an adjective," I said. "And I told you not to get in that van. I told you."

"You also told me that your coat was falling apart, and now we have money for a nice new one." She wadded up a bloody napkin and tossed it into the back. "You're welcome."

"You went too far this time. What if this guy goes to the police?"

"Then he gets to explain to them how he sexually assaulted a tiny Asian chick before she grew claws and wrote her name on his chest." She sat up abruptly. "Ooh, do you think he'll tell them how I tased him with my mouth?"

"It's not funny, Kay."

"No, it's freakin' hilarious. You're the one who said nobody believes in dragons, Rosa. If people are gonna go around pretending I don't exist, they're gonna face the consequences."

I had to pry my hands off the wheel to use the turn signal. "He pulled a gun on you."

"It's not like he's the first one."

"But he could've been the last one," I snapped, turning to glare at her. "It only takes one shot, Kay. That's it. And then you're gone." I forced my eyes back onto the road. "You could've died."

I couldn't see Arkay, but I felt her watching me like I was one of those Magic Eye images, like if she squinted and turned her head just right she'd be able to see whatever it was I was upset about.

"Yeah, but I didn't," she said. "You had my back. I knew that."

"And if he shot you before I hit him?" I asked. "What if I ran you over?"

She shrugged. "That's what hospitals are for, isn't it?"

"That isn't always an option, and they can't always…" God, what was the point? "Just… be careful, alright?"

She gave my shoulder an affectionate squeeze. "Don't worry, Rosa. I'm not going anywhere."

What I wouldn't do to have her confidence.

The stolen credit cards had to be used before the courier had a chance to cancel them, and so we made our way to a twenty-four-hour Super Target to stock up on supplies.

Before I could make a beeline for the camping gear, Arkay dragged me to Ladies' Apparel. It had been a bit since I'd last let her rob anyone completely blind, and in that time our clothes had gotten stained and torn beyond repair.

Reluctantly I picked through the plus-sized section, looking for soft cotton and sturdy denim in muted tones that looked about my size. I didn't want to even try with the dressing room. I could practically feel people's eyes on me, judging how long it had been since I'd bathed and making mental notes about what clothes I'd touched. If they saw me trying anything on, somebody might say something, and then Arkay would jump to my defense, and then we'd have one less place we'd be welcome in. Better to just estimate my size and go as fast as possible.

Besides, I didn't need my reflection to tell me that the clothes wouldn't flatter me, any more than I'd need it to know my face was probably smudged with something, and that my long black hair was full of split ends and halfway out of the braid that fell down my back, or that my dark brown eyes were bloodshot and puffy from lack of sleep. Some things were just obvious.

Arkay didn't seem to have that problem. She skipped in and out of the dressing rooms, draped in brightly colored fabric that was so thin it needed four layers not to be see-through. If I'd tried any of that on, I probably would have looked like a walking pile of laundry, but she managed to look like she was getting ready to go clubbing. Her short dark hair was a mess of hard-gelled spikes, her big brown eyes were bright and wild, and when she smiled, it was so bright you could practically see it from space.

Most of the clothes she rifled through were impossibly impractical, and I'd have to help her get rid of the worst offenders before we left the store. But I still needed to stock up on non-clothing supplies, and while I filled our cart, she could have her fun playing dress-up. I had to admit, Arkay had good timing. Winter was coming fast, and things like thermal sleeping bags and industrial-sized containers of hand warmers didn't come cheap. We piled them high into the back of the van and filled the rest of the remaining space with industrial quantities of soap, pads, diapers, socks, and other basic toiletries. What we couldn't stow in our home base, we brought to a scraggly patch of woods on the south side of town.

The Valley, the city's largest homeless camp, lay deeper behind the trees, nestled in the fork between two railroad tracks. We didn't go as far as the camp. Instead, we left the supplies piled a dozen yards or so past the tree line, the topmost of the packages signed in blue sharpie with our mark. There was no point in leaving more of a note; most of the local homeless community was all too familiar with Arkay's hands-on style of problem solving. We weren't welcome in most of the other camps in the area, so I made sure to send regular gifts to the Valley. Hopefully if we plied them with enough peace offerings, they wouldn't sever ties with us.

We spent the rest of the night camping out in the van. I slept curled up across the bench of the back seat and Arkay nestled tight against me, burying her face in my hair. The van was warm and the steel doors felt refreshingly secure, but we couldn't risk keeping it for a second night. The thing was police bait.

"Good riddance," Arkay said as we set out to get rid of it the next morning. "It's gonna take forever to get the tobacco smell out of my hair. You think Raimo will let me use his shower?"

Raimo Abels was a favorite contact of ours, a mechanic with a talent for making stolen vehicles disappear. He was a burly blond hulk who looked like he'd walked off the set of a Viking docudrama, but as far as I knew, he'd never had to use all that muscle. He had a jovial smile, a reputation for altruism, and a talent with paperwork that bordered on magical. Even if the cops could find something to book him on, nobody really wanted to do him harm.

His shop lay on a wide lot on the southeast side, and he kept it neatly divided between the cars he sold, the cars due for repairs, and the heaps of scrap metal that were beyond saving. Even though he didn't live there, he spent enough time at the shop to justify the shower he'd installed there, and he was free about letting anyone use it, along with the fresh pot of coffee he always kept on hand.

Like I said, he was a popular guy.

Arkay hopped out of the van to pull open the heavy chain-link gate at the edge of his lot. An enormous gray pit bull sprinted across the lot, summoned by the rattle of metal, and lunged at Arkay. Moments later, her face was shiny with slobber from an impromptu tongue bath.

"Hey, there, Rufus," she cooed, rubbing the dog's muscular shoulders. "Who's a good boy? Who's a good boy?"

His owner stepped out of the shop a few moments later, cleaning his hands on a greasy rag.

"Well if it isn't Hiccup and Toothless!" he declared as I pulled the van into the junk yard behind his workshop. "I like the ride. Real FBI chic. Very stylish."

"I think you mean rank," Arkay said, wrinkling her nose.

He winked. "It's called camouflage, Toothless. Nobody'd expect a fed to go around smelling like that."

I opened the driver's side door and Rufus, satisfied that he'd licked every inch of Arkay he could reach, leaped onto my lap before I could slide from the seat.

"Hey to you, too, boy," I said, ruffling his fur while he tried to smother me with kisses.

Raimo grinned wide. "I'm guessing you two are lookin' to sell?"

"Depends," I said, once Rufus had left my lap to prance at his owner's feet. "Are you looking to buy?"

Raimo threw a hand at his chest in fake affront. "Really? Hiccup, Rosie, baby! Have you ever caught me when I wasn't in the mood for a sale?"

I shot him a dirty look.

"Okay, aside from that one time," he said. "But it was just one time! Where's the love?"

"She'll love you a whole lot more if you don't call her 'baby'," Arkay pointed out.

The drama faded from Raimo's expression, leaving behind genuine sympathy. "Hiccup, hon, your mark didn't hurt you, did he?"

Arkay snorted. "If he did, you'd be washing his blood out of the upholstery."

"That's my girl." He ruffled her hair with a hand the size of a shovel, mirroring her savage grin with an affectionate smile.

He let her in to get cleaned up, and offered me a drink while he looked the van over. I'd already run my own sweep, cleaning up Arkay's bloody napkins and searching for a GPS and police bugs. I hadn't found anything interesting except for a metal box that took up most of the back.

"What have ya got there?" Raimo asked when his inspection reached the back of the van.

"No clue," I said, coming around front. "The guy we got this from said he was delivering something."

"Like what, a case of beer?" He tipped the box back a few inches, and it made a wet gravelly sound. "It looks like a cooler."

"Must have been some excellent beer," I said, tapping the padlock that sealed the lid. "You don't get ice boxes like this at Walmart."

An excited grin crossed Raimo's face. "Let's find out, shall we? Give me a second." He vanished into the garage and came out with what I could only describe as a murder weapon. "Watch your fingers, Hiccup."

This wasn't a friendly little set of bolt cutters. It had wicked blades nearly as long as my hands, and they snapped shut around the cooler's lock with a slow hydraulic snarl.

"Isn't that a bit excessive?" I asked.

"I know, right?" he squealed. "I just got her in. Isn't she gorgeous? I'm going to call her Matilda."

"Ooh, did Raimo get a new toy?" Arkay called from inside. "I wanna see!" She bounded out to join us, bits of moisture still dripping down from her damp hair.

The padlock could probably have been pulled off with a solid pull, but Raimo caught the remaining sliver of metal between Matilda's jaws with an almost dainty twist. Another roar, and the pieces fell away.

"All right," Arkay said, taking the lid with both hands. "Let's see what we've got here."

Matilda hit the floor with a solid thunk as Raimo stumbled back. "Jesus Christ!"

It took me a moment longer to make sense of the metallic, meaty smell and the sudden flash of red.

"Jesus— Arkay, don't touch it!" I shouted, grabbing Arkay and yanking her close. Behind me, Raimo retched onto the concrete floor. The smell of sick almost masked the smell of gore. Almost.

Gently, Arkay extracted herself from my grip and approached the van again, climbing into the back to get a better look.

The cooler was lined with half-melted ice, like a seafood counter at a grocery store. It even had the same irregular lumps, each in shades of pink and puce and red.

They weren't fish.

Some of them could have been mistaken for anything. Something unrecognizable. Maybe something innocent.

But there was no mistaking the heart that floated at the top of the slush.

I ripped my gaze away and turned my back on the cooler, trying to swallow the bile that rose in my throat. Awkwardly I patted Raimo's shoulder. "Maybe… maybe they're animal parts. Pigs or something. Cows."

"No." Arkay leaned over the open cooler, breathing deep through her nose. "They're definitely human. And not just one person, either."

Raimo vomited again. I shepherded him away from the growing puddle, trying to focus on him instead of the ringing in my ears or the welling panic in my gut.

"Arkay, can you call the police?" I said.

"No!" Raimo gurgled. "No, you can't do that. Not here. God, if you bring the cops down here with— with a car full of organs— they'll think I— I—" He lurched, and I narrowly escaped another round.

"He's got a point, Rosa." Arkay sealed the lid. "We stole the van. Whatever the hell is going on here, we really don't want to be blamed for it."

"What, do you have a better plan?" I demanded. "This thing belongs to a serial killer, or an organ harvester, or— or I don't even know what. Somebody's got to let people know."

"Not here," Raimo repeated. His face, pale even on a good day, had gone bone white. "Whatever the hell you do, keep me out of it." He swung his arm wildly for emphasis. He would have hit me, except that another hand intercepted it: small and long-fingered, with a stronger grip than such a slender wrist should have been capable of.

Arkay fixed him with an icy stare, and he retreated into himself.

"First," she said, "you're going to calm down. And then you're going to do as I say."

In the end, it took a few hours of frantic pacing, several raised voices, and a homicidal glare from Arkay for us to reach a conclusion.

We brought the cooler to an abandoned parking lot on the west side, out of sight of surveillance cameras and unfriendly eyes. We alerted the police by text— no way of identifying us by our voices that way— then wiped down the stolen cell phone and left it with the cooler. I'd seen enough crime shows to know the police could trace you with those things. Raimo took the van back to his shop to hack it to pieces.

Not exactly a perfect system, but it worked well enough.

Arkay insisted that we check into a motel, and I didn't argue with her.

This one was a familiar haunt to the homeless in the area. The rates were cheap and the owner never asked questions when the name on your credit card didn't match your face. Sure, they gave us hell if we were still around when the card got declined, and Arkay always had to zap the mattress to kill the bed bugs, but it felt good to sleep behind a locked door.

We slept the way we always did, curled tight around each other and jerking awake every time the curtains lit up with the headlight of a passing car. When I finally woke up for good the next morning, it wasn't because of a loud noise or a sudden movement, but because of the subtle tension in the body nestled against mine.

Murky daylight light filtered through the curtains, and the clock on the bedside table read 10:49. We had plenty of time before we had to leave.

"Kay?" I mumbled, still groggy. "What's wrong?"

Her eyes remained on the window. "Someone's coming."

A shot of adrenaline yanked me out of my doze, but I kept my tone soft. "It's okay. It's probably someone going to the room next door or something. We're fine."

A fist pounded on the door.

"Rosario Hernandez!" barked a low female voice from the other side. "Open the door. This is the IMPD. We have a warrant."

Arkay rolled off the bed. Her eyes narrowed and her lips curled into a snarl.

"Wait!" I hissed, scrambling to my feet. At the door I shouted, "Just one second!"

"This is the police," the woman on the other side repeated. "Open this door right now."

The door clicked and squeaked as the doorknob lock unlatched. More clicks, and the deadbolt twisted in place.

I dove at Arkay, grabbing one of her hands in my own as the door opened a few inches. Only a taut length of chain kept it shut.

"Rosario—"

"I'm coming!" I said, raising one hand in front of me. With the other, I held Arkay so tight I thought I might leave bruises. "I'm coming. I'm sorry, you caught me while I was asleep. I'm gonna open the door now. Just don't shoot, okay?"

Arkay pulled aside the blinds with her free hand and sniffed petulantly at the air. "I can handle this, Rosa."

"I'm asking you not to." Taking a deep breath, I unlatched the door and let the chain clatter against the frame. I gave Arkay's hand a warning squeeze, forced a smile onto my face, and turned the handle. "What seems to be the problem?"

I stayed polite while we were searched, handcuffed, questioned, and forced into the back of a police cruiser. I met everything with smiling submission, prefaced every sentence with 'please' and 'thank you'. It wasn't about good manners: five uniformed officers and a detective had come to pick us up, and the latter was the only one with her hands not on a firearm. Beside me, Arkay thrummed with tension, so strong that sparks of static made my hair stand on end. The last thing anyone here needed was an excuse to stop playing nice.

During the ride to the station Arkay's hands curled into wicked claws and clenched again into fists, over and over again. I took her hand, lacing her fingers between my own.

"It's okay," I said. "I'm sure they just want to ask us a few questions. We'll be out of here soon."

She didn't bother pointing out my lie.

It didn't occur to me that we'd be separated until we were being led through a plain, door-lined hallway in the police precinct— and even then, not until one of the officers took me by the shoulder and pushed me toward one of the doors.

Naturally Arkay moved to follow me, but the officer held out a hand. "Not you. You're in there."

She blinked at him, dumbfounded by the idea. "I'm with her," she said, like that explained everything. Which, to her, it probably did.

"You're being questioned separately," he said. "You're in there."

"But I'm—"

The door shut between us, cutting off the rest of her argument.

And then there was silence, and all the gaping, unnerving possibility that came with it.

I tried not to panic.

It wasn't like we were joined at the hip or anything—we didn't exactly chaperone each other's love lives— but in the three years I'd known Arkay, every separation had been deliberate, with specific understandings of how long we'd be gone and where we'd meet up afterward. Even then, I'd spend half my dates worrying that I'd come back to our home base to find a corpse.

But that wouldn't happen here.

Especially not *here*. A few weeks ago, a guy had gotten shot by cops in police custody up in Chicago, and local governments were scrambling to keep people from rioting.

They wouldn't let it happen again.

They wouldn't.

Would they?

I paced the room, trying to take my mind off the possibilities. It didn't take long to make each pass: the interrogation room was small, crowded by a desk and three chairs. The walls were blank and off-white, interrupted only by a camera and a massive one-way mirror. I tried listening at the door, but to no luck.

The only thing that came through was a detective holding a manila folder, after what felt like hours on my own.

She was a strong-looking woman, broad-shouldered and well-muscled, with natural hair pulled into a tight bun. She regarded me with intense brown eyes.

"Miss Hernandez." Her voice was softer, smoother than I'd anticipated it. But then, the last time I'd heard her speak, she'd been hoarse from yelling through the motel door. "My name is Detective Sharp. Could I have you sit down?" It wasn't a request.

"Sure thing," I said, my fallback smile plastered on my face. "I hope my friend hasn't given you any trouble?" Hopefully, if I cooperated, she'd return the favor.

"Your friend," she repeated. "Miss... Plath?" She fixed me with the kind of immovable patience that teachers give misbehaving middle schoolers. "I'll assume her name isn't really Sylvia."

I kept my expression neutral. "No, it isn't."

"And I'll assume it's not Austen, Dickenson, or Bly, either. Do you like to read, Miss Hernandez, or is that just your friend's hobby?"

"We spend a lot of time in libraries," I said.

"Then I'm sure you understand what's happening right now."

I swallowed. I could only imagine what was going on with Arkay. "Actually, I don't. Could you please tell me why you brought us here?"

I had a couple of inches on Detective Sharp, but when she sat down across the desk, she loomed over me. "Miss Hernandez, do you know Ian Driscoll?"

I frowned. It sounded familiar, but I couldn't match it to a face. "Should I?"

"I would hope so." She pulled a piece of paper from the folder and scraped a ball-point pen across it in a succession of straight lines. "Because he had this carved into his chest." She slid it across the desk for me to see, but I'd seen Arkay scratch that symbol into enough surfaces to recognize the motion. "Do you know what this is?"

I didn't say anything.

"We've got reports from almost a dozen men who have the same mark somewhere on their body. Their chest, hands— one on his face."

I remembered that one.

Most of the time they fell for Arkay's flirting and focused their attention on her. This particular guy had tried to grab me instead. I'd had to call an ambulance by the time she finished with him.

Sharp continued: "All of them say they got it from the same person: Asian woman with a pixie cut, late teens to early twenties, five foot two, hundred pounds soaking wet. Always accompanied by a brown woman in her mid-twenties, long hair, six one, two hundred and fifty pounds. In the next hour or so, we're going to have those gentlemen take a look at a line-up. What do you think they're going to tell us?"

I wrung my hands. "They're probably not going to tell you what they were doing right before she did that to them."

Sharp's eyes bored into me. "Explain."

"That mark she cut into them? She doesn't just throw it around," I said, keeping my gaze low. "When she does that to someone, it's because that person's dangerous. Sexual assault, usually. Sometimes people who've pulled a gun on us. It's so the rest of us know to keep away from them."

"'The rest of us' being...?"

"On the street." My words faded into a mumble. The more Sharp loomed, the more I wanted to dissolve into my chair. "Listen, what she does is self-defense. Always. We don't go looking for these guys, we don't start trouble. But when they come after us, we protect ourselves. And..." I bit my lip and looked her in the eye. "And if any of them are going to be pressing charges, then so am I." I tried to at least look confident, but internally I searched my memories of every police procedural show I'd ever seen. Was that actually something I could do?

Sharp's face revealed nothing. "I'm sure Ian Driscoll would feel very threatened by that, if he were still alive."

"He's dead?" Immediately my world went sideways. "I— I don't understand."

Another photograph slid across the desk. "Does that jog your memory?"

The photo was of the courier, his eyes wide open and glassy, a look of horror frozen on his face. His shirt lay in shreds around him. The space below his ribs had been reduced to a bloody, empty cavity, all ragged edges and a single fresh symbol carved into his chest.

"No." I shoved myself away from the desk. Bile rose in my throat. "No— I— no. We didn't do this. Arkay didn't do this."

"You sure about that?" Sharp asked.

I shook my head. "He was alive when we left him. We made sure. He didn't look great, but we didn't…" I couldn't rip my gaze away from the carnage. "We didn't."

"I believe you," Sharp said. "I believe you had nothing to do with this. So let me tell you what I think. This guy, he's a scumbag. You wouldn't be the first person who's said so. So he comes after you, and your friend cuts him up. Only then he gets angry. Maybe he decides he's going to get some payback. Maybe he comes by later when you're alone. Tries to do his thing. And Arkay, she doesn't like that. She's your friend, after all. She doesn't want anything bad to happen to you. So she stops this guy the only way she knows how. And she doesn't want you to get upset, so she hides it from you. But friends, they always know. Even if you don't want to believe it, you know. Don't you?"

I shook my head. "No. No, that's not possible."

"We both know that's not true." Her voice was soft. Confident that she'd won.

"No, I mean it," I said. "Between when we saw him and now, the longest Arkay and I have been apart has been to shower. I don't care what you think she's capable of, she physically couldn't have done what you're saying."

A crash interrupted me before I could go on. I didn't hear it so much as I felt it through the table and chairs.

"What the hell was that?" I asked.

Apparently Sharp wondered the same thing, because she got up and rushed out the door. In the moments before the door slammed shut, a crowd of uniformed officers rushed past, a few shouting at each other, one calling for backup on his walkie-talkie. I didn't catch much of what he said, but I didn't need to.

"— *the hell is she?*"

The world moved in a blur. I was on my feet and across the room, grabbing uselessly at the door handle.

Oh God.

I whirled away from the door and flattened myself against the one-way mirror, cupping my hands around my eyes to see into the darkened room on the other side.

Thank God, there were still shadows in the observation room, though they were turned away from me.

"Hey!" I shouted, slamming my fists into the glass. "Hey! Is that Arkay? Is she doing this?"

Movement. Hopefully they'd noticed me.

I pounded on the glass again. "Please, if that's Arkay, you need to let me see her. Please don't hurt her. Whatever she's doing, you need to let me see her!"

Another sharp crash rattled the floor under my feet.

"Listen!" I shouted. "I get that you people have procedures or whatever, but that's not going to work. Please, just let me talk to her."

The door burst open. Sharp stormed in, rumpled and disheveled, blood flowing from a gash above her hairline.

She looked like she'd been thrown.

"*You.*" She pointed at me. "What the *hell* is she on?"

"N-nothing."

"That woman is trying to smash her way through cinder block. *And it's working.*"

Another crash, this one punctuated by a shout of pain.

"Let me in there with her," I said.

"Like hell," she said, grabbing me by the shoulder and forcibly dragging me from the room. "We're evacuating before she kills someone."

That shouldn't have come as a relief, but it did—because it meant she *hadn't* killed anyone.

Yet.

"This is going to keep getting worse until she calms down," I said. "I can do that, I swear."

"We've got this under control," she said. A knee-jerk response.

"If she were anyone else, I'd believe you. But you've never dealt with someone like her before. She's not hopped up on PCP, or bath salts, or whatever the hell you think is going on with her." She kept dragging me down the hall, and I dug my heels in. "Do you really want to explain to the press why you shot a handcuffed woman in your interrogation room? Because that's what it's going to take to stop her if you don't let me in there."

She stared me down, on that narrow ledge between uncertainty and determination.

And then a scream threw her over the edge.

"You better know what you're talking about," she muttered, turning around and dragging me back toward the crowd.

"Everyone back!" she snapped. "Let us through!"

At least a dozen police officers had gathered in the hallway, their weapons drawn. Another half dozen moved along the walls of the interrogation room like a pack of wolves, watching for an opening in Arkay's defenses.

34

My dragon crouched in the corner, snarling like an animal. The interrogation table had been torn into pieces and hurled through the one-way mirror. The ground was strewn with pulverized cinderblock and silvery crumbles of broken glass. Arkay's handcuffs had been ripped apart, and the broken metal cut into her skin. Blood poured from her wrists, staining the twisted metal bar she brandished like a club.

One of the officers, a six-foot white guy who looked like he could bench press a horse, charged forward. She rushed forward to meet him, bending low to grab him by a thigh that was nearly as thick around as her waist. So fast I could barely follow it, she yanked him up and over her back, using his own momentum to hurl him into a wall. Blood darkened the fabric around his leg. I couldn't tell if it was hers or his.

She hissed, and I ran past the last line of police into the tiny room. I stumbled between her and the fallen man, my hands outstretched.

"Arkay, it's me!" I inched closer. She angled her body toward me, but her eyes kept darting to the officers around her. "See? They let me in. Everything's okay now."

She grabbed me by the wrist and yanked me into the corner behind her with a growl.

Half a dozen handguns snapped into the air, echoed by a dozen shouts of "put her down!"

"Don't shoot!" I threw my hands over Arkay's shoulder. "Don't shoot! I'm not hurt. Just... everybody just calm down." I lowered my voice. "Detective Sharp, please. She's trying to protect me. It's what she does when she freaks out, and your guys are freaking her out. If they leave, she'll start to calm down."

Sharp stared Arkay down, and the dragon met her with a growl.

"She hasn't hurt me yet, Detective Sharp," I said. "And she's not going to. Please. You need to trust me here. We're not going anywhere."

Slowly, Sharp's eyes rose to meet mine.

"Please," I repeated.

"Stand down," she said finally. "Kurtz, Green, into the hallway."

Two of the officers exchanged glances, but they holstered their weapons, backing slowly through the open door. Arkay's body shifted slightly, following their movements, but she didn't fully relax.

"It's all right," I said gently. I withdrew my cuffed hands to rub soothing circles on her back. "Everything's gonna be okay, see? I'm here now."

Arkay relaxed visibly, though I couldn't be sure whether that had more to do with the slow, gentle touches, or with the fact another two policemen retreated into the hall.

I carefully worked my way down her arm. "Let me see your wrist, Arkay. Did you do this?" I could have been reading a dictionary for all she cared. When Arkay got angry enough, she didn't just stop talking, she stopped responding to words entirely, beyond volume and tone. Sometimes when it got bad, she didn't even seem to recognize my voice. But she always responded to touch.

With one hand she still brandished the table leg, but she let me tug her other arm up so I could get a closer look. The metal had bitten deep gouges into her wrist, probably when she'd snapped the cuffs. The broken twists of metal still dangled uselessly around her arm.

36

"That looks painful," I said. "How about you let me get you cleaned up? We don't want this to get infected." I looked to the only other person left in the room. "Detective Sharp, could I please have a first aid kit or something? I think it'll help."

I wasn't stalling. Something about the ritual of first aid helped calm Arkay down. It meant that the danger was over, the fight was won, and everyone was safe. She needed that right now.

Sharp said something into the hallway, but I couldn't catch it. Most of my attention remained focused on Arkay, and the slow uncoil of her muscles. A few moments later a uniformed officer handed Sharp the first aid kit. Arkay tensed at the intrusion, but I stroked at her shoulders, easing Arkay's attention back to me.

There was another jolt of tension as Sharp extended the kit to me, but she didn't lash out as I accepted it and picked up one of the downed chairs.

"Thank you, Detective Sharp. Arkay, I want you to sit down right here. Let me have a look at you." She didn't respond to the command, but she didn't resist when I guided her into the chair.

"I'll give you credit," Sharp said, her voice guarded. "You got her calm. Think you can keep her that way?"

"Yeah." I soaked a cotton ball with ointment and started dabbing it across the cuts. Arkay twitched, but didn't jerk out of my reach.

"I want you to keep doing what you're doing, then. We've got a transport on its way to pick you both up."

I swallowed, but I kept my face blank, keeping my eyes focused on the gauze pad I was unwrapping. "Why? Where are you taking us?"

"Someplace better equipped to handle her," she said. *Good luck with that.*

"She didn't kill Ian Driscoll," I said quietly.

"Maybe not, but she's too dangerous to be on the streets. Look at her. Look at this room. She's a danger to herself and everyone around her. She's a danger to you."

I pulled Arkay close against my chest so she couldn't see my face anymore. "No, she's not. Not to me."

"Huh." I could feel Sharp's gaze boring into my back. "I heard a lot of people use that line, back when I worked as a beat cop. Want to guess how many of them turned out to be wrong?"

There was a knock at the door, and a man in uniform signaled for Sharp. She stepped outside.

Arkay pulled away to watch her leave.

"Asshole," Arkay muttered once the door shut.

"I take it you're talking again?" I smoothed her hair. "Mind telling me how all this happened?"

She leaned into the touch. "You know how in movies, when two people are getting into a heated argument, and one tells the other to do something, and the other one says 'make me', it usually ends with a makeout session?"

"Oh my god."

"Yeah. Turns out that doesn't happen in real life."

"Please tell me you didn't—"

"He tried to shove me into the chair. Things escalated."

I buried my face in my hands.

In case I needed any more reasons to get anxious about leaving her alone.

Another knock on the door announced Detective Sharp's return, but I didn't raise my head.

"Everything all right in here?" she asked, as if it didn't look like a bomb had gone off in here.

"Peachy," I muttered.

"The transport's arrived. Officer Troy will be taking the two of you to a secure facility." She paused. "I've already told them not to separate you, so hopefully that won't be an issue again. It's all I can do."

"I appreciate it," I said, finally rising to look her in the eye. "Thank you for your help."

She eyed Arkay warily. "Will she be able to be restrained?"

Arkay leaned forward, resting her elbows on her knees. "Do you really want to find out?"

I tugged her back to me. "It's not a good idea, no. But I'll keep her from causing any trouble. Promise."

Sharp pinched the bridge of her nose. "God help me. Take off your coat, then."

The tension fell out of Arkay's frame, replaced by puzzlement. "Huh?"

"Your coat," the detective repeated. "Take it off and fold it over your arms. You've got half the station spooked, and they're expecting you to walk out of this room handcuffed. Keep your wrists covered, and they can go on thinking what they like."

I was surprised by the allowance. But then, Arkay had already proved how little handcuffs mattered if she really wanted to hurt somebody.

"Thanks," I said, rising to help Arkay get the sleeves off over her mangled wrists.

"Don't thank me." She looked grim. "I'm probably going to lose my badge over this."

I cringed. I hated seeing people get hurt for trying to help. "For what it's worth, that guy Driscoll said he was making a delivery."

"Yeah?" she asked wearily.

"He had a cooler in the back of his van," I said. "I don't know who it was meant for, but we called it in."

Sharp's eyes snapped open. "Wait. That was you?"

"Cooler full of human organs, about yea big?" Arkay mimed a massive box. "Yeah. We sent that to you. Didja like it?"

"And Driscoll had it in his van?"

"He said it was for a client," I said. "I don't know who that was, but anyone who special orders that kind of thing has to be bad news. If they didn't kill Driscoll themselves, I bet they know who did."

"Wait, van guy's dead?" Arkay asked.

Sharp ignored her. "Did he say anything else?"

"No," I said. "It didn't seem like he knew what was in there. But I hope that helps."

"You mentioned a van," she said. "Do you know where it is? Or even what it looks like?"

Arkay snorted.

"Sorry," I said. "We sold it to a chop shop."

"Which one?"

40

I shook my head. No way was I dragging Raimo into this, too. "It doesn't matter. It's long gone. But it was a big white van— like church bus meets pedo van." I shot Arkay a preemptive glare before she could open her mouth. "I know it's not a lot, but maybe it'll help."

"Here's hoping."

Maybe I imagined it, but she looked almost sympathetic as she led us to our escort.

As soon as I turned the corner and looked at the new arrival, I stumbled.

Officer Troy, according to her name plate, had dark skin and delicate features, with full lips she chewed when she was anxious. I knew, because I'd watched her doing exactly that for nearly an hour at Stella's a few nights back. I'd almost asked for her phone number.

Arkay stared at her as we approached, but she didn't say anything as we were led past the equally uncomfortable glares of several dozen cops. I kept my head down. Somebody had to.

Arkay didn't say a word until we were being loaded into yet another white van, this one outfitted with a steel interior to discourage restless prisoners.

"Okay, I give up," Arkay said as we settled into the benches on one side of the van, and Officer Troy perched in the other. "What are you?"

Troy frowned. I buried my face in my cuffed hands. The woman looked like she might have been mixed race, but that didn't matter. It wasn't my business, and it wasn't Arkay's either. I'd taught her better than that.

"I mean it," Arkay continued. "You're not human, and you're not like me. So what the hell are you?"

Troy froze. "You're insane," she said, but her whole body said otherwise.

"You wouldn't be the first person to say that." Arkay shrugged. "But I'm not. Just not as blind as everyone else around here." She jerked her head to the front of the van. "Do they know you're not human?"

Troy shut the van door, locking herself inside with us.

"That's a no, then?"

"Arkay," I said quietly. "Stop." Whatever she was getting at, it wouldn't end well for us.

"Does it work both ways, though?" she asked. "Do you know what I am?"

"Arkay, please don't antagonize the nice cop."

"But she's not a cop." Arkay's eyes never left the woman. "That's not her uniform. It smells like someone else. A human. And fresh blood, too. I'm guessing you killed the real Officer Troy and took her uniform, right?"

My stomach dropped. What had we gotten ourselves into?

"You need to stop," the imposter said.

"So if you're not Officer Troy," I said. "Who are you? What's your name?"

"That's not something you need to know," she said.

"No, but I'd like to," I said. "It makes things a bit more comfortable, you know?"

She didn't reply.

I tried again: "Where are you taking us?"

"You'll find out when we get there," she said.

"It's not like we can do anything about it." I curled into myself, trying to look soft and pitiful. "Please?"

"Stop asking questions," she said again. "This isn't my call."

"I get that," I said. "You're just doing your job."

A minute nod. Maybe this was working.

"You don't mean to hurt us," I continued. "You're not a bad person." Arkay cast me a sidelong glance. "You don't seem like one, anyway."

"Sorry," she said. "It's still out of my hands."

"Can you just tell us why?" I asked. "It's not going to make a difference to anyone out there, but I'd still like to know why this is happening to us."

"It's not like you're giving anything away," Arkay said after a moment, her voice soft and subdued. "I already know you people killed the courier."

The woman jerked upright. "You do?"

That was news to me.

"His blood's all over you," Arkay said. "Like Troy's. It's not deep, though. I don't think you're the one who did it. But you were there. Maybe they had you help move the body."

The imposter grimaced.

"Sounds like things have been getting out of hand for you lately," I said. "That sucks."

"Out of hand is putting it lightly," she said. "You don't know the guy I'm working with."

I tilted my head a few degrees to the side, the way Arkay did when she was paying attention. "That bad, huh?"

"He seemed fine when this whole thing started, but now he's killing people— killing cops—" She shook her head. "I didn't sign on for this. For any of this."

"What happened?" I asked. One thing I'd noticed over the years: people really, really liked talking about their problems.

The imposter shook her head again. "At first he just asked me for a couple favors. Something simple, help him get in touch with some people, figure things out. And I figure, fine, whatever. We were friends. I thought we were friends."

I flashed a sympathetic smile and nodded for her to go on.

"Only then he started getting weird. Twitchy. And I knew that was going to happen. I knew. I mean, that's what happens when you play around with necromancy. That stuff's worse than meth, the way it gets into your head…" She shuddered.

"Did he do something?" I asked gently.

"Threatened to out me if I didn't keep helping him," she said. "Not just me, either. Friends of mine. Family."

"Bastard," Arkay said, and it got the faintest hint of a smile from the woman.

"How did he find out?" I asked. I didn't want to ask what she'd been outed as; I didn't want to risk her remembering that she didn't actually trust us.

She gave a bitter chuckle. "Stupid. We worked together, you know? At the county morgue. And one day he caught me sneaking out pieces to take home."

She couldn't be serious. "Pieces of… equipment?" I offered.

"Bodies. Kidneys, slices of liver— you know, the kind of things they'd never miss at the funeral. And it wasn't like they were going to use it anymore. And there are people starving out there. I can't just let perfectly good food go to waste."

I blinked, trying to process what I'd just heard. Or better yet, to unhear it entirely.

"Of course not," I said faintly.

"Don't you get all judgmental," she snapped. "I'm a medical examiner. I know how those people died, and a lot of how they lived. I know their names. I respect them. Do you give that much attention to the cows that make your burgers?"

"Do you? Eat cow, I mean." Arkay asked, apparently unperturbed. "Or are you a straight up vegetarian when you're not nomming on the soylent green?"

"I have to be," she said. "I'm a ghoul." Her gaze darted ceilingward when she caught our nonplussed expressions. "It's not like eating human is cheap. Not like I can just run down to Kroger and pick up a few pounds of Chuck. But if I don't, I'll die. And it's not like I can substitute it out for beef or whatever, either. You know how they say you are what you eat? That's literal for people like me. There are stories about ghouls who got hungry enough, they started eating beef, pork, that kind of thing. And you'd be able to see it. Day by day, they'd get bigger and dumber, as they turned more feral, more animal, until they barely know their own names."

"That's awful," I said softly.

The ghoul jerked in surprise. Apparently she hadn't expected that reaction. "Yeah. It is."

"And I'm guessing they don't serve human in prison," I said. "If this guy'd turned you in…"

"I'd either starve to death or go feral," she said. "I can't go out that way. I can't."

"Of course not." I reached across the aisle and gave her hand a squeeze. She returned the gesture, but halfheartedly. Her eyes lingered on my handcuffs, and she bit her lip.

"I'm sorry," she said. "About what's going to happen to you. If I had a choice about it…"

"It's okay. I get it." I gave her another reassuring squeeze. "But can you tell us what it's going to be? Please? I just…" I ducked my head. "The worst part is not knowing."

She bit her lip, but nodded. "Matheson, my boss, he's doing a ritual, and he needs certain organs. Special ones. They have to have been properly sacrificed, or else we would have just snuck them out of the morgue with the other bodies. He tried buying a set from a supplier up in Chicago, but…"

"But then we happened," I said softly.

"We'd try buying them again, but he's out of money and out of time. And…" She frowned. "And he's not himself anymore. There are ways around what he's doing. I've tried to tell him, but he won't listen. He's not rational anymore." She lowered her head. "But that's what he wants you for. To replace what he lost."

The car made more frequent turns as we neared our destination. We didn't have much time left.

"What's your name?" I asked.

"Danielle," she mumbled.

"I'm Rosario," I said. "This is Arkay."

"Yeah. I know your names." The van slowed and finally came to a stop. "Come on. Let's get this over with. Stand up, please."

She extended a hand to help me to my feet as the doors opened.

I'd expected a warehouse, or a parking lot, or an evil underground facility. Not the inside of a vaguely crowded one-car garage. The van's driver stood outside to meet us, shifting his weight uneasily and averting his eyes away from us. The other man had to be Matheson. He leaned toward us, watching us like we were his next hit. I could see what Danielle had meant, comparing necromancy to a drug. He was pale-faced and red-eyed behind horn-rimmed glasses, with wispy ash-blond hair that looked like it had been pulled at too often. His fingernails were bloody from being bitten and picked at. His dress shirt hung awkwardly on his frame.

I recognized him— or maybe I'd seen a hundred guys just like him, but not quite as far gone. He had a forgettable face, bland enough to fade into the background if not for the obvious decay. In the corner of my eye, Arkay tensed.

"I've got them," Danielle muttered, nudging me forward.

"Good," the necromancer said. "Excellent. You've done well."

I stood my ground. "I'm sorry," I said, "Were you going for Emperor Palpatine just now? Because you really need the black cloak to pull that off. Great job on the face, though." I flashed a thumbs up.

Matheson jerked like he'd been smacked. The other man, another blackmailed ghoul, maybe, straightened. Perhaps he'd expected me to grovel or cry. He'd get neither.

"Excuse you?" Matheson demanded. "How dare you, you—"

"If you say 'insolent', I get bingo." I winked. Arkay snickered behind me, and I shifted my weight to hide her from view. "Oh! If I guess your evil overlord name, do we get to go? Because my first guess is totally 'he who—'"

Matheson lunged at me, and I ducked. Arkay vaulted over me like a gymnast, both hands on my back as she kicked Danielle out of the van and into the driver. The grace ran out just in time for her to smash headlong into Matheson. He hit the ground hard, but so did she.

I jumped out of the back of the van and rushed to lift the garage door, but it wouldn't budge. A shiny new lock gleamed on the side of the door.

Apparently these weren't the complete idiot brand of bad guys, after all.

"Arkay?" I called, throwing my shoulder into it without any luck. "A little help here?"

She staggered to her feet, but so did Danielle and the driver. We had to get out of here.

I grabbed Arkay by her elbow and dragged her upright as I ran for the other door. This one was unlocked, and I yanked Arkay through, slamming it behind us and fumbling with the deadbolt.

"What was that?" a man's voice called from somewhere deeper inside.

Of course they weren't alone. That would have been too easy.

We stood in the kitchen of what looked like a foreclosure. The linoleum floor was cracked and the wallpaper peeling, but the counters were free of grime, and shiny new drip pans glinted under the heating coils on the stove.

"Shh," I signaled for Arkay to follow as I tiptoed toward the next room, holding my hands carefully apart so the handcuffs wouldn't rattle. Hopefully we could sneak out the front door before anyone else in the house noticed us.

It would have been a great plan, if the people we'd locked in the garage hadn't started pounding at the door.

"Matheson?" called the voice from upstairs.

"What's going on?" asked another.

Footsteps joined the noise of the banging door, one set hurrying down a flight of stairs, another heading toward us.

"New plan," I hissed, rushing for the first door I could see and jumping inside before I could register the darkness.

My feet found nothing underneath them. My stomach leaped into my throat as I dropped into empty space. I grabbed for a handrail, but my cuffed hands couldn't reach that far. My heel hit rickety wood and promptly skidded forward, and I slid down the steps. The sharp edges of the stairs jabbed at my rear and grated along the small of my back, and I bit back a yell of surprise and pain.

"Rosa?" Arkay called. There was a fumbling thud and a light flickered on. She stood at the top of a flight of stairs.

"I'm fine," I said. "Shut the door!"

She obeyed, and hurriedly locked it behind her. And kept locking it.

Gingerly I rolled to my feet, wiggling my toes. No spinal damage from what I could tell. "Who the hell puts a lock on their basement door?"

"Is that not normal?" Arkay asked, finally coming down to check on me.

"It's not usual."

"So does that mean seven locks are really unusual?"

I peered up at the door. "Yeah, that's a bit weird."

"Are you sure you're alright?" Arkay bounded down the stairs to help me up.

"My ass is gonna be black and blue for a month," I groaned. "But I'll live. Didn't even twist my ankle. Any blood?"

She pulled at my shirt to check. "Nothing I can see."

Okay. Next order of business. "There's no way they don't know we're down here," I said. "And even seven locks won't hold them off forever. Do you think you can break these handcuffs?"

Arkay grabbed one silver bracelet in each hand and pulled them apart, but it was no use. Her hands shook from the effort. Everything past her forearms was dark and swollen, and fresh blood seeped through the bandages on her wrists.

"That's fine," I said, tugging my hands out of her grip before she could hurt herself. "Are you alright, Arkay?"

"Tired," she said.

"Do you need to sit down for a minute?"

Upstairs the door rattled against its many locks, and a muffled swear seeped through the crack.

"I don't think we've got time," she said.

"Then how about we look for a way out of here, and then we can find someplace nice and comfy and you can sleep until summer."

She flashed a thin smile. "Sounds like a plan."

She ducked through another lock-covered doorway into another basement room, while I searched through the one I'd landed in. The only light came from small, grimy windows that squeezed in close to the ceiling. Dust and litter scattered

50

unevenly on a cracked concrete floor that was covered in deep gouges and splattered with stains.

Arkay and I had broken into similar houses, when winters had gotten particularly bad. We'd probably be doing the same this year, if we couldn't panhandle and steal enough cash to book a motel when the temperatures dropped.

And, you know, assuming we survived the homicidal necromancer upstairs.

I found a few slivers of wood from the ceiling boards, but they splintered when I tried to pick the cuffs with them. In the corner, I found a crumpled coke can. It took some doing, but I managed to wrench the metal apart, peeling off a piece of sticky aluminum. I wedged it between the teeth of the cuffs and the locking mechanism, and finally the cuffs slid open.

"Kay?" I called, following her into the second room. "I found a way to get these things off me."

"Good," she said. "I think I found something, too."

Oh yes she did.

The room was lined with dozens, maybe hundreds, of unlit candles in shades of white and red and black. The line of candles only stopped at a bookshelf full of old, leather-bound tomes and even older-looking brass weapons. An iron circle had been pounded into the concrete floor, which had been liberally smeared with rust-brown stains. The far wall was shiny and steel with a big door that looked like a walk-in refrigerator, the kind you'd find in a restaurant kitchen.

Arkay had apparently ignored Occult 'R' Us entirely, except to stack the old books under a window and try to pry open the glass with a rune-covered dagger. "Think you can fit?"

"I'll suck it in," I said.

"Then give me just a minute. I've almost got it."

So during that minute, I did The Thing. You know, that one thing you usually see people in horror movies doing. The one that makes you facepalm and shake your head at the sheer stupidity.

Because Arkay was busy with the window, and Matheson and his goons were scratching at the door with what sounded like a screwdriver, and I had nothing else occupying my time or my mind.

Nothing but that giant freakin' door in the shiny metal wall, just begging to be opened.

Three guesses what I did.

The door was vacuum sealed, and it sucked at the wall when I yanked it open. A wave of stale, cold air flooded out, along with a sterile white light.

"Oh my God!" I yelped, slamming it shut.

Arkay was on the floor in an instant, ducking under my arm to get in front of me.

"What is it?" she demanded. Curling forward for an attack, she wrapped her hand around the handle and pulled open the massive door. The dagger in her other hand was out and ready to kill.

But the people inside were already dead.

They were bodies. At least a dozen, all ashen and unmoving. Some of them were whole, others carved up like something you'd see in a butcher shop.

I wanted to throw up.

"Guess she wasn't kidding about the whole necromancer thing," Arkay said. "You alright, Rosa?"

No. No way in hell was I alright. "F-fine."

"Okay. Let's focus on getting out of here, then. I think I've got it." I'd expected her to try actually opening the window. Instead she had carved through the rotting frame and pulled the glass onto the floor, careful to avoid breaking it. "You want a leg up, or do you want more books to stand on?"

I grimaced at the shaky pile she'd been standing on all this time. It didn't exactly inspire confidence. "You know, I think I trust you more."

She gave me a light smile and crouched down, cupping her hands.

Let me repeat here that I'm well over six feet tall and built like a fertility goddess in training, and Arkay is five-something and could pass for a pixie.

Let me also repeat here that she punched through solid cinderblock when she'd gotten pissed off at the police.

She hoisted me into the air like I was made of cardboard and tissue paper. It took a bit of wriggling to get through the narrow window, but she had no problem pushing me through. She didn't even need the stack of books to climb up after me: a handhold, a twist, and she was dusting herself off beside me.

The necromancer had made his hideout in a crappy neighborhood, but tonight that worked to our advantage. We slid like shadows between the houses, some of them glowing with light, others boarded up and empty. If the necromancer wanted to chase us, he'd probably do it by car, and so we zigzagged, cutting through unfenced yards and hiding among overgrown bushes.

Soon I started recognizing the area. It was the east side of town, not too far from Stella's, or from The Valley.

"This way." I grabbed Arkay and steered her south. When we couldn't run any further, we slowed to a walk, staying in the trees and darting out of sight when headlights flared up on the road. We were still too far east, but once we reached the train track we could follow it all the way to the camp.

As soon as I turned onto the track, Arkay slowed. "Seriously? We're going to the Valley?"

"We don't exactly have a lot of options," I said.

"Sure we do," she said. "We've got about a million options. There's plenty of bridges. Or trees. Or parks. We can sleep in shifts."

"I'm exhausted and so are you," I said. "They can help us hide until this all blows over."

"Or they'll help you hide and kick me out. They hate me, remember?"

"Don't be petty, Kay."

"I'm not," she snapped. "Just because they say they're going to protect you doesn't mean they actually plan to do it."

God, not this again. Not now. "Arkay, it's fine."

Her feet dug into the gravel of the track. "And just because they're protecting you from Mr. Reanimator over there doesn't mean they'll save you from anyone on their side."

"Kay!"

"I don't go there for a reason, Rosa."

"No, you don't go there because you broke Rudy's arm. Of course they're going to be scared of you."

"The hell I did!" Her lips peeled back into a snarl. "The way he was grabbing you, he was lucky I didn't snap his neck!"

"He was drunk," I said. "And this isn't the time. Get over it."

"How the hell am I supposed to get over it?" she demanded. "How the hell are you over it?"

"Because this is survival," I snapped. "Sometimes you have to deal with the bad to avoid getting killed. It's a tradeoff."

"It's a tradeoff you don't need to make anymore," she said. "It's not okay."

"It's necessary."

"No, it's not!"

"Kay, please." I took her by the shoulders and looked her in the eyes. "One night. Just try to hold it in for one night, and then we're out of there. Please, Kay. Just one."

Arkay's brows were still furrowed, her mouth in a thin line, but she lowered her eyes. "One night. I'll keep my hands to myself if they do."

The last hours of daylight had dissolved into darkness by the time we reached the Valley. We approached slowly through the trees, telegraphing our presence, but as soon as we stepped into the glow of the campfires, an uneasy silence washed over the camp. I pasted a timid smile onto my face. Arkay glowered, but she kept her mouth shut.

More than two dozen pairs of eyes followed us as we moved closer. A few retreated into their tents. I couldn't exactly blame them. I'd lived here, once, and after I'd found Arkay I'd brought her here to stay with me. Thing is, Arkay had broken more than an arm before we'd been sent away. A lot of guys around here thought that doing me a favor entitled them to cop a feel, and Arkay had taken issue with that. It had even cost me a few potential girlfriends. Just because I promised she wouldn't hurt them didn't mean they believed me.

I searched the crowd, praying the mayor of the camp was around. I probably couldn't convince the entire camp to let us stay, but he was reasonable. Honorable. And almost more importantly, the others would listen to him.

Apparently God decided to give us a break, because a tent toward the back of the camp opened with the squeak of a zipper, and the mayor emerged. His name was Mike Jones, a lean man with weathered hands and gray-streaked dreads that fell around his face like a lion's mane.

"Rosario," he said, clasping my hands. "It's been a long time. How have you been? And Arkay." His tone changed, less warm and more respectful. He had good instincts. That was probably the smartest way to deal with a dragon.

"Mike." She tipped her chin at him.

He extended a hand to her, too, but didn't clasp it. "I hope the two of you are doing well?"

"Actually," I said. "I was wondering if we could ask you for a favor."

We didn't offer much information, and Mike didn't ask. He just offered us his tent to sleep in for the night, and let us know that he'd be minding the fire if we needed him. It was a good strategy on his part. It kept us away from anyone Arkay might fight with, and it let him keep an eye on us in case of trouble.

His tent had a particular smell about it. All tents do, after you spend enough nights in them, but it wasn't an odor I'd ever found offensive. If anything, it had always seemed overwhelmingly human: sweat, earth, old books, and a faint note of nostalgic tobacco.

I lay on my stomach to take the pressure off my bruised back, and Arkay tucked a pile of blankets around me, burrowing in at my side.

Every time I tried to sleep, I woke up to visions of blood and corpses. Arkay was still too far gone for my squirming to wake her, but she still nestled closer against me.

"It's gonna be alright," I whispered, stroking her hair. "Everything's gonna be alright." She couldn't hear me, but it made me feel better to tell her so.

It made it easier to believe.

By dawn I'd given up on actual sleep. Instead I dozed, absently listening to the camp waking up: the slither of tents shifting, the rip of opening zippers, the shuffle of feet, the grunts and mumbles of morning greetings, and through it all, the background notes of birdsong. I hadn't realized how much I missed being here.

The peace of it started to pull me under when a new sound snapped me awake. Feet pounded on dirt, twigs snapping underfoot as a body rushed frantically through the woods toward the camp.

"Mike!" shouted a woman's voice. "Somebody! Oh God, somebody help—"

I disentangled myself from Arkay and crawled out of the tent to get a look. Around me, the rest of the camp shuddered and shivered as its more permanent residents got up to do the same.

A heavyset woman burst through the trees, stumbling and gasping for breath. Thorns had chewed up the legs of her pants, but it didn't look like that was the source of the blood that had soaked through the denim below her knees. More red stained the palms of her hands, though already it was flaking off like rust.

Mike rushed out to meet her, catching her by the shoulders before she fell. "Sue! Susan, it's me. I gotcha, Susan. What happened?"

"There was— Oh God," she sobbed between panting breaths. "There was so much blood."

"Is this your blood?" He gently took her wrist. "Is any of this yours?"

She shook her head so hard her hair whipped at Mike's face, but he didn't seem to notice. "It's— oh God. She's dead. They're all dead. Ripped open, all empty inside, and…"

My stomach churned, and I stepped closer.

"Who's dead?" Mike asked gently. "Do you know? Did any of them look familiar?"

She shook, staring at Mike with big, round eyes. "A cop," she said. "A good one. Friendly. Used to let me sleep a couple extra hours in the morning. She was good people, Mike. She didn't deserve to die."

"Who?" I whispered, and Mike asked the same question. "Who was it?"

"Troy," she said. "Officer Dana Troy."

My stomach gave up churning and dropped straight through the soles of my feet.

"She wasn't alone, neither. There were two people with her. Cops, too, I think. I mean, they had the hair, and… but they were naked, and ripped open, and— if I didn't know Dana…"

I stepped closer. Maybe the movement caught her attention, but Susan looked up like she'd been slapped, and her eyes met mine.

She screamed, hurling herself away from Mike like he was covered in spiders. "It's them! For the love of God, get them away!"

Mike stepped between her and me, raising his hands to calm her. "That's just Rosa," he said softly. "She's cool. You know that. Came by a few days ago to drop off supplies."

"It was all over!" Susan cried, backing away. "Everywhere! On the walls in their blood and cut into their skin! Over and over and over again, the mark of the beast!"

Two dozen faces turned to me, and two dozen bodies pulled violently away. Parents held their children close. Men pulled their partners behind them.

Hands reached for weapons.

"It wasn't us." I could barely hear the protest in my own ears. "We didn't do this. We couldn't have done it. We were here all night."

But Officer Troy hadn't been killed last night. She'd been murdered the night before, her uniform stolen so Danielle could abduct Arkay and me from the station.

"What's going on?" Arkay emerged from the tent. Her gaze swept the crowd, and already her body curled into a protective stance as she moved closer to me.

"You let them in here?" came a man's voice. Rudy. Fantastic. "The hell is wrong with you, Mike?"

"Get her away!" Sue threw herself backward. She disappeared into the crowd, but I could still hear her screaming. "That thing's a monster! A murderer!"

"I thought you're supposed to protect us," Rudy continued. "And you go letting those— those crazy bitches back in here? The fuck were you thinking?"

"Arkay, we're leaving," I said.

"The hell you are!" Rudy snapped, stepping closer.

Arkay jumped between him and me, her face twisting into a feral snarl.

I grabbed her by the shoulder. "We're leaving," I repeated, raising my voice. "We don't want any trouble here, so we're just gonna go."

"I want everybody to calm down," Mike's shout was a roar, but for once it didn't stun the camp into obedience.

"You gonna let them just walk away?" Rudy demanded, whirling on Mike. "The cops see those tags, and they'll think it was one of us done killed their people. And what the hell do you think they'll do to us then, Mike?" He took another step forward, and he wasn't the only one.

"Mike, please." I pulled Arkay tight against me. "You know how this ends. Don't let it."

Mike looked me in the eye, cutting through the crowd. Thinking. Deciding.

"Rosa, Arkay, you're going to come with me," he declared. "I'm gonna walk you to the road, and I'm gonna watch you walk away. And then I'm gonna call the police, and I'm gonna tell them that we have no part in all this. Do you understand?"

60

Arkay's face twitched, a growl vibrating in her chest. I tightened my grip on her. "Yeah. We get it."

"Do you understand?" he repeated, louder this time. "You, all of you, are going to keep your hands to yourselves and let these women pass. This camp is our home. Don't you ever bring violence into it."

He extended a hand to us, silently challenging anyone else to intervene. I lowered my eyes and followed him. Arkay marched at my side like an empress in exile.

"We didn't do this," I said quietly, once we'd passed out of view of the rest of the camp. "We couldn't possibly have done this. We've already talked to the police once, and..."

"It doesn't matter, Rosa," Arkay said quietly. "He doesn't care. Just like the cops didn't care. Ever notice that they didn't have a problem with my violent tendencies when we were giving out free shit?"

"It's nothing personal," Mike said. "I've got to protect my own. You do the same."

"So you're throwing us to the wolves," Arkay said. "Thanks for that."

"Wolves can howl awfully loud," he said. "But I've seen you bite. Even if you're not the ones who did this, you could. And you will, if Rosa's in danger. Which means whoever it is that's out there killing people, they're the ones who need to be scared of you, not the other way around. But whatever it is that's going down, I don't want my people in the crossfire."

"Yeah, I get that," I said, cutting off Arkay before she could say anything else. We'd reached the edge of the trees, and pavement rose up past a border of gravel. "And thank you. I know you're doing what you can."

"You two take care of yourselves," he said. "I can give you a couple of hours before I call the police. If I were you, I'd work on getting out of town."

"We'll get right on that," I said.

We didn't bother getting onto the road. It would be too easy to follow us by car, and too easy to see us from far away. Instead we climbed up the steep slope across the street and into the tree-lined railroad track. My feet slid and skidded on the loose chunks of tar-black gravel, but Arkay climbed the raised hill with ease, weaving between the scraggly trees like a pro and pulling me along behind her.

We walked away from the camp for a good while before I'd had enough of the unnerving silence.

"So, those ghouls," I said finally. "You could tell they weren't human."

She glanced at me like I was a puzzle that needed to be solved. Apparently she figured me out, because she shrugged. "They smelled funny. Different."

"Have you ever smelled anything like that before?" I asked.

"I don't know. Maybe?" She shrugged again, and I heard something in her back pop. "We see a lot of people in a day. I don't usually pay all that much attention to them."

"But they weren't human," I said.

"Neither am I."

I frowned to myself. "You said you were the only person like you," I said.

"Only dragon, sure," she said. "If we ever met another one, I'd know."

"The only not-human, I mean. You said you didn't know about any other..." I searched for the words.

"The word the courier used was 'freaks'," she said, and I flinched. "I didn't know about any others. Still don't, aside from ghouls now. But you didn't know dragons existed before you met me, and here I am. Just because you haven't personally seen something doesn't mean it doesn't exist."

The ground rose up to meet the track and flattened out. It occurred to me that we were going east. If we kept up on this route, we'd be pretty close to Stella's.

We'd be close to where we met the courier.

I wrapped my arms around myself. "You're not a freak, Arkay. No matter what anybody says."

"I know that."

"I know you know," I said. "And... so do I. I just don't have a word for what you are."

"You mean aside from 'dragon'?" she asked.

"For everything. For people who aren't... muggles, like me. I mean, all this time, I just kind of assumed you were some kind of a cosmic exception to the laws of the universe. And that's wrong of me, because you're not. You're not. Are you?"

Arkay stopped, her face turned to the sun.

"You know," I continued. "Some days I still wonder if I made you up. If you're just some huge hallucination, and I haven't just been talking to myself all this time. I'd kind of hate that, though. I like having you here as my friend. I do. Even if I don't understand you all the—"

Arkay turned back to me, her eyes flashing. "There's someone out there."

"Where?" I whirled, searching through the trees. Was that someone coming toward us, or was that just the wind? "Why didn't you shut me up?"

"It looks like an ambush," she said. "It's not like they didn't already know we were here. Might as well finish your thought."

"Do you think someone in the Valley sold us out?"

"Probably," she said.

"Can you see who's out there?"

She shook her head. "I can smell them. Ghouls, mostly. Some humans, too, I think."

"You think?"

"They don't smell right. Not like the ghouls, but... stale. Rotten." She fidgeted with the bandages around her wrists. "You didn't happen to grab a knife or something while we were in the Valley, did you?"

"No," I said.

"That's okay." She cracked her knuckles. "There's always the old-fashioned way. They're gonna try to come at us from all sides, but try to stay behind me. If we run—"

"Run where?" I asked. We were too far away to make it to our bridge from here, and even if we weren't, home base was dangerously close to the police station. We couldn't exactly go back to the Valley, either. Besides, running wasn't my strong suit, even when I was scared. Big feet and disintegrating shoes made for easy tripping, large breasts weren't exactly helpful, and the gravel underfoot didn't make things even slightly better. I'd be on my ass faster than the sexy chick in a zombie movie.

Which, it turned out, was an apt comparison.

More than a dozen of the walking dead burst through the trees all at once, moving faster than their raggedy shamble should have allowed. I recognized some of them: gray-faced and open-mouthed, they were the same bodies I'd found in the giant walk-in freezer in Matheson's basement.

The first lunged for us, and Arkay sent it sprawling with a punch that unhinged its jaw. It gargled and writhed, but it didn't get back up.

"On your left!" I shouted, and she twisted to throw another punch.

The others were getting closer, coming in from all sides. Staying behind Arkay stopped being an option.

I turned to face the nearest one, knocking it down with a stomp to the stomach.

Another figure lingered in the back, barely visible through the trees. She watched us with remorseful eyes, anxiously chewing her lip.

"Danielle!" I rammed another zombie to the floor with my elbow and tried to ignore the sudden flare of pain from my funny bone. "We could use a little help over here!"

She looked to another figure behind the trees, and shook her head frantically. I couldn't hear what she said, but I didn't need to: she was denying she knew us.

"Danielle, please!" I shouted. Another zombie reached for me, but Arkay grabbed it by an arm and swung it into a tree trunk. "You don't have to be a part of this. We can still get you out. But we need—"

Another zombie jumped out from behind me. I moved to kick it away, but I couldn't lift my leg. One of the zombies I'd knocked down caught my foot in its grip.

And it wasn't alone.

The ground at my feet writhed with fallen bodies. Before I could dislodge the first one from my foot, a second hand wrapped around my other leg. A third caught the inside of my knee, and I plunged to the ground with a cry.

"Rosa?" Arkay's voice cut through the horde, but I couldn't see her. The corpses swarmed around me, blocking her from view.

I flailed, but even more hands wrapped around me. They grabbed my arms, my hair, my throat. Jagged nails snagged on my clothes and scraped my skin. Mindless groans filled my ears. I gasped for breath, and the little air I could suck in tasted like antiseptic and rotting meat.

I couldn't move.

"Rosario!" Arkay's voice rose above the moans.

I tried to call out to her, but I couldn't breathe. My lungs burned. My vision swam. I gagged, but nothing got past the vice around my throat.

"Rosario!" she howled. And then she said something that wasn't a word at all, formed by a mouth that wasn't remotely human.

The watery gray of the sky was blotted out by blue scales and white fangs, and one of the zombies was ripped away. Another was hurled back, its broken nails carving through my jacket before it went flying. Another one fell back, its arm caught in an enormous set of jaws and flung away so violently that the arm was ripped from its socket. The swarm dissolved into salsa, and only the beast remained.

It loomed above me, forty feet long and as thick around as an oil drum. Mottled blue scales swept down its serpentine body, from the tip of muzzle to the end of its tufted tail.

Sharpened antlers rose from its skull. Wide gashes ringed both its forelegs, at least an inch wide and just as deep. The dragon bore down on me, and talons the size of tire irons sliced through the decaying flesh mere inches around my body. The arms that had been holding me down fell limp, no longer attached to anything that could give them leverage, and I wheezed for breath, choking on the taste of the sewage and ozone that filled the air.

The dragon turned away from me, but it wasn't finished. It zigzagged between the trees like a bolt of lightning, knocking down the stragglers and ripping them to shreds. Most only moaned, but one scrambled away, tripping on disembodied limbs and spilled entrails in her rush to escape.

The dragon saw, and it pursued. In an instant it was on top of the fleeing woman. It caught her in its long antlers and hurled her through the air.

Danielle's scream cut short when she hit a tree and tumbled to the ground.

Stay down, I thought, dragging myself upright and rushing toward her. *For the love of God, stay down.*

She didn't.

She scrambled backward, clutching one arm to her chest.

"Please," she sobbed. "Please don't— I'm sorry— I'm so sorry—"

The dragon advanced through the trees. It rose to its full height, its mouth open wide to show off gleaming fangs.

"Oh God, no!" She curled into a ball and screamed as the dragon lunged—

—and then stopped short, to avoid crashing headfirst into me. Wicked jaws snapped shut mere inches from my skin.

"Arkay, stop." I sounded like a chain smoker, but at least I got the syllables out in the right order.

The dragon's head was bigger than my torso. It could swallow me whole, but instead it gnashed its teeth and twisted to move around me.

I grabbed it by the antlers and dragged its head back. "I said stop."

It hissed, its enormous brown eyes narrowing into slits.

"Don't you start," I said. "She's begging for her life. Good guys don't go around killing people who beg them to stop. That's a villain thing."

The dragon growled again, but it was a petulant growl: the grumble of a teenager who didn't want to do her homework.

"She's not going to hurt us," I said. "Are you, Danielle?"

"N-no!" the ghoul yelped behind me.

"See? You've made your point. So let her go."

The dragon moved faster than my eyes could follow: one moment it was in front of me, the next it had me wrapped in its coils, its whiskered muzzle tracing up and down my limbs, so close that sparks of static crackled between its flicking tongue and my ruined coat. Its muzzle came to a rest at my left arm. The polyester sleeve hung in crimson tatters around my elbow. Blood dripped down my hand. Long gashes crawled along my arm, interrupted by two deep, jagged crescents.

The dragon huffed a deep breath onto the wound, and I inhaled the sharp tang of ozone.

Everything had happened so fast, I hadn't even noticed the bite.

I laid my other hand on Arkay's nose. "It's— it's fine. I'll be fine." I took another deep breath. "Everything's gonna be okay."

The dragon gazed up at me, its large eyes wide. We'd watched zombie movies together on swindled pay-per-view and stolen cell phones. She knew what a bite meant.

"L-listen, Kay," I said. "It's fine. Really. But if it isn't—"

"It is." She was small and human-looking once more, still wrapped protectively around me. "It will be. We'll get you to a hospital and everything's going to be fine."

"No," I said. "No hospitals. They won't know what they're dealing with, and they won't believe it if we try to tell them. If somebody catches it—"

"If they catch it, they can go to some other hospital," she spat. "You need help, Rosa."

"No." I grabbed her arm and tried to ignore how much my hand trembled. "No. We deal with this here. Just you and me. And if things…" I swallowed. "If things turn ugly, then we deal with that, too. Or I can deal with it. Or…"

"Um…" Danielle mumbled. "Are you two—"

"Keep out of this," Arkay snarled. "I'm not done with you."

"Yes, you are," I said. "Kay, don't you dare take this out on her."

"The hell I will! She's involved with this. She helped them do this to you."

"I don't care," I said. "Don't go all Sith on me, Arkay. You're better than that." I tilted her head back to me so I could look her in the eyes. "And I hope you think I'm better than that, too."

"I just want to make sure you aren't assuming you're going to turn into a zombie or anything," Danielle said in a rush. "Because it doesn't actually work like that."

We both turned to face her. I kept my face carefully blank. Arkay's was a mask of outrage.

Danielle swallowed. "I mean, you should still get that looked at. It's not very sanitary or anything. But those things— they were raised with magic. Necromancy. It isn't contagious."

I exhaled so hard my knees wobbled.

Arkay drew closer to keep me steady. "Do you need to sit?" she asked gently. I shook my head, but she eased me down against the nearest tree regardless. "Take off your coat. Let me take a look at you."

She helped me peel off the heavy coat and the sweatshirt beneath that. Thank God for layers. The zombies had managed to gouge some nasty scratches into my skin, but most were superficial. Arkay yanked off her own coat and wrapped her long-sleeved shirt around my mutilated arm. She didn't have a chance to tie the sleeves into place before the blue cotton soaked through.

"Hey, you," she jerked her head at Danielle, "call an ambulance. We need to get her to a hospital."

"An ambulance?" I asked. "What do you think they're going to do when they see that pile of bodies? We're already wanted by the cops, and people think we killed four people—"

"Thanks for that, by the way." Arkay glared at Danielle.

"What we need to do right now is lay low," I said. "We've got some bandages and disinfectant spray back at home base."

"This isn't something we can fix with Neosporin," she said. "This is just begging for infection."

"Then we'll go to a hospital somewhere else," I said. "Muncie. Cincinnati. Or we go to a clinic or something and pick up antibiotics. But we do it later. Not now, and not here."

"You," Arkay said, pointing at Danielle. "You're coming."

The ghoul stammered. "I— can I just go home?"

"No, you can't," Arkay said. "Because that makes you a witness, and we don't want you ratting us out to your boss. So you can either come with us, or I can go all Titus Andronicus on your ass."

I glared at Arkay, but Danielle just stared from her to me, completely nonplussed.

"It's from Shakespeare," I explained.

Arkay rolled her eyes. "Nobody reads anymore. Geez. You're coming with us, and that's final."

"It's obvious you don't want to be involved in all of this," I said. "If your boss gets cranky, you can tell him you've been captured by a homicidal dragon. Which shouldn't be too hard to believe, since I didn't see any other non-zombies around. It looks like the rest of your crew took off when things got bad."

Danielle's shoulders sagged. "They did."

"Then you're our hostage," I said, not unkindly. "Or prisoner, or whatever. You can make a token resistance if you see any of your guys coming."

"Just like that?" Danielle pointed at Arkay. "She tried to kill me all of ten minutes ago."

"It's nothing personal," I said. "Is it, Arkay?"

"Let's just get you cleaned up, okay?" Arkay muttered. We had to move quickly, and every step sent a painful pulse through my injured arm. Arkay stayed close as we walked, giving me a hand to squeeze when it hurt, and my arm hurt a lot, once the adrenaline started to work its way out of my system. Pain burned in my arm, and it brought to mind uncomfortable thoughts of infection and disease, gangrene and amputation. By the time we reached our mural-covered overpass, I was breathing hard and gritting my teeth.

"You sit," Arkay commanded, easing me down in the brush on the side of the road, just out of sight. "I'll be right down." She turned her eyes to Danielle, and her stare carried the weight of a judge's gavel. "And you. Don't go anywhere." The unspoken 'or else' lingered in the air while Arkay scampered off, leaving the two of us alone.

"So," Danielle said as she watched Arkay climb. "You two. You're... um... close?"

"Yeah," I said carefully.

"Like... 'together' close?"

If she'd asked me the same thing three days ago, I'd have been ecstatic. Now I just felt exhausted. "Is there a reason you're asking?"

"You kept her from ripping me into confetti," Danielle said. "I just figure I should know where everyone stands."

72

Arkay and I were partners. Not 'partner' partners, not exactly, but not exactly not, either. We'd been sleeping together on and off, early on. But then, that was kind of traditional, given the circumstances. The streets were dangerous at the best of times, and exponentially more so for a woman. The best way to stay safe was to pair off with someone who could watch your back and protect you, and a lot of times that was paid for with sex, whether you were actually interested or not. At least Arkay was a woman, even if she wasn't a human one.

When I'd told Arkay about it, she'd been furious. She said taking care of me was her duty. Her responsibility. That I thought she needed to be bribed or persuaded to do that job was the highest form of insult. It had taken more than a week for that fury to fade, and I'd spent most of that time terrified that she'd storm off and leave me entirely.

She never did.

There was still sex sometimes, but it was more casual after that, usually when the stars aligned and I was rebounding while she was going through a dry spell.

But were we *together*?

"It's complicated," I said at last.

"Well, I guess it would be," Danielle said. "Dragon and all."

I raised an eyebrow. "You know a lot of dragons?"

"I've heard rumors," she said. "Usually they stay away from places like this. You hear about them living in the mountains, or in national parks, that sort of thing. I've never heard of a dragon living in the city."

"That doesn't really surprise me," I said. "Your food options are either fish from a polluted river or McDonalds. Not exactly great for a growing lizard."

"You guys know I can hear you, right?" Arkay jumped from the ceiling of the underpass and landed in a crouch, a duffel bag clutched in her arms.

"I know," I said. "And city fish still isn't good for you."

"One time!" she grumbled. "One stupid case of food poisoning, and suddenly it's a big deal. People can learn from their mistakes, you know."

"And you did," I said.

"Damn straight." Arkay unzipped the pack and dug through it.

Danielle blinked in surprise. "You guys have a lot of stuff in there."

"She makes a living beating the crap out of armed strangers," I pointed out. "It pays to be prepared."

Apparently Arkay had found what she needed, because she'd started unwrapping her shirt from around my arm. The fabric stuck to the wounds where the blood had clotted, and the bleeding started again as she peeled it away.

"Okay, this is gonna sting. So just bear with me, okay?" She didn't give me a chance to respond before she doused my arm in hydrogen peroxide. It bubbled and hissed as it came into contact with the blood, dripping from my elbow in pinkish-yellow foam. I gasped in pain, my face scrunching up as I tried not to shout. I used to use peroxide to rescue my favorite clothes from awkward stains, and I remembered watching it froth and foam as it dissolved the blood. Now it felt like it was dissolving my entire arm. Irrationally, I wondered if there'd be anything left below my elbow by the time she was done.

"You're doing great, Rosa," Arkay cooed. "You're doing just fine. Just think of titties. Big, bouncy titties. It'll help take your mind off things."

Behind her, Danielle choked.

Arkay ignored her, dousing a cotton ball in even more peroxide and cleaning the cuts with delicate care. "That's my girl."

"Titties?" I asked through clenched teeth. "Is that seriously how you deal with it?"

"I like other anatomy, too," she said. "But that's not going to help you very much, I think."

"Seriously?"

"Sexy thoughts can be very distracting." She tossed the last soiled cotton ball over her shoulder and retrieved a fresh one, soaking it in ointment and applying it to the wounds. "So can thoughts like 'I'm going to eviscerate the person who did this to me', but that kind of thinking usually just makes the claws come out." Another cotton ball flew over her shoulder. "Besides, that's really not your style."

I'll give credit where it's due: Arkay worked efficiently, and the mortifying conversation we were having in front of a beautiful woman made it easier not to focus on my arm. She layered gauze pads on the wounds, wrapping them in bandages and then sealing it in place with colorful sports tape.

"How's that?" she asked. "As good as yours?"

I ruffled her hair with my uninjured hand. "You've learned well, padawan."

She grinned, but it was a strained grin. "So, have you figured out where we're going from here?"

"Was that my job?" I asked. "I'm the injured one, remember?"

"You're also the one who said we're not going to a hospital," she said. "Which I still think we should do, by the way. And she doesn't get a vote." She jerked her head at Danielle. "So you get to think up an alternative."

I groaned, falling back on the weed-strewn ground. Cold seeped through my jeans.

This Matheson guy had burned our bridges with the homeless community, so there'd be no help from them. We might be able to take a bus out of town, but that was a gamble. If the police thought they still had us in custody, we'd be fine, but if Mike had already called them, or if they'd found the remains of the real Officer Troy, we'd be walking into an ambush.

What we needed was a car.

And I knew where to get one.

"Raimo," I said at last. "We go to him, borrow a car, and get the hell out of Dodge."

"You sure he'll front us?" Arkay asked.

"Doesn't matter," I said. "If he doesn't, we hotwire one off his lot. It's not like he can report us to the police." Unlike any of a million civilians off the street. I didn't like the idea of stealing from Raimo, but at least I could predict his actions.

We kept off the main roads, weaving through yards and ducking through foreclosures, making sure to give Matheson's hideout a wide berth as we made our way to Raimo's. It was slow going. The fight had worn Arkay out, and I felt lightheaded and dizzy, and Raimo's lot wasn't exactly in the middle of downtown. We almost always drove to see him, and he usually dropped us off at our home base when we finished our business there. By the time we reached the barbed wire fence that surrounded his secluded lot, the sun had started to dip close to the horizon and my feet ached almost as much as my arm.

Arkay slowed, tugging at my shoulder to drag me to a halt beside her. "Wait. Something's wrong."

"What is it?" Danielle asked.

"You don't smell it?" Arkay asked.

"Wait," I said. A prickle washed down my spine. "There's no barking. Where's Rufus?"

"Who's Rufus?" Danielle asked. "And what exactly am I supposed to smell?"

Arkay peered through the chain link. "Blood."

No.

Oh God, no.

Without thinking, I wrenched myself out of Arkay's grip and rushed to the back entrance.

Arkay shouted after me, but her words were lost to the roaring in my ears.

The door gaped open. A bullet hole yawned through the remnants of the lock.

"Raimo!" I shouted. "Raimo, are you okay?"

My feet splashed on the linoleum floor of the back office. It was wet. Slippery. The air smelled like metal and raw sewage.

"Dammit, Rosa!" Arkay's hiss sounded like it came through radio static. "What the hell do you think you're doing?"

I didn't answer. I couldn't.

"Whoever broke in could still be here," she continued. "At least you could've let me go in first."

Something touched me. Arkay, maybe. It occurred to me that I should look, but everything not directly in front of me had faded into pale gray.

"Rosa?" A note of alarm seeped into her voice. "Rosa, are you alright?"

"The— the light," I stammered, sliding backward and fumbling behind me without turning around. "I need to—" My hands found the switch. I barely blinked as the light gave detail and color to the ruin before me.

Blood pooled on the floor and splattered the walls. A body— mangled, mutilated, but unmistakably huge and blond— lay stretched across the desk, its chest ripped open and hollowed of organs, its mouth and eyes wide with horror.

He'd died in agony.

He'd died screaming.

And everywhere, everywhere, sliced into his face, his arms, his shoulders— on every exposed inch of skin— smeared on the sides of the desk and scrawled on the walls— dripping from the ceiling: RK.

Our tag.

Our mark.

Our fault.

"Arkay." I couldn't tell if I was saying her name or reading the accusation off the walls. My voice came out like a dry wind. "Arkay. He's dead."

"I know. I'm sorry, Rosa." An arm wrapped around my waist and gave it a squeeze that should have been comforting. Instead, it dislodged that last inch of control I had over my stomach. I dropped to my knees and vomited up acid and bile. Blood soaked into my hands and knees, but I stopped caring. There was no escaping it here.

"You," Arkay said somewhere over me. "Did you know about this?"

A dull thud made me look up in a panic. Another body? Was somebody else dead?

Arkay had Danielle pinned to the wall, but they were both alive. Still whole.

Danielle looked at me, her mouth opening and shutting soundlessly. "I'm sorry," she said at last. "I didn't know this would happen."

"He was a friend," Arkay said quietly. Cold, but without menace. "He wasn't involved in any of this. There was no reason to do this to him."

"His name was in the case file we took from the precinct," Danielle said. "His fingerprints were on some of the evidence. The police were already investigating him."

It was getting hard to process the words. The smell was everywhere. I was drowning in it. Smothered by it. The world was going blurry, but I could still see Arkay pulling away from Danielle.

"Hey." My dragon was suddenly at my side, and I jumped. She flattened herself against me, one arm wrapped around my shoulders, the other around my waist, and eased me back to my feet. "No more of that. We're gonna grab a car and get the hell out of here. And then we're gonna get you to some help. And then we're gonna figure out what to do about all this."

It sounded nice. Easy.

This was how we did things: I handled the mundane human stuff, and she dealt with the freaky panic-inducing horror. We were going to be okay. She would take care of me.

We had to be okay.

"Delia, help me get her out of here," she said.

"It's Danielle."

"It's gonna be going bovine in a prison cell if you don't help me get her out of here before the cops show up. And it's gonna be extra crispy if you even think about leaving us here."

A second pair of arms helped pull me upright. Arkay's diminutive form nestled under my injured arm, and Danielle settled under the other.

Normally, I'd be protesting right about now that I was too heavy, that I'd squish Danielle if they weren't careful. It was an old habit, deeply ingrained and tough to break even after Arkay had become the exception. But I couldn't say a word.

My voice lodged in my throat, even when I saw a shadow cross the door and the barrel of a gun rise to meet us.

"Police," came a snapping voice. A familiar voice. Detective Sharp. "Get on the floor and put your hands on your head."

Arkay ducked closer to me, her body curling into mine, all hard angles and bared teeth.

"I said get on the floor," Sharp repeated.

"I heard you the first time, Detective." Arkay's voice hardened into a steel edge as she peeled herself off my side. I tried to hold her back, but my arms felt as limp as the lettuce you find in a dumpster. She broke out of my grip with ease and stepped in front of me, throwing her hands in the air with a grand gesture. "See? Just like you said."

Oh yes. Taunt the freaked-out cop all alone right outside a crime scene. That couldn't possibly go wrong.

"Kay, don't," I said.

Sharp raised her gun at Arkay's head. "Stay right where you are."

"A bit of an overreaction, don't you think?" Arkay asked with that low, languid tone that she used on designated victims. "I'm not doing anything. Just standing here. Go right ahead and cuff me, Detect…" Her head snapped to the side, her nose in the air. A slight wind fluttered through the door and disturbed my hair. "Rosa, get down."

"Don't move," Sharp repeated, and Arkay's lips peeled back into a growl.

"You can stay put for all I care. Danielle, get Rosa behind cover."

"What is it?" Danielle asked. "Arkay, what do you… Oh God."

Even I could smell it now, so potent that it overwhelmed even the reek of fresh gore: antiseptic and decay and rotting meat.

Sharp's face twisted into revulsion as it hit her nose, but she didn't understand what it meant.

More zombies.

"Okay," I said quickly, staggering forward. "Arrest us already. Just take us to your squad car and do it there."

Sharp's eyes narrowed in confusion.

"Something's coming," I told her, offering my hands for her cuffs. "I don't want to be here when they get here, and neither do you. So please, let's just skip the catfight and go before we—"

"Don't move!" Sharp shouted, suddenly training her handgun away from us. "Sir, get back down. I can have paramedics here in a few minutes."

Paramedics...?

Everything inside me told me to stay put, but I turned slowly to follow the detective's horrified stare.

Raimo pushed himself up off the desk. His arms strained to raise his upper torso, unsupported by the shredded flaps of muscle that had once been his abs.

"You!" Danielle commanded. "Stop. Don't come any closer. I said stop!" The corpse slid off the desk and tottered toward us. Danielle backed closer to me and Arkay. "Sorry. Worth a shot."

"Sir, you're in shock," Sharp said.

"For the love of fuck," Arkay snapped. "You can see his spine from here. Could you please paddle your ass out of denial for a second and shoot him already?" She pulled me closer. "Here's a hint: headshots work on zombies."

Sharp shook her head, but her hand remained steady on the gun. "No. No way. This is impossible."

"For the love of—"

Raimo's corpse staggered closer, extending one hand to reach for us. His eyes were draining of color. Air whistled through a mouth that hung open, still fixed in its dying scream.

Arkay moved to meet it, but she didn't get a chance.

Three gunshots rang out, deafening in the small office, and the corpse fell to the ground. Three new holes bloomed on his forehead and burst out the back of his skull.

"About damn time," Arkay growled, repositioning herself under my arm. "C'mon, Rosa. Let's get out of here before— shit!"

I caught a glimpse of more shapes swaying outside the door before Arkay slammed it shut. She pulled away from me and grabbed a filing cabinet off the wall, dragging it in front of the broken lock. When she released it, her fingers left indentations in the metal.

"We're trapped," Danielle breathed.

"No, we're not," I said. My voice shook, but adrenaline was forcing me out of my shock. I pulled myself out of Arkay's grip and staggered toward the pegboard on the wall, grabbing as many keys off the hooks as my trembling hands could hold. "Sa-same plan. We go to the front, find a car that works, and get the hell out of here."

"Works for me," Arkay said, crossing the office to open the door that led to the garage— and slammed it shut just as fast. "Fuck. Never mind."

"What?"

"Garage door's open. They're everywhere." A dull crash shook the door behind her.

Sharp shook her head. "I'm calling for backup."

The filing cabinet shuddered as fists banged on the back door.

"Do you think they can get here before the doors give out?" I asked.

"If we can keep holding them—"

A gunshot split the air, and the door's lock erupted into a burst of splinters. The door burst open, swarming with bodies on the other side. Arkay gave a shout, throwing herself against the door to wedge it shut.

"Arkay, get away from there!" I shouted.

"Kinda busy here!"

There was someone with a gun on the other side, and if they shot again— oh God, if they shot again—

"Get the desk," I called to the others, and Danielle and Sharp rushed to help me drag the gore-covered surface in front of the door.

Another crack of gunfire, and a second hole appeared in the door.

"How long before backup arrives?" Arkay asked.

I could read the answer on Sharp's face: too long.

"We can lock ourselves into the bathroom," I said. "It might buy us a little more time."

But not enough. And then we'd be backed into a corner.

Arkay caught my eye.

"No," I said. "Don't you dare."

"It might work," she said. "Our biggest problem is the person with the gun. I take them out, we can handle the rest."

"Assuming you don't get shot first," I said.

She batted away my argument like a mosquito. "It'll be a flesh wound, at worst. I'm one of the good guys, remember? I'm practically bulletproof." Her grin didn't quite reach her eyes. "Barricade the door as soon as I'm through, and then get into the bathroom. Okay?"

"Arkay, wait!" I started. "Don't—"

She didn't give me a chance to refuse. She grabbed the desk and shoved one corner aside. The door clattered open, pressed against the desk by a wall of grasping limbs. She was already on top of the desk, grabbing the nearest zombie by the head and using it to vault over the others.

"Shut the door!" Sharp threw her weight against the barricade, and Danielle joined her an instant later.

For a moment the swarm of bodies wedged the door open, but a series of crashes rattled on the other side and the door slammed shut with only minor resistance.

I stared at the wall that separated us from the zombie horde outside. I wanted x-ray vision so I could see what was going on out there, but all I could do was hear.

More gunshots.

Wet squelches.

Hollow thuds as bodies hit the concrete floor.

Sharp grabbed me by the shoulder. "Come on," she said. "We need to get to cover."

I shook my head and pulled out of her grip. "How many more bullets do you have left in your gun?"

"I'll make them count," she said. "But they're gonna go a lot farther if we're not trying to defend from two sides. Now let's go."

She moved to grab me again, and I stepped back. "How many?"

"Nine, and another couple of magazines if I need them," she said. "Now let's go."

"Can you show me how to reload?" I asked.

"You're not touching my firearm," she said. "Now get into the bathroom by yourself, or I'm going to put you in there by force. This is not a game."

"No, it's not." I backed up further. "Arkay's out there by herself. She's going to need help, and I really don't want to try fighting off a bunch of zombies with a monkey wrench."

"No, you're staying put. Help is on the way."

"I know," I said. "And when they arrive, you'll have God knows how many cops here, shooting down zombies, and Arkay won't be able to tell them apart from the person she went out there to kill."

Uncertainty broke into Sharp's expression, but she quickly schooled her face back into a look of command. "And if we go out there packing heat, what makes you think she'll see us any differently?"

"Not us," I said. "Just me. No matter what happens, she won't hurt me. She knows I've got her back."

A few minutes later I burst through the door, and Sharp and Danielle slammed it shut behind me. They needn't have bothered: the zombies swarmed at the mouth of the garage, surrounding a spiral of scales and teeth. The dragon spat flashes of lightning into the crowd, and each crack lit up the garage like a strobe light, igniting oil stains on the floor. Sickly sweet smoke joined the reek of ozone and rotting flesh, and I struggled not to retch.

The dragon was huge, but there were dozens of zombies, clinging to its body and dragging it down. One was tangled in its antlers, and the weight dragged at its head. No wonder the dragon wasn't getting anywhere with all that lightning: it could barely stay upright, let alone aim.

I grabbed the nearest zombie and jammed the barrel of the gun under its jaw.

It was a woman. Her pale skin had gone gray, her blond hair was tangled, and her eyes had faded into blank white.

She was already dead.

I pulled the trigger, and she crumpled at my feet, the inside of her head painting the wall and ceiling behind me. My stomach wanted to crawl out my throat, but I had bigger problems: the dragon had twisted around to follow the sound of the gunshot.

"If you could hold off on the lightning, that would be great," I said, grabbing another zombie off her foreleg and putting a bullet through his— its— head.

The dragon grunted, but grabbed another corpse between its teeth and snapped it in half.

"Don't you start," I said. "I never agreed to hide in the bathroom." I tried to keep my tone light. Cheerful. Like I wasn't desecrating the remains of innocent human beings. If I let myself think too deeply about what I was doing, I would wind up in a fetal position in the corner. "So which pile of squishy bits was the shooter?"

I don't know if Arkay even heard the end of that sentence.

Tires squealed. The zombies parted like a wave, giving just enough room for a flatbed truck to ram into us. The impact threw me to the ground, but it was the dragon that took most of the damage. It slammed into the wall of the garage so hard that it collapsed, taking part of the ceiling with it. I threw myself under a workbench, curling into a ball as bricks and concrete rained down around us.

For nearly a minute, there was chaos: the snarl of a mangled engine, the crash of falling debris, the moans of crushed zombies, the high twinkle of shattering glass, the clang of bricks hitting metal.

And then silence.

Dust hung thick in the air as I crawled out of my shelter. "Kay?" I croaked. "Arkay?"

The dragon lay in a heap at the mouth of the garage, wrapped around the crumpled engine block and half-buried in rubble. The blood that splattered the hood of the car was thick and sludgy with dirt. The dragon didn't move.

My knees buckled.

She wasn't gone.

She couldn't be. Not like that.

The truck's front airbag deflated abruptly, and the driver's side door creaked open.

Matheson staggered out and stared at the wreckage. In his hand, golden metal caught the light of the dying sun: a massive dagger, etched with runes.

"Dragon," he said to himself. "An actual dragon. Ha!" The laugh was cut short by a coughing fit as he inhaled a lungful of brick dust. He doubled over, hacking and wheezing, before he finally forced himself upright. He limped to Arkay's head and nudged it with one foot. "Look at you. Look at you. Small. Juvenile?" He grabbed her muzzle and pulled the edges of her mouth back from her gums. "Not with those teeth. What do you think?" he called over his shoulder. "Pygmy dragon?"

A pair of ghouls crept into sight, sticking close to the ruined walls. They stared at Arkay's body with wide eyes. They looked frightened. Sad.

Matheson let go of Arkay's mouth. "Still too big, though. No way could I fit this in a car. Not in one piece."

He snapped his fingers. "You. Get a tarp. And you, find me something that can—" His face bloomed into a look of delighted surprise. "Oh! That'll do."

One of the zombies shuddered upright and shuffled to the array of power tools at the back of the garage. When it returned, it was dragging Raimo's brand new hydraulic cutters.

Matheson hefted it in his hands and studied it intently. He flipped a switch, and it filled the air with a roar like a chainsaw. Six-inch blades gnashed shut and slowly opened again.

He turned back to Arkay and patted her like she was some kind of dog. "Let's make you travel size."

I don't remember pulling the gun or climbing to my feet. One moment I was prone on the ground, the next I stood at the edge of the pile of rubble, the gun in my hand, my finger on the trigger. "Get. The fuck. Away from her."

"Or you're going to shoot me?" Matheson laughed. He hadn't even looked surprised to see me. "Don't you know who I am, little girl?" The air filled with shuffles and groans as half a dozen zombies climbed to their feet. "I have conquered death."

"Then you can go ahead and conquer the hole I'm about to put in your head," I said. "Back off or I shoot."

"Will you? Really?" He laughed and spread his arms, presenting himself to me. "Go right ahead."

I hesitated.

He started moving forward, slow and theatrical. "Having trouble deciding? The heart is a classic, isn't it? So poetic. But remarkably difficult to hit accurately, what with all those ribs.

The head makes for a much more reliable target. Care to give it a try, little girl?" He was standing right in front of me. "Care to look me in the eyes?" He grabbed the barrel of the gun and pulled it to his face.

I jerked back with a yelp and yanked it away. My palms were slick with sweat. My fingers bent to avoid the trigger. It only took a moment's fumbling, and the gun fell to the ground more than a foot away.

He laughed again. "Of course not. You have a big mouth, but you don't have the guts to kill a man." His grin was wide and sickle-sharp. "I bet you think this is all a game. One of your cartoons or your comic books or your movies, where bad guys wear black and good guys never spill a drop of blood and everybody lives happily ever after. But the world doesn't work that way."

He was right.

Shooting zombies was one thing, but I'd never killed anyone. I didn't think I could. Not even a man like him.

But he was right about other things, too: the world doesn't work like it does in movies.

Because in real life, people don't have to sit still during the villain's monologue.

I grabbed Matheson by the shoulders and smashed my head into his, driving my knee into his groin. He went down, but his fingers dug into my shoulders and brought me down with him.

I threw my whole weight into pinning him, grinding his face into the concrete with one hand while I grabbed the cutters away from him with the other.

He grabbed me by the hair and yanked my head back. I jolted, and he took the opportunity to punch me in the eye.

The world blazed white and I fell back, and suddenly he was on top of me.

And he'd drawn his knife.

He started chanting— something low and guttural, in a language I'd never heard before. My eyes ached. My ears hurt. It was getting hard to focus.

He made a shape in the air with his knife, and the last flecks of sunlight glinted off the blade. That bright reflection seemed to linger overhead even after the knife had moved on.

I reached up to stop him, but my hands felt like they'd been weighed down with bricks. I couldn't move. I couldn't think.

Something roared in my ears, a grinding, awful sound. Matheson pulled away, turning to look with an expression of horror.

The spell shattered.

A pair of powerful jaws closed around Matheson's chest and yanked him off me. An enormous muzzle clamped tight around him and shook, thrashing him from side to side like a dog shredding a chew toy. Razor teeth carved through flesh and bone. Blood splashed my face. An arm fell one way, a head fell the other. The legs and lower torso hit the ground just inches away from where I lay, the pieces connected by a few broken tatters of flesh.

A dozen animated corpses collapsed. Only the ghouls remained standing, alone and obvious without the zombies to keep them hidden.

For a moment they remained frozen, blinking in shock at the panting dragon.

And then one of them turned to flee.

The dragon lunged after her, roaring and enraged. The mound of bricks crumbled as it struggled to dislodge itself.

The other ghouls scattered, running and screaming, each one a new target.

"No," I coughed, crawling to my hands and knees. "Arkay, please—"

A hand settled on my shoulder. "Don't make a sound," Sharp said.

I looked up. She stood over me, gray-faced and shaking. The office door hung open behind her. The discarded gun was steady in her hand. She raised it. Tightened her grip.

"Wait, no!"

The dragon whipped around. Sharp froze like a stray cat in the headlights of an oncoming car. But the dragon wasn't looking at her.

It was looking at me.

Its eyes were flat. Animal. Soulless. Its jaws hung wide, dripping gore, its lips pulled back to show its teeth. There was no softness there, no recognition: just a mindless beast that had been brutalized and forced into a corner.

I raised my hands, palms out and empty, still on my knees. "It's alright, Arkay. He's gone. The zombies are gone. We're safe now."

I tried to rise to my feet, and the dragon growled so loud that I had to look back to make sure the cutters hadn't turned back on.

Slowly I forced my gaze back. "You're scared, Arkay. I get it. You're scared and you're hurt. But I'm here now. We can get you to a hospital. Everything's going to be okay."

"Dammit, Hernandez, that thing's going to kill you," Sharp muttered, and the dragon snarled at her.

"Hey!" I shouted, and its attention returned to me. "Hey. It's okay. Don't worry about her, Arkay. She's just worried. She doesn't mean anything by it." I took a step forward, and the dragon advanced, a massive knot of muscle and scales, as much crimson as blue.

A splinter of bone was wedged between two of its teeth, digging into the gums. I recognized the curved end of a rib.

"Looks like you've got something there." I reached out one hand toward jaws that could rip off my arm.

"Oh my god—" Sharp started. "Don't you dare—"

"Look at me, Kay!" I said, before the dragon could turn its attention back to her. I was another step closer, my hand so close to those fangs that I could smell ozone and iron. Static made the hairs of my arm stand on end. "Look at me. I'm right here."

I reached into that mouth and seized the shard of human bone. The dragon twitched as I gave it a tug, the jaws threatening to snap shut around my elbow. Then the bone came free. I pulled my hand out just as slowly as I'd put it in, and held it out for the dragon to examine. Massive eyes almost crossed as it struggled to focus on the shape in my hand. "See? It can't hurt you anymore. Everything's fine. You're safe now." I dropped the scrap of bone and laid one hand on either side of that enormous muzzle, rubbing gently back and forth. "You're safe, Arkay."

Clarity returned to those eyes, and before I could register, the dragon was gone, and a human figure stood in its place. Her face was pale in my hands, her eyes glazed and unfocused. She looked like she might have collapsed if I wasn't holding her upright.

"Come here, Kay," I said gently, gathering her into my arms. She flinched, but didn't fight as her head fell against my shoulder.

I looked around. Danielle clung to the frame of the office door. Two of the other ghouls had stayed behind, watching us in stunned silence.

I raised my voice. "Please tell me one of you still has a working car."

One of the ghouls nodded shakily.

"Then go get it. The police are on their way."

Detective Sharp stepped back in front of me. "You don't seriously think you're walking away from this."

Arkay tensed in my arms.

"Yes, I am." I scooped up my dragon, ignoring the pain in my arm. "And you aren't going to stop me."

Sharp looked me in the eyes. She still had a loaded gun in her hands. I held her stare.

A blue four-door sedan rolled up to the entrance of the garage, a nervous looking ghoul fidgeting behind the steering wheel. A second sat in the back. Danielle stepped past me to open the passenger door.

Unblinking, I turned away from the detective and climbed inside, Arkay cradled in my lap.

Detective Sharp made no move to stop us as we pulled onto the road.

I couldn't make much sense of what happened after that point. Shock and exhaustion had finally caught up with me, and my awareness shuttered and skipped like a scratched DVD.

The moon hung high overhead when the car finally pulled to a stop before a two-story house, tucked into the fringes of a college town an hour north of Indy.

Danielle and the other ghouls helped me and Arkay out of the car and into the house. I'm not sure how many times Danielle explained it to me before I grasped that this was her home.

Snow was falling thick outside the window when I woke up. I stared, hazy, certain I had to be dreaming. I couldn't remember the last time I'd woken up to snow and been warm. It was nice, like something out of a movie.

I was wrapped in a thick quilt, with Arkay nestled against my side. She was clean and dressed in unfamiliar clothes, with fresh bandages around her wrists; apparently I'd received similar treatment.

It was nearly two in the afternoon, according to the digital clock that perched on the bedside table. I carefully extracted myself from Arkay's hold, wincing as my back shifted positions. It was still bruised and sore from that tumble down the stairs, but my biological needs were more pressing.

I opened the bedroom door as silently as I could and crept down the hallway, looking for a bathroom. The house was warm and smelled of vanilla and cinnamon, but I still felt wary. On edge.

A rumbling buzz nearly made me wet myself. It took me a moment to realize that it was a vibrating cell phone, and not the sound of hydraulic cutters in the distance. At least, I didn't think so.

I shuddered, and forced myself to follow the sound. I had to be sure.

I found the offending phone on a kitchen table beside two others. Danielle sat at the table, along with the two other ghouls from the garage. All three of them stared nervously at the ringing phone.

"Aren't you going to answer it?" My voice scratched out from the inside of my throat.

Danielle looked up at me, and soon two more gazes followed hers. They watched me carefully. Expectantly.

"Who is it?" I croaked, moving down the stairs. "Do you know?"

"That detective from…" Danielle trailed off.

It hurt when I swallowed. "You gave her your number?"

"It's not my phone," Danielle said quietly. "That was— that belonged to the… the woman. I took it with her uniform."

Officer Troy.

"And those other two?" I asked. "Are they from the same place?"

Danielle nodded. "She's been calling all three phones. One after another. It's been happening for maybe an hour now."

To hell with that.

I crossed to the table as quickly as my aching legs could carry me and snatched the ringing phone off the table, swiping the screen to answer.

There was a long silence on the other side. Finally: "Didn't drop the call. You're not the answering machine, either."

"No," I said.

Detective Sharp made a derisive sound. "And here I thought you'd have dumped the phones by now."

"If you really thought that, you wouldn't keep calling," I said. "But thanks for the idea. We'll make sure to do that. Bye."

Before I could pull the phone from my ear, she snapped, "Wait!"

I paused. "What?"

"I want to know how you did it."

"Did what?"

"How did you hack into our servers?" she demanded. "We had redundancies in the system. All the paper files, all the data— it's all gone. What the hell did you do?"

"I didn't do anything," I said.

"You know this doesn't change anything," she said. "Three cops are dead. You're hiding out with their killers. You can't just walk away from this."

"The man who killed your officers is in pieces in that garage. Or the morgue. Or wherever you put dead people." I frowned. Something didn't add up. Or maybe it did, but not to the right conclusion. "Is there a reason you're calling this number over and over again instead of, I don't know, tracing the phone? Seems kind of low budget, don't you think?"

"Don't worry, the local authorities are on their way." There was an edge to her voice. I knew it all too well.

"I'm sure they are," I said quietly. "A word of advice from the crazy homeless lady: the next time you see a dragon and a bunch of zombies, you might want to try keeping it to yourself."

"Fuck you."

"You have a nice day, too," I said. "Let me know when they give you back your badge."

I ended the call, and methodically disassembled the phone, tossing the battery and SIM card onto the table before I did the same to the next, and the next.

Footsteps creaked closer. When I looked up, Arkay was standing on staircase, peeking out from within the folds of her borrowed clothes.

"So what was that all about?" she asked.

"Don't worry about it," I said with a small, grim smile. "I think, for now, we're safe."

Book 2:

Shadow and Steel

Rosario

The stuffy quiet of the Goodwill was split by an unholy shriek.

Maybe it was because we were in a broke college town, because this was a Goodwill, or because the entire local population was just *that* exhausted from finals and jobs and life in general, but nobody seemed to care.

Seconds later, Arkay came sprinting between two rows of plus-sized jeans and skidded to a stop at my feet. She was a tiny thing— five-foot-something when she stood still long enough to be measured, maybe another inch when her short black hair was up in spikes— and I was a *bona fide* Amazonian

Amazon, but she would knock me down like a bowling pin if she came at me at top speed.

"Rosa! Holy crap, Rosa, you have to see this!" she squealed, grabbing my hand and dragging me to the back of the store, leaving my shopping cart abandoned in the aisle. "Rosa, I want it!"

"Wait, what?" I asked. This was less of a furniture section than it was a Tetris-style arrangement of sofas, ottomans and chairs in various states of repair. "Which 'it' are we talking about here, Kay?"

"Look at it!" She swan-dived into the ugliest armchair I had ever seen—a huge, plushy, overstuffed monstrosity, with upholstery such an alarming shade of pink that I was pretty sure it would glow in the dark. "Rosa, look! It's so big and pretty and bright. I want it."

I shut my eyes. If I stared at the thing any longer, the image would be burned into my retinas. "Yes, it's definitely… bright."

She sprawled across the armrests. "Isn't it gorgeous? And look! It's on sale! Can I have it? Please?"

"I… I don't know," I said. "It's kind of…" *Loud* was the word I was looking for. "Big. I don't know if it would fit in Danielle's car." And more than that, I didn't feel too great about asking Danielle for yet another favor. She'd helped us skip town a few months back, helped me get a job at a local diner, and let us stay at her house in Muncie until we could afford a place of our own. Asking her to help us transport new furniture into said place now that we got it… well, that felt like pushing it.

Danielle was a nice person, really, and she claimed she didn't mind helping us out. But it still felt too much like extortion to keep asking. Sure, I wasn't forcing her to commit multiple homicides, like the last guy who found out her secret, but imposing on her still made me feel like scum.

"We don't have to use Danielle's car," Arkay said. "We can ask Kindra to help. She has a truck, right?"

"Oh God." I covered my face with my hands. "We are not asking my coworker to help us move furniture."

"Come on. You've been wanting an excuse to get to know her better. She can help us bring this home, and you can pay her back with dinner. Or more than dinner."

I swatted at her arm. "Stop."

I wasn't even looking for a girlfriend right now. We'd only just gotten our lives back on track. Priorities and all that.

"C'mon, Rosa," Arkay whined. "How can you see something this perfect and let it pass you by?"

Because the last time I let myself get sucked in by something bizarre and confusing, I wound up with a dragon.

"Tell you what," I said. "We'll ask them to hold it for us. I'll talk to Kindra at work and see what I can do."

"Sweet!" Without further warning, Arkay launched herself off the mutant monstrosity that was the armchair and threw her arms around me.

I caught her easily—dragon or not, she weighed next to nothing when she wasn't all big and scaly—and lurching back to the clothing department. "Hey, I'm not making any promises here. I'm only going to see if she'll help. Got it?"

She snuggled into my shoulder in reply. And God bless thrift shops in college towns, nobody even gave us a sideways glance.

Arkay

The chair was a good find. Beyond the fact that it was absolutely glorious and loud and perfect—the prospect of actually having it was the first thing I'd actually looked forward to since we'd left Indianapolis.

Okay, so I didn't mind having a shower and a bed and climate control whenever we wanted it—the lack thereof had always been the worst part of living on the streets. But I'd lived my whole life without those things, and it had never bothered me all that much.

Honestly, I had a hard time seeing the appeal of settling down. Sure, the new house had enough space to put awesome new furniture in, but at what cost? I'm not even talking about the rent and utilities and myriad other expenses that meant Rosa had to be away at work all the time.

Every time we stayed in one place more than a few days, we got shackled with *rules*. In the Valley at least, there was stuff like 'keep quiet after midnight' and 'play nice with others' where I could argue it out half the time. At the shelters it was stuff like 'lights out at ten' and 'don't flirt with other women' and 'don't remove anyone's fingers when they try to grope you', and every single stipulation came iron-clad with a zero-tolerance policy. At Danielle's it got even more arbitrary, with minutia about the refrigerator and the bathroom and leaving windows open at night.

No matter where you went, the consequences were always the same: if you broke the rules, you were back out on your ass. That was just fine with me. I'd rather have my freedom and forego the place to store my stuff—and if it was just me, I probably would have up and left a long time ago. But it wasn't just about me. Rosa wanted stability and consistency and central heating, and she was willing to trade long hours serving drinks to ungrateful assholes in order to get it. If it was that important to her, then I'd learn to cope.

I wound up getting a job that I could actually stand— partly to give us a second source of income, and partly to give me something to do while she was away. I threw myself into the décor, and really tried to appreciate the not-broken windows and the solid door that looked like it had only been kicked in twice. And it was… nice. But it felt less like settling down than it did like *settling*.

But it was for Rosa. I would settle for Rosa.

Rosario

We'd picked a good time to go on a supply run. The last spring showers left over from April had rained themselves out a week ago. The earth had hardened into solid ground, instead of the squelching mud that sucked at our feet while we walked. Not that I minded mud all that much—especially now that I had a clean shower to look forward to afterward—but I didn't like the idea of slipping and tripping while weighted down with shopping bags full of paper-wrapped plates. Arkay would take them to our new house after she dropped me off.

Arkay walked me to work every day, and she walked me home every night. She was friendly enough with my coworkers these days, but for the first few weeks she'd been nothing but raised hackles and stormy glares, especially at the customers who tried getting a little too friendly with me. The incidents had left me mortified, but I didn't ask her to stop. I felt safe with Arkay around to protect me, and I needed that more here than I had in Indianapolis. It wasn't just that the bar I worked at was south of the river and in a patently shady part of town. It was the quiet around here. The houses were all too far apart, and the roads seemed to wind on forever before they hit an intersection, and between it all were buildings in various shades of dereliction. Anything could sneak up on you, and you'd never know until it was too late. I'd once seen the living dead crawl out of buildings like these. Endless crowds of corpses, hidden in a giant walk-in refrigerator until they woke up, and then they had swarmed, and—

"Rosa. *Rosa*. Rosa, you still with me?"

"Yeah, I'm here." I blinked away the gray static from the edges of my vision. "Thanks."

"If you're not feeling up to working today, we can always head home. We'll tell them you're sick."

"That won't be necessary."

"You did say you've got some sick days saved up."

"It's alright, Arkay."

"You don't even have to go inside to talk to Kindra. She's right there."

"What?" I looked more closely at the approaching building.

One of the other waitresses sat on the edge of the uneven sidewalk taking her pre-lunch smoke break, probably a bit closer to the back door than the regulation eight feet, and she waved us over. As we approached, my heart stopped pounding with the remnants of anxiety, and started racing for other reasons entirely.

Her name was Kindra Douglas, and she was pretty in a way my teenage self would never have been brave enough to admit: bold, heavy makeup; braided ropes of bleached blond hair that contrasted strikingly against her dark skin; and more piercings than I had fingers.

"Hey you two," she said. "Get some good shopping done?"

She quirked her sharp black eyebrow, and the captive ring looped around it glittered in the light. That's the only reason I stared so long at her eyes. Promise.

Arkay covered for me with a dramatic sigh. "Ugh. Yes. Seriously, how much stuff does a house actually need to have? This is like the third shopping trip in a week."

"And tomorrow you're gonna be sittin' on the john and remember something else you need." Kindra gave a sage nod and rolled her cigarette between her fingers. "You alright carrying all that?"

"I'm fine with this stuff." Arkay's face lit up like someone had flipped a switch. "But if you're offering, we saw this really amazing chair—"

"You know what, I should probably go ahead and clock in," I said quickly, handing Arkay my set of shopping bags. "How about you go home?"

"Actually, you might want to hold up a sec." Kindra climbed to her feet. "A guy came by earlier. Says he knows you."

"Really? Huh." I tried to look nonchalant, but Arkay stiffened. All the pixie-stick giddiness vanished, and now every inch of her frame coiled with tension.

"He's still in there," Kindra said. "Dan got to him before I did, told him you had a shift later today. Which is why Dan's gonna be rolling your silverware tonight, so don't let him get out of that." She leaned in slightly, her big brown eyes wide and sincere. "Rosa, if you need any help with this guy, you say the word, okay?"

"Thanks," I said, and I meant it. "But let me take a look at this guy before you two start searching for places to dump the body."

Kindra flashed an encouraging smile. "Who says I need to look?"

I tried to look confident as I stepped in the front door, but I could feel half the staff watching me.

When I first applied for this job, I'd been trying to hide some nasty bruises, and my hands were covered in the long, thin scars of dozens of scratching fingernails. People asked, of course, but I kept my mouth shut, and enough stormy glares from Arkay convinced them not to push it. Almost six months later, they still didn't know where I'd come from, only that Arkay and I left in a hurry.

I'd heard some theories. My manager thought I was on the run from an evil ex. Dan, the bartender, put his money on a drug problem gone bad. The dishwasher swore up and down that I was in Witness Protection, and Arkay was my FBI-assigned bodyguard.

So far, nobody guessed we'd skipped town after a fight with a necromancer and his zombie horde. Mostly because none of my coworkers were actively delusional. It wasn't exactly common knowledge that necromancers, ghouls, and dragons existed outside of D&D and Syfy miniseries. According to Danielle, most non-humans went out of their way to keep hidden, and they covered their tracks at the first sign of being discovered—and even when something did slip, most people just took it for a hoax. I'd only ever found out about Arkay by accident, and telling people about her got me branded as delusional, with heaping sides of stigma and isolation.

I wasn't going back to that again. Not if I could help it. Which is why I needed my visitor taken care of fast.

A slender black man sat in the corner booth, nursing a cup of coffee. Fresh streaks of gray colored the dreadlocks that fell like a mane around his narrow shoulders. He made an obvious effort to keep his back straight and his head up, but there was no hiding the new creases lining his face or the exhaustion ringing his eyes. His name was Mike Jones, and he was the mayor of the homeless camp where I used to live.

"Hey, Mike," I said, sitting down across from him.

"Rosario. Hey." He fidgeted with his mug. Mike Jones didn't fidget. "Susan's in town—says she saw you working here—and I wanted to say hi. How are you doing? I haven't seen you in a while."

He wanted to say hi? An hour's drive away from his home turf, and God only knew how long by bus? How much had that ride cost him? More than he had lying around, I knew that much.

"I'm fine. Living here now." I floundered in the awkwardness. What was I supposed to say? "Just signed a lease on a house."

"That's good," he said. "Real good. I'm glad to hear it. You… you look good."

"Wish I could say the same," I said. "Mike, are you okay?"

He rubbed one hand across the back of his neck. "No. I can't say I am. Rosa, do you have a minute to talk?"

Four strained shopping bags hit the table with a sharp clatter. Apparently Arkay had decided to accompany me in the talk. "You're kidding, right?"

And eavesdrop.

Mike's gaze remained steady on me. "No, I am not."

"That's hilarious." Arkay slid into the booth beside me, wedging tight against my side. "Because last time I saw you, you were kicking us out into the cold. We really could've used *a minute to talk* back then."

The fact that we'd gotten attacked by an honest-to-God zombie swarm less than an hour later didn't help her opinion of him.

"I'm real sorry about that," Mike said. "I wish there was a way to take it back. Really, I do. But I didn't have any choice. It's my job to take care of the camp. The whole camp. And if someone's endangering the others—"

Arkay threw her head back in a laugh, but it sounded more like a snarl. "You sure picked a convenient time to start being picky about that. I could give you a list a mile long of people you've let in and out without a problem— people you've *seen* pulling shit. But god forbid there's a *rumor*—"

"Kay, stop it," I said quietly.

"Why are you even giving him the time of day?"

"There's no harm in hearing him out," I said, and then angled my body toward Mike. "So what's up?"

He wrapped his hands around the mug. "I know how the two of you feel about me and the Valley—"

"Oh good," Arkay said. "And here I was worried I was being too subtle." I couldn't exactly blame her for being upset. Her priority was my safety, and his was the entirety of the Valley. They didn't always overlap.

"I wouldn't come to you with this, but we're out of options. And honestly, it seems like your kind of problem."

"Exactly what kind of problem is 'our kind'?" I asked.

"The kind like her." He nodded at Arkay, but kept his eyes on me. "There was a time when you came to me and said she wasn't human. I figured that was all talk, you know? People get funny ideas about each other all the time, especially strangers. But since then…"

Since then, Arkay had snapped a man's arm the way I might snap a pencil. Since then, three police officers had been murdered and their bodies had been carved up with her tag. Whether he believed in dragons was moot; he knew something was seriously off about Arkay, and he was still coming to us for help.

He took a long drink. "Our people have been disappearing these last few weeks. It was only one or two at first. But then it started being one or two a day. And it keeps happening. People are getting scared, running to other camps, trying to hide out alone, but that makes it that much harder to keep track of everyone."

"Meaning even more people could be disappearing and you wouldn't know," I said.

"Exactly. We have no idea what's going on, or who's behind it, or why this is happening. We've gone to the police, but they just say to head to the shelters."

Advice like that assumed a lot. That you could get into the shelters at all, for one. That there were enough beds. That you didn't have a family, which could make it nearly impossible to find spots for everyone. That you were straight. That you were more worried about what would happen to you on the street than what might happen to you inside its walls.

"Fuckers," Arkay muttered.

Mike spread his hands, conceding defeat. "Like I said, we've got nowhere else to turn. So I'm asking you."

"For what, though?" I asked. "I still don't know what you want us to do."

"Help me keep my people safe," he said. "Find out what's doing this, and if you can't stop them, then at least let us know what we're dealing with so we can figure out what to do. I'm not asking for miracles, Rosario. I just need help."

I glanced at Arkay, her eyes black and scalding. "Give me a second," I told Mike, shooting Arkay a meaningful look. I got up, and she followed me into the bathroom.

"You think we should help him," she said, as soon as we'd checked under the stalls for eavesdroppers.

"You're not wrong," I said.

"Even though you don't owe him anything."

"That's debatable."

"You don't."

"Even if I don't," I said. "People are getting hurt. That's more than enough reason to try to help them."

"There's such a thing as going too far with the whole 'good Samaritan' thing," she said. "That Christ guy got nailed to a block of wood for his trouble."

I gave her a look. All those Masses I'd dragged her to never quite took the way I had hoped. I let it go. "I'm surprised. Usually you're all gung-ho about chasing down bad guys."

"Those bad guys are perverts and assholes. What Mike's talking about is a serial killer, if we're being optimistic. We've dealt with that type before, Rosa. You almost got killed."

My hand traced over the bite mark on my right arm. I hadn't forgotten. "And if it's not a serial killer?"

"Then I know better than to poke around in another predator's territory. Especially if it's picking off two people a day. An appetite like that means it's probably big and it doesn't mind attracting attention. If you go after something like that, it's going to retaliate. And that means somebody isn't going to walk out of that confrontation alive. Which is why you're staying right here."

That caught me off guard. I'd always taken Arkay's enthusiasm for granted, when she wasn't holding a grudge against someone. It hadn't occurred to me that anything could scare her. "Arkay, I didn't mean… You don't have to come…"

She huffed. "What are you talking about? Of course I'm coming. There's a freaky who-knows-what running around in my old town. Which is why *you* need to stay here where it's safe." She gave an indignant sniff. "Besides, you've got work."

My shoulders sagged. My beautiful, ridiculous dragon. "I'll see if Kindra can cover for me. If I let you go alone, you'll wind up chasing half the camp out of town."

"Only if they deserve it." She shrugged daintily.

I took her by the shoulders. "Besides, somebody's got to watch your back."

We took a bus to Indianapolis, our tickets purchased by Arkay with a handful of small bills from dubious origins. Most likely she made her extra spending money the old-fashioned way, by luring in depraved strangers with her doe-eyed damsel routine and then robbing them blind while they lay unconscious in a back alley. I used to keep her aggressions corralled to the kind of creeps who really deserved it, but babysitting Arkay was a full-time occupation, and it didn't exactly mesh well with waitressing. Hopefully she'd internalized at least some of what I'd tried to tell her.

"By the way," Arkay said, trying to cram the leftover bills back into her wallet as we picked out our seats. "I keep forgetting to ask you— can we go to the bank sometime soon? I need to make a deposit."

I glanced at the wad of cash. Anybody else would have been more discreet about waving around that much money, but she didn't seem to notice. "What did you do, rob a guy on his way to a strip club?"

"Nah," she said. "Most of the time I only get them on their way out, and by then they don't really have a lot of money on them anymore."

Wait. "So who did you get it all from?"

"I don't really get names off them or anything. They're not exactly good tippers." She pointed out the excess of singles.

116

There were so many levels of Does Not Compute at hand, I didn't know where to start. "People gave you this money? Willingly?"

She blinked. "...Yeah?"

"Without any threats of violence?"

"Well, there is this one guy who keeps wanting me to hit him, but he pays in fifties."

"Arkay?" My voice jumped an octave. "Where are you getting this money?"

"Our Lady of White River. You know the place. We've walked by there a few times."

"*The strip club?*" Forget Does Not Compute. I was veering into a straight-up Blue Screen of Death. She nodded, all cheerful and chipper, like it was no big deal. "Since when?"

"About a month after you started working at the bar. Where do you think I go while you're at work?"

I *thought* she'd been out doing her Hard Candy Robin Hood routine. This was—this was—better? Worse? I didn't even know. "Is there a reason you've been keeping this from me?"

The question seemed to confuse her. "It never really came up. And you were having problems with bad tips, so I wasn't going to rub it in or anything. But that's how I paid that deposit, remember?"

"God, Kay—" Good thing we were already sitting down, because otherwise I would have fallen over. "I know money's important right now, but we're not... we're not desperate or anything. If you don't feel comfortable with anything—*anything*—I want you to get out of there ASAP, all right?"

"I guess?" She cocked her head to one side. "Rosa, are you feeling okay?"

No, I wanted to say. *Because I just found out my best friend is a stripper.*

The wrongness of that thought hit me like a slap. I'd had less of a freak-out moment when I'd learned dragons were real. How was that less bizarre than the fact that she took off her clothes for money? She was an adult, after all. Obviously she didn't see any problem with her line of work. And honestly, it was probably some of the best money she could make without a birth certificate or a social security number.

So who the hell was I to judge?

"Fine," I said slowly. "I'm fine. Just... recalibrating, okay? Give me a minute."

"Take all the time you need." She curled up on the seat beside me and laid her head on my lap. "We've got an hour, right?"

"Yeah." Already my pulse was settling back into a reasonable pattern. Arkay's confidence was contagious. "Want me to wake you when we get there?"

She snuggled deeper against my lap. "That'd be nice." Slowly her breathing evened and she seemed to doze.

We used to do this sort of thing a lot—catching a ride on the longest bus route we could and staying until the driver made us leave. Often enough they were sympathetic, especially on late-night routes in the dead of winter. I never could get used to sleeping on busses, no matter how tired I got, but Arkay would curl up and sleep for ages if I let her.

Old habits die hard, I guess.

I watched her in silence for several long minutes, only looking up when Mike settled into the seat in front of ours.

"She asleep already?" Mike asked. The bus had started moving a while back; apparently he'd waited until we'd finished our conversation before coming to join us. I appreciated his discretion.

"This is as close as she gets to sitting still," I said. "Most people call it napping."

He watched her for a few long moments, lost in thought. "I don't know how you do it," he said at last.

"Do what?"

"I remember when you first brought her in, she didn't even talk, just growled and hissed and hated everything. And now…" He gestured to my dragon, curled up like a sleeping kitten on my lap. "You've got a gift, Rosa. You really do."

"Nah, Arkay just likes me." I petted her fluffy hair. It had grown out of her pixie cut; she'd need to get it cut again soon. "Let's see if we can talk sense into whatever's giving you a hard time, and then you can decide if I'm gifted."

The nostalgia left Mike's face, replaced by something darker. "So you do you think it's… like her?"

"You're allowed to call her a dragon," I said. "It's not a racist metaphor or whatever. When she gets all big and scaly, she seriously does look like the picture on a box of Lo Mein."

Arkay elbowed my hip without opening her eyes, but she had a smirk on her face.

"Honestly, we don't know what's going after your people," I said. "But she should be able to tell you whether it's human or not once we've had a look around." I hoped so, anyway. Arkay had figured out that Danielle was a ghoul based on her smell. Hopefully, she could do the same with whatever this was. "Is there anything else you can tell us?"

"There's no pattern in time of day or anything like that," he said. "I tried setting up a curfew when I started noticing disappearances, but then they happened in the daylight hours. People would wander off for a few minutes and then never come back."

"You sure they didn't... you know, move on?"

"And leave all their stuff behind?"

I conceded the point.

"It's not just that," he said, lowering his voice. "I've seen people head toward the train tracks, and they looked all... out of it."

"Could they be taking a new drug or something?"

"I've never seen a drug make people act like this. They're almost stoned one minute, but once you shake 'em a bit, they're fine, and they say they're clean."

"People lie."

"Not like this." He shook his head. "Some of them go wandering off again. And the ones who do, they never come back."

"I take it you haven't sent anyone looking for bodies, then."

"I sent two," he said. "They didn't come back, either."

We were halfway through the month of May, and the days seemed to stretch into the late night— so you'd think we would have plenty of daylight while we investigated. Unfortunately, it took us half of forever to get back to Indy, and nearly as long to get from the bus hub at the courthouse to the East Side. By the time we arrived at The Valley, the sun had fallen low on the horizon.

As we broke through the trees encircling the camp, a few regulars raised their hands to greet us. More cast sidelong glances at Arkay and kept their heads down.

The Valley was Indy's largest homeless camp; even depleted, it held maybe fifty people in at least thirty tents, some of which were draped with old rugs or heavy blankets for extra warmth and privacy. In the center of the camp lay a small, makeshift library, a dry-erase community bulletin, and a fire pit that sent a plume of smoke through the surrounding trees. Outside the communal area, the space between the tents was piled high with garbage— an unavoidable consequence of living off scraps, especially when you couldn't exactly pay for weekly pickups from a garbage truck. Back when I'd lived there, Mike had made arrangements with a local church to dump the trash that was beyond saving. Either that tradition ended since we'd left town, or the next dump was way overdue, because the piles were especially high today.

I recognized the pungent odor of old diapers and felt a pang. This life was hard on little kids, even when there weren't monsters on the loose.

"We've been doing everything we can to keep people close by," Mike continued. "But it's not enough." He gestured at a figure moving through the camp, a blond woman who tapped softly at the front flaps of a tent. I caught snatches of conversation between her and the people inside. At one of the tents she used signs, and I caught snippets of 'is everyone here?' and 'how many?'

I'd picked up a little ASL over the years. Deaf and hard of hearing people weren't exactly uncommon among the homeless.

"You said you saw some people wandering off," I said, dragging my focus back to the conversation at hand. "Were they going anywhere in particular? The road, or..."

"Always up to the train track," he said, pointing the way. "Toward downtown."

I frowned. If they were heading downtown, there were easier ways to get there. The tracks that converged on either side of the Valley lay at the top of steep slopes, covered with oversized gravel and thick with undergrowth. The road would be faster, easier to navigate, and a lot more subtle.

The only places easier to reach by train track would be things already on the railroad line.

The blond woman moved toward us. "Hey Mike, we've got a problem," she said. "Allison's gone. Nobody's seen her in at least an hour."

"That's our cue," Arkay said flatly. "Show me which tent is hers, and I'll see what I can do."

That was one of the perks of having a dragon on your side. Reptiles had an impressive sense of smell, especially when it came to things like pheromones. She couldn't exactly track a person bloodhound-style, but some days it seemed damn close. Once she had Allison's scent memorized, she started toward the train track, bounding up the loose rocks like a mountain goat. Halfway up, she paused to look back at me.

"Coming, Rosa?"

I didn't even realize I'd hesitated. The last time we'd gone up this path, I'd nearly been eaten by the undead.

I could stay behind. I could interview the others, find out what they knew about what was going on, and let Arkay track down the actual monster and beat it into next Tuesday. She wouldn't mind.

But whatever it was had been taking its victims from this camp. I was no safer here than I was up on the track. At least there, I'd have Arkay to protect me.

"Wait up, you overgrown lizard."

The rocks slid under my feet as I climbed after her, and I grabbed onto wrist-thick saplings to steady myself. As soon as I got within arm's reach, Arkay caught my hand and pulled me up, pushing aside bushes and low branches until we'd reached the plateau of the track. The sounds and smells of the camp faded, the city lights dyed the sky the color of an old bruise. Distant traffic blended into the rustling of barren branches in a cold night wind. The trees were all warped here, beaten and bowed by the wind tunnel of the railroad and the second-hand gale of every passing train. They seemed to be reaching for us.

How encouraging.

"Smell anything?" I asked.

She tilted her head back and shut her eyes, and I could practically see her sifting through her senses. The wind shifted, and she stilled. She stood like that for nearly a minute, tasting and sorting what the shallow breeze brought her way.

"Yeah," she said at last, not moving. "Blood, but it's faint. Either there's not a lot, or it's far away. And fresh earth, like gardening, but not so alive. More dusty."

At least we were on the right track. So to speak.

"So if you were gonna kidnap a whole bunch of people, where would you put them?" Arkay asked.

"I'd probably ship them all to a country with halfway decent health care."

She rolled her eyes. "A little less Rosa, a little more evil, please."

"How about over there, then?" A rainbow of chipped paint peeked through the trees that lined the track to one side. "Lure people into the junkyard, kill them, and hide their bodies in the trunks. A different car for every victim."

"That's more like it." She started down the slope, darting easily from one solid foothold to another, while I scrambled after her. She grabbed a handful of the chain link fence. "I think I see a good spot to climb over. You think if I give you a leg up—"

A mass of fur and fangs lunged at the fence, and she jumped back. The snarling creature looked more like a bear than a dog.

"Excuse you," Arkay grumbled, kicking at the fence. The dog only barked louder. "New hypothesis: if I wanted to kill someone, I'd throw them to Fido over there. But there's no way anybody came in here quietly."

"This isn't the only junkyard in the area," I said.

"Do you think they all have dogs like this?"

"This close to a homeless camp? I'm positive."

Land in this area was cheap, relatively speaking, thanks to an old coking plant that stood on the other side of the tracks. It had operated for most of a century before it got shut down, and all that time it had spewed lead and mercury and who knew what else into the air and water. It had been slated for cleanup for years before I got to Indy, and word on the street was that it would take at least another decade to clean up the poisoned soil.

Three guesses why the city never tried too hard to bulldoze the Valley.

Arkay made her way to the track. "So we could check every single junkyard in the area to make sure that they're all stocked up with guard dogs. Or we could try another angle and save the junkyards for last."

I sighed. "You want to check out the factory, don't you?"

Even though the Valley was within spitting distance of the factory, the homeless population had generally stayed away. It was too open and too thoroughly rusted to make a decent shelter from the wind, too frequently patrolled by police to be any good as a stash, and in winter the steel walls and floor sucked the warmth right out of you.

And besides, the massive ruin was creepy.

"What?" Arkay said innocently. "You mean that old rust heap you never let me climb on?"

She, of course, only ever saw it as a super-sized jungle gym, complete with slides and all sorts of dark places to explore.

"You still haven't had your tetanus shots."

She fluttered her eyelashes at me. "It's for a good cause."

Yes, it was. It was also big enough and deserted enough to hide a few dozen dead bodies.

Dammit.

"Fine." I started walking, and Arkay fell into stride beside me. "But you only get to take the moral high ground if you're actually trying to help. No goofing off."

We walked for half a mile along the grooves of packed gravel beside the tracks where maintenance cars still drove for their regular checkups. A barbed wire fence separated us from the empty wasteland beside us. Arkay could probably scale it within a few seconds, but she stuck close beside me, looking for the kind of holes in the fence I could cross without her having to lift me over.

It didn't take us too long to find a path leading down to a break in the chain link. The denizens of the Valley didn't come this way much, but that didn't mean it was entirely forgotten. Teenagers came by to explore sometimes, and they left graffiti and garbage behind. Apparently it was a favorite hangout, because the path had been used so frequently the earth was packed smooth, and I had to hold onto Arkay and handfuls of saplings to keep from slipping.

Beyond a mesh of tall grasses and scraggly weeds, the grounds flattened out into eighty acres of ruins and barren wasteland. The ground was scored with old train tracks, some covered with sheets of steel, others half-filled in with dirt and debris, only to open up into pools of stagnant water a few yards further on.

The old coking plant had taken up most of the land at one point, though half its structures had since been demolished, leaving behind a patchwork of cracked foundations and broken roads on a vast field of scraggly pioneer grasses. The parts still standing were massive exoskeletons of old warehouses and boilers, stitched together with networks of pipes, chains, and catwalks that stretched from building to building like jungle vines.

The carcass of an old conveyor belt hung overhead, feeding into an enormous boiler to our left. Below it stood a brick-covered control room. Mounds of grit and coal dust barricaded the door, but together we managed to crack it enough for Arkay to sniff the stale air inside.

"Anything?" I asked.

She grimaced. "I'm pretty sure a bird or two died in there, but that was ages ago. Nothing fresh."

Blocked from any active roads, the empty spaces became a great big echo chamber. What might have been the uneven beat of dripping water bounced between cracked cement and metal walls, growing and twisting and doubling in on itself until it sounded more like the clatter of footsteps.

"Do you hear that?" Arkay asked, stopping short.

I wanted to say 'it's probably nothing,' but swallowed it back. Reassuring lies like that are the reason why people in horror movies don't live to see the credits.

If I'd had my way, we would have woven between the enormous abandoned rust-heaps that hadn't been up to code for at least a decade. But I was with Arkay and she was following her nose, which meant we were taking the most direct route— which, naturally, was the most dangerous. I could only guess how she could smell anything. My own nose was overwhelmed with the lingering fumes of diesel and petroleum, and the constant, oily chalk smell of coal dust.

A rectangular hole yawned open in the far corner of the loading bay. The fading sunlight didn't reach into its depths.

The sound of dripping continued, but mixed among the drops were other sounds: the rhythmic scrape of metal on dirt and the softer rustle of falling earth.

Someone was digging.

Arkay looked me in the eye and started slipping out of her shoes.

"What are you doing?" I asked.

She pointed to a dilapidated mass of bricks— the power house, according to a yellowed sign over one door. A rickety scaffolding clung to the brick, beginning with a ladder and turning into an elevated walkway that branched off to the higher reaches of several other buildings.

"You stay here," she said. "I'm going up. Gonna get this thing from above."

"It's going to hear you from a mile away."

"Not if I go barefoot."

I grabbed her arm before she could take a step. "The hell you are. Do you have any idea how much broken glass we've stepped on in the past five minutes? I'm not pulling rusty nails out of your feet."

She scowled, but put her shoes back on. "An ambush would work better."

"First rule of horror movies, Arkay. We're sticking together."

The sounds of shoveling grew clearer with every step. On the other side of what looked like a hellish jungle gym, I spotted movement. We picked our way around the tangle that marked the edge of the industrial complex and its concrete floor.

In the distance hunched a lone figure with long, matted hair, emaciated but definitely male. Barbed wire coiled around his limbs and chest, wrapping with particular savagery around his neck and forehead.

He was chanting, the low tones almost drowned out by the scrape of the shovel. At his feet lay a mound, a good three feet wide and six feet long. Beside it lay another, and another— more than a dozen in all, arranged in uneven rows.

"I'm gonna go out on a limb and say we've found our guy," Arkay said. She wasn't particularly quiet about it, but the digging man didn't turn around. He didn't even pause in his work. "Alright, guy." She raised her voice, stepping between me and the digging man. "This is where you put down the shovel and turn around. Hands on your head, yadda yadda yadda."

He kept chanting. Only as we approached, I recognized the words: *"Eternal rest grant unto her, O Lord, and let perpetual light shine upon her. May the souls of all the faithful departed, through the mercy of God, rest in peace."*

I frowned. "Arkay. He's praying for them."

"I don't give an okapi's ass what he's doing," she said. "Religious nuts can be serial killers as easily as anybody else. The important thing is he's creeping me the fuck out."

The wind shifted, bringing with it the faint sharp smell of a freshly lit match. The man straightened, but not before Arkay grabbed the shovel and wrenched it violently out of his hands.

He whipped around. His eyes went wide and his mouth dropped open. He stumbled backward so fast that he tripped over the fresh grave, and his hands wrapped around the barbed wire at his throat the way other men might clutch a rosary.

The chanting became too rushed and stuttered for me to make out the words anymore. He managed to climb to his knees, but got no further, rocking back and forth, crossing himself over and over again.

"This isn't normal," I murmured.

"No shit." Arkay brandished the shovel, and the man flinched. "Serial killer, remember?"

"I don't think he is."

His face and hands were caked with grime. Patches of skin were raised and swollen, dark with infection and streaked from attempts at cleansing the wound. With peroxide, if I had to guess. In those rare spots of cleanliness, his face was so ashen it almost seemed gray.

He looked like hell, but he didn't look like a killer. He didn't even look dangerous.

He looked *scared*.

I lowered myself to my knees. "Hey." I gave a small, friendly wave. "It's okay. We're not here to hurt you."

His eyes darted madly from me to Arkay. The chanting didn't stop. I caught what might have been a few snatches of the Lord's Prayer in Spanish.

"I'm gonna come forward, okay?" I inched closer on my knees, my hands out. "Let me know if it isn't." I repeated the words in Spanish. Still no response.

"Rosario, he's covered in blood."

Arkay was right. Rust-brown stains splattered his clothes. Some of them still looked wet and bright.

"And that's why I'm glad to have you here," I said evenly. "You can stop him if he tries to hurt me. But until he does, let me try to talk to him." I scooted a little further forward and lowered my voice. "Hey, it's okay. I'm Catholic, too. Catholic-ish. Haven't been to church in a while. But I'm safe, see?" Slowly I crossed myself. "I'm not going to hurt you."

Apparently that show of solidarity finally got through to him. His hands dragged in their frantic gestures. The chanting slowed, ending after a hoarse 'amen'.

I smiled. "Are we good, then?"

Emotion crossed his face in a rapid cascade: relief, realization, and then a freezing horror.

He lunged forward and grabbed me by the arm.

"Hands off!" Arkay snarled, brandishing the shovel.

The man ignored her. "You have to come with me," he said in heavily accented English. "Please. It's not safe out here."

"You touch her again and you'll find out exactly how not safe it can get," Arkay said.

"I can explain when we get you to shelter, but first you must come with me. Your life depends on it." His voice rose and broke.

Nobody I knew could fake that kind of desperation. And besides, if he was faking and this was all some kind of trap, Arkay would rip his arms off.

"All right," I said, letting him pull me to my feet. "But you're going to tell us exactly what's going on."

He dragged me behind him and Arkay followed. The three of us climbed up a grated staircase so old and rusty that it threatened to collapse under our combined weight. It rose into a tangle of pipes and rebar that wrapped around a row of smoke stacks, like thorn bushes twining around old trees. Wide sheets of metal had been dragged into the structure over a patch of grate walkways, forming something like a roof.

As abruptly as he'd grabbed me, the man released my arm and darted around a corner.

"You're the expert on humans," Arkay said to me. "Mind telling me what the hell is going on?"

"When I figure it out, you'll be the first to know."

The man returned with the sound of a clatter. For a moment, I thought the noise was because of the structure coming apart underneath us, but no. He was carrying an armful of iron chains.

"Put these on," he said hastily. "They'll keep you safe."

Arkay gave me another look. "He's not even trying anymore."

"Please," he said. "It can't touch steel. I don't know why, but it cannot touch steel."

"And I'm sure whatever it is absolutely *can't stand* the smell of chloroform, right? Not like you'd be able to smell it over the rotten eggs."

I looked down at her. Before, the scent had been subtle, blending into the petroleum odors that clung to the site. But in the past few minutes it had gotten stronger. Not yet overpowering, but now that I was paying attention, it couldn't be ignored.

But the man didn't respond to her remark. His eyes kept darting around, searching for something on the ground below.

I picked up one of the chains and draped it over my shoulder to calm him down. "You said you'd explain what's going on. I'm holding you to that."

His brow furrowed. His eyes focused on my mouth.

I knew that look. He was trying to read my lips.

"You can't hear me, can you?" The gestures I made were a pathetic hodgepodge of ASL and pantomime, but finally I caught a glimpse of clarity in the man's eyes. He shook his head.

"No." His shoulders sagged. "I… it was whispering to me. Trying to tempt me to come down. To come out of safety so it could…" He shuddered. "I couldn't keep listening or I would give in. So I…" He cringed, like the memory still hurt to think about. "It's a small price to pay, isn't it? Lose your hearing to keep your soul?"

Smears of old blood stained his shoulders and collar. Crusted flakes still clung in places to his ears.

My stomach turned. Just poking my ear drum with a Q-tip was agony. Intentionally deafening himself— I didn't even want to know how he'd pulled it off.

"Do you… um… sign?" I asked. 'You' was easy enough to remember. Either twirling my pointer fingers around each other was the right sign for 'use ASL', or else my attempt was close enough to charades that he could figure it out despite my incompetence.

"No," he said finally. "I— Sorry. I don't know what you're saying."

Okay, then. Plan B.

I pulled out my cell phone. I didn't have cell reception out here, but I didn't need it. I opened a note app and started swiping my fingers across the keypad.

Will this work?

His expression softened. "That's fine, yes. Thank you."

Do you not sign? I typed. *Or was I just way off?*

"I… I don't," he said slowly. "I… I've only been… like this… it hasn't been long. Only a few… I don't even know anymore. Weeks? Months? I don't know."

I'm sorry. That must have been very painful.

He nodded grimly. "It worked, though. That… thing… hasn't taken me yet."

What is it?

He turned his eyes away, scanning the ground in the gathering dark. "I have never been a man of superstition." His voice was a croak. "I always thought the monsters in scripture were… symbolic. Metaphors. But I don't know what else to call this thing except a demon."

I swallowed, but I forced my expression into a look of confidence. At least it wasn't a zombie.

We've handled weird stuff before, I wrote. *Whatever this thing is, we'll take care of it.*

"Wait," Arkay said. "Is this going to be a regular thing now? Can we start charging money?"

I decided not to type out her contribution. *I'm Rosario Hernandez. My friend's name is Arkay. We're here to help.*

"I'm… er… Gabriel Mendoza." He extended a hand, and I fumbled my phone before I could shake it. "Father Gabriel, once. I'm not entirely sure if that has changed."

Do you know why it would?

His eyes dropped from the phone. "Because I'm the one who found that… thing," he said. "I let it out."

Gravel crunched under a footstep.

Arkay advanced up the stairs in a heartbeat, swiping out one arm and yanking me behind her. Her hands curled into claws and her lips pulled back to show razor teeth. Maybe it was the angle, but she looked bigger than before. Longer. More animal.

Below, a woman stepped into view from behind a small shed, bathed in the twilight gloom. Her movements were stiff and aborted, like something you'd see on a badly scratched DVD.

It was hard to make out much detail in the dim light. She had a medium build and twigs tangled in her long hair.

More striking was the smell that flooded the air, like sulfur and rotting meat.

We'd been out here looking for a woman.

"Arkay," I whispered. "Tell me that isn't Allison."

"Not anymore." Sharp teeth and a distended jaw turned the words harsh and inhuman.

Oh God. What happened to her?

Not-Allison staggered forward, so stiff it seemed like a strong breeze could knock it over. My pulse thundered in my chest, and I searched the darkness for more.

One zombie was fine. We could handle that. If there were more—God, if there was another necromancer— we would handle it. I knew we could handle it. But before my eyes flashed the memory of the last one, blood splashing him while Arkay dismembered him her shaking jaws. I couldn't watch her do that again. I couldn't.

The corpse of Allison started climbing the stairs. Its hand brushed the railing, and jerked away with a hiss. The skin that had touched steel was blistered and burned, but it kept climbing.

Focus, Rosa.

I grabbed my cell phone again. *I thought you said it couldn't touch metal?*

Gabriel was already hoisting himself up into the tangle of support beams. "It can't. Not by itself. But humans can." He dragged himself further away from the grate. "Hurry!"

I tried to organize my mind. I'd seen too many zombies clawing their way through the inside of a body shop for them to have an aversion to metal. So what the hell was this, then?

I tested my weight on a heavy crossbeam. It didn't seem ready to fall yet, so I leaned on it and reached out to find another. We were a good fifteen feet off the ground, and I could feel every inch underneath me. If I fell, it wouldn't be straight down, either— I'd probably hit a few of the branching pieces of rebar and pipe on the way down.

"Arkay!" I shouted. She was still on the edge of the stairwell, between me and the advancing… thing. She hadn't budged an inch.

The dead woman kept climbing, staggering and slow.

So very slow.

I could see her lips moving through the gaps in the metal. She was saying something. I couldn't make it out, but I could almost hear it. A wordless chant. A drone. It sounded… nice. Comfortable. As I listened, my mounting panic drained away, leaving only a warm buzz in its place.

The whole world felt like it was moving in fits and starts.

Gabriel shouted from behind me, but his words slurred together into nonsense. He grabbed me around the waist and pulled me backward.

I was wobbling just now, wasn't I?

The bit of metal I'd been standing on was bent almost in half from my weight. Any longer and I probably would have dropped through all that mess to the ground below. The thought should have scared me—it had scared me, a few seconds ago—but now it seemed absurd. It was just a little fall. It couldn't possibly hurt me.

Gabriel clapped his hands over my ears, still shouting.

Farther away, Arkay moved in shudders and starts, like I was seeing her illuminated by a strobe light. She vaulted over the rail of the walkway and leaped through the air in brief, stop-motion flashes, and collided with the possessed woman with bizarre grace. Her momentum carried them both backward. Over the railing. Down, and down, and down until they both hit the cement beneath.

Reality snapped back into focus. The laws of physics sobered instantly, and so did I.

Oh God—what had just happened to me? What had happened to Arkay?

I wrenched out of Gabriel's grip, nearly falling off the perch in my hurry to reach her, but he grabbed me back.

"She's all right!" Gabriel shouted, tightening his hold on me. "She isn't hurt!" He flashed a thumbs-up, and suddenly I realized that I wasn't the one he was trying to reassure. Arkay was on the ground, already on her feet again, nodding at Gabriel with a grunt.

"Don't listen to it," Gabriel told me too loudly. "Whatever you do, don't listen to it. Its voice. That's how it gets you."

The demon started to rise, but it didn't have a chance to scrape itself off the ground before Arkay picked it up and hurled it away from our shelter. The demon rolled, and Arkay chased after it with single-minded fury.

The demon had tried to hurt me. Nobody ever hurt me in Arkay's presence and walked away in one piece.

A kick to its abdomen echoed with the sickening crack of broken bones. A second kick sent it sprawling backward several feet. A third sent it out of sight entirely.

I started after them, desperate to keep Arkay in view.

"No!" Gabriel pulled me back. "It isn't safe down there."

I fumbled for my phone, but my hands were shaking. I couldn't type.

"I have to see them!" I said, pointing from my eyes to Arkay. "I'm not letting her go alone."

He pointed up. The rickety staircase continued higher, branching off into the same catwalk Arkay had wanted to use earlier to sneak up on Gabriel.

That would work.

The rusting metal clattered underfoot as I rushed up and over. Somewhere in the back of my mind, I noted how high we'd climbed, how badly the catwalk shook, how long it had gone unmaintained, how easy it would be to lose my footing in the dark, but those facts got shoved into the corner that was usually reserved for gameshow trivia. Arkay was fighting a demon. That took precedence.

The clatters turned to low echoes as we crossed onto the roof of the power house. Another all-metal surface, but this one might have been tin, rather than solid steel, and I leaned my weight on the brick ledge surrounding the roof.

Hopefully the demon wouldn't figure that out.

Below, the demon grabbed Arkay by the arm and hurled her into a metal shed, which crumpled on impact. Arkay scraped herself out of the wreckage and lunged. The demon moved to block her assault, but Arkay dove low, throwing her weight onto her arms and swiping her heel across the demon's face. While she was down, she grabbed a length of rebar and cracked it against the demon's thigh.

Its femur buckled with another echoing crunch. The demon went down hard, splinters of bone jutting through its upper leg.

"Kay!" I shouted, and Arkay looked up. Her eyes were feral and uncomprehending, but her focus rested entirely on me. "Arkay, that's enough. She can't hurt you anymore. You can stop now."

I moved toward the ladder, but Gabriel caught my arm. "Don't go down there," he said.

I tried to calm my pulse enough to type properly. *She won the fight. I need to calm Arkay down before she kills Allison.*

Resignation pulled at the creases on Gabriel's face. "That poor woman is already dead. She was as good as dead the moment the demon took her."

I looked back to the ground. The possessed woman twitched and flailed madly. Arkay circled her, knocking her back down every time she tried to rise. Blood pooled under the broken leg, but she didn't look beyond saving.

"She doesn't have much longer," Gabriel said. "I've never seen a vessel last more than an hour before it starts to break down. The demon is corrosive, Rosario. It's rotting her away from the inside."

"Oh God," I whispered. Below, her movements started to slow. Arkay sent her sprawling, and she didn't try to get up again. *Can she feel it? What's happening to her?*

"I don't know," Gabriel admitted softly. "I dearly hope not. But you need to call your friend. It isn't safe down there."

The woman's body spasmed and finally fell still.

"Arkay!" I shouted, and waved her closer. "Come on up." She moved to obey— and then stopped.

A thick blackness pooled around the unmoving body, spreading like blood. But there was no reflection in it, no mass, no real substance, only shadows. The dark was dappled and uneven, like the cover of a thick canopy of leaves. Except there were no trees for at least a hundred yards in every direction. The flecks of moonlight surrounded rusty nails and scraps of rebar and clung to the tangled mass of Gabriel's shelter. Darkness pooled on brick and concrete, dirt and weeds and the flesh of a broken body.

Arkay grabbed her weapon and sliced it across the ground like an amateur golfer. Sparks leapt where steel met concrete, and the shadow fled the assault. But only briefly.

Then it came surging back in around her, even thicker and darker than before. She backed away, but it closed her in on every side.

"Arkay!" I rushed to the edge of the rooftop, throwing my hand over the ledge to give her a hand up. It was high—a good twenty feet at least, more than even she could jump. But she didn't need to make it up all that way. I yanked the length of chain off my shoulders and threw one end down to her. "Climb up!"

She didn't need to understand English to know what I wanted. The shadow fled from the clanking links, and with a running leap, Arkay caught the other end. The sudden pull of her weight nearly sent me over, but Gabriel was behind me, his arms around my waist, keeping me steady.

Arkay was halfway up the wall, moving quickly. Then she looked up at me and froze.

The shadow was crawling up the brick like ivy. She was moving fast, but it was faster.

On the metal roof, on the catwalk, I would have been fine, but I had all my weight braced against the outcropping of brick. I couldn't move. Not without dropping her.

"Hurry!" I shouted.

She looked me in the eyes. The draconic fury was gone. In its place was pure cold calculation.

And then she let go of the chain.

Gabriel and I fell backwards, compensating for a weight that suddenly wasn't there. I untangled myself and scrambled back to the wall, peering frantically over the side.

Arkay lay below, supine in a pool of boiling tar. The shadow wrapped around her outstretched hand, encasing it like a glove. It slid up her skin and under her clothes, shrouding her in darkness before it blended seamlessly into the natural ochre of her skin. It drained into her and left nothing behind but cold, white moonlight.

I stared, frozen.

She moved. Twitched. Rolled over, and then kept rolling. It wasn't the awkward soreness from the fall— she was twisting. Writhing. Contorting into shapes that a human body shouldn't be able to take.

Mindlessly I turned and ran for the stairs. An arm closed on my wrist and jerked me so hard I fell to my knees. Gabriel stared at me, wide-eyed and horrified and so very *sorry*.

He pulled me away, and I pulled right back. "No!" I snapped, letting my body language translate for me. "I need to get to Arkay! She's hurt, she's having a seizure, she's—"

"It has her." His voice was hoarse, but steady. Resigned. "You can't help her now. It's too late."

No. No no no no no.

"She's gone."

I tried to twist out of his grip, but he held me tight, pinning both arms to my sides. I could only watch as Arkay stopped shaking and went deathly still.

"Arkay, get up!" I shouted. "You have to get up!" She had to be okay. She had to. She'd gotten hit by a truck and walked away. A fall like this shouldn't hurt her, and neither should a stupid shadow. She didn't even believe in God— how the hell did she get off being murdered by a fucking demon?

One hand twitched. Her fingers flexed as they dug into the dirt.

My whole body sagged. "Thank God. She's all right."

Another hand braced against the ground, and Arkay pulled herself to her knees. But it was an unnatural motion, stiff and careful, like it hurt to move her back. It was all wrong for someone so compulsively bendy.

Her head turned like it was on a ball joint, twisting dangerously far to the left, to the right.

She looked up at me, and my breath lodged in my throat.

That wasn't Arkay.

Arkay

My leg twisted as I hit the ground. Something would probably be sprained later.

Overhead, Rosario fell backward, away from the demon that crawled up the wall. She was out of harm's reach, along with the priest. Safe, then. Even if the priest meant her harm, he would have made a real shitty serial killer.

I tried to get up, but something wrapped around me, and it was cold and dark—

No, that wasn't right. Two different sensations at the same time, warm and cold: Rosa was squeezing me closer, but in the process she'd dislodged the blanket. A semi rumbled across the bridge overhead, and its roar echoed around me. I'd been dreaming just now, hadn't I?

"Arkay, get up," I heard a faint whisper. "You have to get up."

"Can't sleep?" I whispered, burrowing closer to her warmth.

"Maybe a little." Her face was lit half in silver moonlight, half in the yellow glow of a street lamp. "And don't say it."

I politely withheld my 'I told you so'. "So this doesn't have anything to do with those creepypastas you've been reading, then?"

"I told you not to say it." She gave me a playful shove, but I nestled against her. She always regretted reading all those scary stories online, but that never actually stopped her from reading them.

"Was it the balloon one again?" I asked.

She groaned. "You had to bring up the balloon one."

"Was it the Rake?" I guessed.

"Ugh. Stop already!"

"Ooh! Was it the one with the haunted Zelda game? That one was awesome."

"For the love of—" She pulled her pillow out from under her head and smacked me with it. "No more out of you. Stop."

"Not until you tell me," I singsonged. It wasn't nearly as mean as it sounded, either. Rosario was good at getting into other people's heads and seeing the world the way they did, but things like logic and reason didn't always get to come along for the ride. Talking through it was the fastest way of getting her out of the story and thinking critically again.

144

"Fine," she said. "But only if you shut up."

I drew my fingers across my lips.

"ThreeClaw, okay?"

I tilted my head, inviting her to continue.

"The story was about this thing called ThreeClaw. It sneaks up on you when you're desperate, you know? Scared. Lonely. And then it promises to take away all the bad parts of your life. Only then it takes you."

I drew another invisible line over my throat and stuck out my tongue for effect.

"Actually, it doesn't kill you," she said. "It... it erases you. Takes away everything you are. It's still your body, but all your memories, your personality—everything that makes you *you*—is gone. You're a stranger. And that's..." She shuddered. A cloud passed over the moon and cast us into deep blue shadows.

"That's not gonna happen," I said. "You know why?"

"Because it's a made-up story on the internet."

"Nope." I stuffed her pillow back under her head, careful not to snag her long braid. "Because if I ever meet this ThreeClaw thing, I'm gonna kick its ass all the way to Lake Michigan. Let the Canadians deal with it. Same with Slenderman, same with the Rake, same with Bloody Mary, and the balloon guy, and that Ben thing."

"Canada's gonna have one hell of a ghost problem, huh?"

I grinned. "No boogieman's gonna lay a hand on you, Rosa. Ever. That's a promise."

She buried her face in her pillow and laughed—only it wasn't her laugh. It wasn't her voice. The nearby streetlight flickered and went out, and we were shrouded in black.

"Unless it gets you first."

I lunged to cover Rosario, but she was gone. The dirty-laundry pillow under her head was gone. The blanket we'd been lying on was gone. Fuck, even the concrete and the moonlight and the trucks were all gone.

"Rosa?" I shouted, leaping to my feet and swinging my arms wide to catch her. "Rosario!"

"She can't hear you," whispered the voice in the dark. *"She's gone—"*

I leaped, claws out, but I couldn't find the source of the sound. It was in front of me and behind me and above and below, taunting me in stereo.

"If you fucking hurt her, I'll rip you apart!" I lunged again. My claws must have caught something, because they suddenly ached with a sharp, throbbing pain, like I'd slammed both my hands in a car door.

The demon only laughed.

Rosario

Arkay's eyes were empty. Cavernous.

The creature behind them stared at me like it had to think back to remember what it was looking at. It pushed off the ground and rose unsteadily to its feet, staggering, but not the way it had in Allison's body. It was less jerky, and more unsteady. Like its limbs had fallen asleep. Like it was learning to walk for the first time.

It stumbled toward the power house we were standing on. And when it reached the wall, it climbed.

Arkay had always had an odd elegance in the way she scaled walls. She'd skim her hands over a sheer surface and find the tiniest crevices she could cling to. The demon tore right into the wall and hauled itself up, fast and brutally efficient. Brick groaned as it crumbled into dust under the demon's claws.

I grabbed for Gabriel's hand and backed away from the ledge. "We need to get out of here. Like, *now*." The warning went unheard, but it wasn't needed. We both took off at a run, our footsteps reverberating through the metal roof. The echo was so loud that I didn't even notice when the steady crunching changed directions.

Gabriel ran faster than I did, and so he reached the catwalk before me. He was looking ahead to the next turn, and not down. He didn't hear the squeal of twisting metal. When his feet hit the walkway, he fully expected it to hold his weight. Instead it dropped out from underneath him, and he dropped right with it.

I still had his hand in mine, but our palms were slick and clammy. For an eternal moment he dangled by the single point of contact, sliding apart an inch at a time. I grabbed his wrist with my other hand, ignoring the bright stab of pain as the barbed wire around his arm dug into my palms. At least it gave me some traction. With an animal grunt, I dug in and threw all my weight backward. His kicking feet found broken brick, and he scrambled over the ledge.

I didn't get a chance to catch my breath before the crunch of pulverized stone began again, growing closer with every pace.

I hurried to look over the edge. The ladder that led down had been torn from the wall, along with the support beams that once buttressed the catwalk. Climbing the wreckage was a small woman with the eyes of a demon.

Arkay would never look at me like that.

I scrambled away from the ledge and pulled Gabriel to his feet. "We need to find another way down." I signed it as best I could and hoped he could follow along, but he wasn't looking at my hands.

"The light of God surrounds me." His voice shook as he tugged me back with him to the opposite edge of the roof. *"The love of God enfolds me."* With a free hand he crossed himself, over and over again.

The demon stepped down from the ruined ledge. Its shoulders were rigid and even. Its back was perfectly straight. It looked almost professional, if you added in an extra dose of rigor mortis. The only thing non-regulation about it was the sardonic tilt of its head.

It opened its mouth, and I clapped my hands over my ears. But what came out wasn't the hypnotic chant from before.

"Good evening," it purred. A few more steps and it could reach out and touch me. "Potnia Theron, my most *magnanimous* benefactor."

I cringed. It spoke with Arkay's voice, but it was all wrong— too low, too slow.

"Get out of my friend," I whispered.

"But why?" Its expression shifted into a cartoonish caricature of surprise. It spread its arms wide, like it was showing off a new coat. "It fits so beautifully."

I tasted vomit, tainted with the matchstick sulfur soaking the air.

She. Not it. **She.**

"I said, get *the fuck* out of my friend."

"Language." It tsked. "There's a priest present, my dear."

Yeah, that was classy. I had a few guesses what 'Potnia Theron' meant, and none of them were G-rated.

Beside me, Gabriel moved on to a different prayer: *"Lord Jesus Christ, I place myself at the foot of Your cross and ask You to cover me..."*

"A token of my appreciation for your generous gift," the demon said, gesturing to one side. "You have my permission to leave unmolested. Go home, Potnia Theron. You've waited so long to have one. Go home to that nice little house you're renting, to the cute little waitress with the pierced eyebrows and the charming laugh. Go home to see to your business, and I shall see to mine."

I'd been hoping the 'psychic demon' thing had been one of those things they made up for horror movies.

"Yeah, I don't take promises from demons," I said. "Nothing personal or anything, but the whole 'damned' thing is hell on your credibility."

It actually twitched at that. Maybe if all else failed, I could pun it to death.

Assuming it didn't kill me first.

The demon shrugged gracefully. "Always a pity to see a boon rejected." It extended a clawed hand to caress my cheek, and I flinched away. "But we will not both be ungrateful. You will die quickly." The last words lost some of their effect when the demon had to raise its voice to be heard over a mechanical roar.

It had started distant, but now the snarl of an engine bounced off the factory walls, and high beams flickered between the cracks of buildings. A black SUV skidded over the tiled foundation of an old corporate office and swerved to a halt. Even when the engine cut off, the roar continued, not from the vehicle itself, but from the chanting of hundreds of voices blasted through oversized speakers on the roof of the car.

The demon had stopped in its tracks. Its face twitched again, ticking in agitation. Its clawed hands opened and shut compulsively. It wasn't just distracted, it was in pain. I would have taken the moment to run, but we were boxed in.

"Arkay," I said. "Arkay, if you're in there—"

I didn't have a chance to finish the motivational speech.

A man climbed out from the driver's side. He looked like a soldier: broad-shouldered and muscular, with an assault rifle in one hand and a silver token in the other that glinted in the moonlight. His mouth was moving, but his voice got swallowed by the torrent of voices.

The demon snarled and tore away at a sprint. When it hit the edge of the roof it took a running leap. The would-be-exorcist grabbed his rifle and shot at the demon mid-flight, but if the bullets hit, they didn't stop it. The demon hit the ground with a gymnastic roll and sprang to its feet less than a yard from the car.

The exorcist readjusted his aim, but before he could fire, the demon slashed at him with clawed hands. He blocked the assault with the rifle, but the first swipe was enough to tear the weapon out of his grip. A second blow bore down, and he ducked out of the way. The exorcist was taller than the demon, his legs longer, and he managed to keep out of reach as the demon swung at him again and again.

It stopped swinging. Its stiff posture loosened, sagged, like suddenly the demon was heavier and more flexible than it had been a moment before.

I rushed toward the ledge. "Run!" I shouted. "Get out of there!" But I was drowned out by the sounds of Latin chanting. Frantically I waved my arms, and for a moment I caught his eye. The exorcist looked from me to the demon and back, unnerved and inching away.

Not fast enough.

Because that's when the demon changed.

I'd seen Arkay do it dozens of times since I'd known her, but her changes had always been so fast they seemed almost instant: one second she was deceptively small and human, the next she was big and scaly. Maybe the demon didn't have her control, or maybe it had more patience for performance. Blue scales washed across its body. Hair rippled down its back in a long mane. Antlers speared from its head in a backward arc. Limbs corded with muscle and rearranged themselves into savage claws. It grew taller, more distorted and reptilian, until it looked more lizard than human, and then more serpent than lizard. And then the small woman was replaced entirely by forty feet of dragon.

It arced over the SUV like a low-flying comet, crushing the sound system and dragging the car into a sideways roll. The chanting cut out, abruptly replaced with the shriek of shattered glass and the groan of collapsing metal.

The exorcist was already running.

A hiss from behind me made me jump.

"Rosario!" Gabriel hissed again. "Hurry!"

I looked up. While I'd been watching the demon, Gabriel had fastened the length of chain to a twisted remnant of the old catwalk.

"Gabe, you're a genius," I said, tapping my middle finger to my forehead and twisting it in the air. Hopefully he could guess what that meant, because we didn't have the time for me to type out the praise.

He climbed down the chain like it was one of those ropes in high school gym class. You know, the kind that people like me never managed to climb for more than three feet before we fell on our asses in front of everybody. Turns out that even when the alternative was getting eviscerated by a demon, adrenaline still didn't kick in enough to keep me from sucking at it. I managed to get halfway down before my grip slipped and I slid the rest of the way, wrapping my arms and legs around the chain and holding on for dear life. As soon as I was loose, Gabriel pulled me into the narrow space between the wall and what looked like a silo of some kind. It was too tight a space for the dragon to slip through, at least not without changing back into a smaller form.

A snarl echoed behind us. I whirled to face it, but we were alone. The demon was still going after the exorcist.

"Hurry," Gabriel whispered, pulling at my sleeve. "We have to hide."

He was right. If the demon found us again, it wouldn't give us another chance to escape.

But I couldn't run and hide while a man was murdered.

"Wait here." I held out my hand. "Give me a minute. I'll be— just give me a minute."

I could only hope he understood, and I took off running toward the sounds of a fight.

Arkay

My brain was cloudy and fogged with pain. Even with a roll to break my momentum, leaping off the roof of a building had sent stabbing, cracking pain through all my joints and left my whole body throbbing. I wanted to lay down and hold myself for a little while, but I couldn't.

I couldn't.

I'd used up everything I had on that rooftop.

It had wanted to make her jump. To wind its spells around her will and send her diving off the roof like it was the deep end of a swimming pool. And all the while it opened my eyes and made me watch.

I roared and snarled and spat against its whispers. I clawed at my own throat—better to tear out my voice box than use it to kill my Rosa—but my claws wouldn't even twitch.

I think the demon found it funny, because it stopped. It taunted Rosa, smearing her with syrupy backhanded compliments in my voice, and all the while it laughed. I could barely hear them talking over its sick, twisted laugh.

It reached inside my mind and sifted through my thoughts and memories, plucking out little morsels of information just to hurt her.

And it touched her, just to hear me scream. It caressed her face like a lover, silently reminding me that it could gouge out her eyes with a flick of its claws, that it could rip off her jaw with the slightest pull, that it could tear the scalp off her skull with one good yank at her braided hair. I threw all my weight against it. I dragged my arm back with all my might. I would rip it out of my fucking shoulder if I had to. Everything I had, everything I was, I threw it all into fighting the demon.

And all of it for nothing.

It didn't even budge, except to toy with me. It didn't seem to feel me at all until the guy with the tricked-out car came riding in.

In the wake of his chanting I could feel the demon's attention divided. And while it was distracted, I spotted what might have been wisps of substance in that oily nothingness. And if I could just grab it—

But I couldn't. I was too spent to try, then too distracted by my own agony. Before I could muster my strength, the

156

speakers were crushed and the opportunity dissolved like just another dream.

The soldier-boy ran, and the demon pursued… but it didn't kill him. It knocked his legs out from underneath him with a sweep of my talons, then reared up and waited. A blink of an eye was enough for him to get back on his feet and run again, buoyed by the faintest sliver of hope.

Then it gathered the electricity from within my bones and sent him to the ground with an arc of lightning. He fell, singed and twitching. The air reeked of fear and charred hair. But he still wasn't dead. The demon wasn't finished taunting him yet.

He got up. Ran. And then fell again, convulsing from another shock. And then he got up again. And he would keep getting up and he would keep getting knocked back down, batted around like a mouse between a cat's paws, until his heart gave out.

It was sadistic. Cruel. An outrageous abuse of my body and powers.

I didn't care. The longer it tortured him, the more time Rosa had to escape.

Rosario

A bright flash split the night and left silhouettes dancing in my vision.

The exorcist hadn't gotten far. He lay on the ground, spasming from a sudden surge of electricity. His rifle lay useless a few yards away. The demon loomed above him, still draconic and swaying like a cobra. Another burst of lightning crackled between its fangs. The demon could have killed the exorcist with one blast, but it hadn't. It was playing with him. Torturing him.

Meanwhile it was distracted. And I was right behind it.

It leaned close to the ground to unleash another attack, and I leaped at the back of its head. The bolt of lightning sailed wide, striking a nearby outbuilding with a blast that charred the bricks. The demon snarled and tried to shake me off, but I grabbed onto the antlers and held tight.

Arkay had always been strong, and the demon took the power and magnified it. But horses were strong, too, and they could be steered with a four-inch piece of metal. No matter what it was— horse, dog, human, or dragon— if you could control its head, you controlled where it went.

The demon tried to claw me off, but its forelegs couldn't reach me. It threw its head to the ground in an effort to scrape me off on the concrete, but I tucked myself inside the cage of its antlers. The demon snarled and writhed, trying to coil one of its hind legs in close enough to get at me. I almost laughed. How many times had I helped Arkay scratch an itch on the back of her neck?

The antlers in my hands grew abruptly thinner and started retreating back into the demon's skull. The body beneath me grew smaller, condensing and shrinking beneath me. Where I had been on top of a dragon, suddenly I was sitting on a woman's back, clutching handfuls of short black hair. The demon drew its knees under it and threw me off like I weighed next to nothing. I hit the ground with a choking gasp.

The demon righted itself and rose above me. A snarl curled its lips back from razor teeth.

A sound roared close by, like the bark of an enormous dog. For half a second, I thought the demon might have made it, but it lunged aside as another bark echoed off the buildings.

The exorcist stepped into the moonlight, his assault rifle a solid patch of black in his hands. He lined up another shot, but the demon was already sliding into the shadows with a long, low hiss.

"Thanks for that," he grunted, searching the darkness for the demon.

"Yeah. Same to you." I coughed. My throat felt raw and bloody, hopefully from the run over. I really didn't want to think about what else it could be. Fresh bruises and torn muscles ached underneath my skin. The cut on my hand had torn wider and was pouring fresh blood.

The exorcist offered me a hand up. "You alright?"

"Yeah." I spat onto the concrete. The runoff from my hand was the only blood on the ground; if that bullet had hit, it hadn't actually gotten through Arkay's scales. "You?"

"I'll live."

"You sure about that?" I asked.

He was muscular and dressed in the kind of clothes you'd find in a military surplus store, but he didn't look any older than me. Right then, short and shivering, he didn't even look old enough to drink.

Now that I had a chance to see him properly, he seemed pale. Not washed out by the moonlight, not white-boy pasty, but bloodless. Sickly. His eyes were wide with either excitement or panic. Possibly both.

"That was a dragon." It took him obvious effort to keep his voice steady.

"Yeah," I said. It was never a good sign when professionals freaked out about a situation.

"A demon is possessing a dragon."

"Yeah."

"That doesn't happen."

Right about now, Arkay would be rolling her eyes and suggesting he tell that to the demon.

But Arkay wasn't here.

"So that really is a demon. Good to know." I glanced back the way I came. "Are you good to run? Or jog, anyway? My friend Gabriel's still out there."

"Right." His posture tightened. Abruptly he was all business, every inch of him focused on the task. "Lead the way."

Maybe jogging hadn't been the best suggestion. I wasn't exactly athletic on my best days, and wrestling a demonic dragon had tapped me dry. The exorcist followed me step for step, deviating only to check on the wreckage of his car.

"Oh, come on," he hissed. The black SUV looked like it had been through a monster truck rally.

"Think you'll be able to drive it again?" I asked when he got back.

"Only if somebody pries the roof off the driver's seat." He tapped a dark shape on his belt. "Managed to salvage some ammo, though."

I swallowed. "Those are some big bullets." Each one was easily as long as my thumb.

".300 Blackouts," he said, with that twinge of excitement that all gun nuts got when they talked about things that go boom. At least he wasn't shaking anymore. "Cold iron core. Might not do much while it's shifted, but three or four in the chest should make a pretty big impression."

The mental image sent a chill down my spine. "But you're going to try to exorcise her first, right?"

"What?"

"Before you go with the shooting thing. You're going to try to exorcise her first, right?"

He blinked. "Maybe you weren't paying attention before," he said. "But I already tried that. Hell of a lot of good it did me."

I signaled for him to be quiet. We'd reached the silo where I'd left Gabriel.

The last gloom of twilight had faded, leaving the factory shrouded in shades of black and gray. The abandoned structures blended into one another, melting into a single amorphous mass of concrete and brick and steel.

A jolt of doubt gnawed the back of my mind. Had the demon gotten him?

I considered calling out to Gabriel, and quickly stifled the thought. That was a stupid idea. Instead I pulled out my phone and turned it away from me. The glow of the screen reflected dully on scratched metal.

"Morse code?" the exorcist asked, barely audible.

"Nope. Just a phone."

Maybe it was the illumination, but he looked a bit put out by that answer.

The light bounced off a face that hadn't been there before. I jumped, and the exorcist raised his weapon to shoot.

"Wait," I whispered, pulling him back. "It's alright. That's Gabe." I lowered the brightness on my phone and flashed a thumbs up. Hopefully a face full of phone glare hadn't completely wiped out Gabriel's night vision.

He hurried toward me, laying his hands on my shoulders. "Are you alright?" Even hoarse, his voice sounded too loud.

I nodded hastily and started typing. *We need to find a place to hide.*

"I know a place. Watch your step." He took my hand and plunged into the dark. We moved in the shadows between buildings, without even moonlight to light our steps. I felt a faint vibration under my feet as we crept along. Not movement, but echoes. We were walking on something hollow. I must have veered too far to the side, because Gabriel pulled me sharply back. I stumbled, and the exorcist crashed into my back.

Fumbling upright, I turned on my phone, pointing it down to illuminate my path.

The dim light showed nothing, but a flicker of white blinked at me, no bigger than a postage stamp. I stared at it for a long time, trying to make sense of the looming darkness— and then it hit me.

The floor had dropped off a few inches from where I stood. Beyond lay a pit, maybe fifteen or twenty feet deep. The light of my phone reflected back at me off the surface of the oil-black water below.

Gabriel gave my hand another, gentler tug, and led me around the edge of the pit.

We passed over a metal plate that shifted and echoed as we crossed over it— apparently it had been laid over another pit, or a ditch or something. No wonder he'd picked this route. It might as well have been booby-trapped.

A creaking metal staircase brought us to a doorway on the second story of a narrow gray building. A web of catwalks and ladders converged around us, branching off to reach the surrounding structures. Inside, one wall of the room was covered almost floor to ceiling with rusted filing cabinets; a pile of computer towers had been thrown into a tangled heap in the corner, along with the rotted remains of an old computer desk. Moonlight leaked through patches of glass block near the roof.

The exorcist grunted. "High ground. Multiple exits, none of them silent. Solid vantage point. You really know your defense."

He says you picked a good spot, I typed.

"Sending for help?" The exorcist nodded at my phone.

"Why, are you getting any reception out here?" I flashed a grim smile. Even if I could call for help, I didn't have anyone who would answer. There was no point in calling the police. We were on the grounds of an abandoned factory, less than a mile from a well-known homeless camp. If I called in ranting about demons, I'd get laughed off the line. I had no idea if Danielle or one of her friends knew anything about this sort of thing, and even if they did, they were more than an hour away by car.

We were on our own.

I tamped down the thought. That way lay madness.

"Gabriel can't hear," I said. "If you want to have a conversation, one of us is going to have to type."

"Oh." I could hear the fluster in the exorcist's voice. "I'm sorry."

"No point telling me," I said. "Got a phone?"

"In the car and probably in several pieces by now." He sighed. "Can I use yours?"

I handed it over. "I'm Rosario, by the way."

"Adam. Adam Smith." His name appeared on the screen as his thumb skated over the keyboard. "I'm with the Order of Saint Michael of the Sun."

"Gabriel Mendoza." Gabriel extended his hand.

"Does that make you a professional exorcist or something?" I asked, after they finished shaking.

"Something like that," Adam said.

A cool wind whistled through the pipes somewhere outside, and the metal groaned. I wrapped my arms around my chest.

Somewhere out there, the demon was hunting us.

"Did either of you see that back there?" Gabriel asked. "Did— did she really turn into a…"

Adam nodded, and reluctantly, so did I. Habit told me to pretend I hadn't seen anything, but there was no point in denying it now.

"It didn't turn into a dragon," Adam said, typing as he spoke. "That's what it was from the beginning. They only look human."

"She," I corrected automatically. I didn't know what gender the demon used—and frankly, I didn't care right now—but like hell was I letting him talk about Arkay like she wasn't even a person. "And I know."

Adam frowned. "You do?"

I gave a small nod. "That's why we came here in the first place. Something was killing people and it definitely wasn't human, so we got asked to look into it. I didn't think this would happen."

Adam's frown deepened into a look of scrutiny. "Are you…?"

"Human," I finished for him, trying not to be annoyed he'd asked. It was probably relevant, but it felt too much like being back in high school, with all the fumbling unspoken questions about my sexuality, every one of them phrased in variations of 'are you… you know…?'.

I snatched the phone back.

I'm human, Arkay's a dragon, she's perfectly friendly when she's not possessed, and you're not going crazy.

My declaration would have carried more punch, but I had to stop twice to correct typos. Adam's eyes followed the words on the screen.

And we're not shooting her, I added. *Not if there's any alternative.*

Gabriel looked between Adam and me, clearly confused.

Adam snatched the phone back. *There aren't a whole lot. This was supposed to be a low-level demon—*

"Low level?" Gabriel repeated.

It should have been.

I took the phone. *Have you actually done this before?*

He hesitated to take back the phone.

"Have you?" I asked aloud.

He looked uncomfortable. "I've assisted with other exorcisms."

"But this is your first time alone."

No wonder the demon wiped the floor with him.

"I'm very well versed in the theory. And even if I did have more field experience, this is unprecedented. I wouldn't have been prepared to handle a demon with a dragon body. Besides, all my supplies are rubble right now. We've got what I have on me. That's it."

"Which is?" I asked, gesturing for him to show his hand.

He stared at me for a moment, a bit confused, but then emptied his pockets. "A loaded AR-15, half empty; a magazine with a little over thirty iron Blackout rounds; a Saint Benedictine Medal; six cold iron knives—"

"Six?" I repeated, staring at the orderly rows of deadly weapons. "Overkill much?"

"Demons don't like getting stabbed any more than humans do," he said. "And they're a whole lot better at disarming you. Six is conservative."

We're not stabbing Arkay, either, I wrote. *Can you do an exorcism with what you've got?*

"Dammit, woman!" he snapped. His voice echoed back at me from around the room, and I flinched. "Were you not paying attention when she almost killed me just now? I know he's deaf, but are you blind, or crazy, or just plain stupid?"

My arm slipped back around my waist, and I looked away.

It's funny how fast you can lose a thick skin. Right after I came out, I'd dealt with a lot of yelling. Even more so after I wound up on the streets. But a lot of that stopped after I met Arkay. She hadn't let people raise their voices at me—not unless I told her to ease off. There was a power in choosing whether or not to listen to another person's vitriol. Shouting lost its sting when I heard it from behind the shelter of an angry dragon.

Only I didn't have Arkay to hide behind anymore. She got possessed to protect me. Now she needed me to protect her.

"Don't shoot her." My whisper barely registered in my own ears. My eyes stung. I felt like a coward for not speaking up more clearly. "Please."

The anger melted out of Adam's expression, and he stared at me in confusion and realization and, slowly, shame. Gabriel laid a comforting hand on my shoulder, though he didn't look much more enlightened than the exorcist.

Adam extended his hand to me, tentatively, like he expected me to explode, and tugged the phone out of my hands.

I'll see what I can do. He tapped out each letter with a deliberate effort. *But I'm going to need more information than what I've got.*

"What kind?" Gabriel asked.

Either of you know the demon's name?

"Not that I can recall," Gabriel said.

I took the phone back. *It kept saying something to me earlier.* I tried typing the name out, but autocorrect kept turning the first word into *petunia.* The second I was fairly certain was the name of some celebrity, but apparently it made sense to Adam.

"Potnia Theron?" Adam repeated.

"Yeah." I nodded frantically. "Could that be it?"

"It's—" He caught himself and started typing again. *It's not a demon name. It means something else. Do you know anything else about it? Where it came from? What it wants?*

I shook my head. "No idea."

Gabriel lowered his hand from my shoulder. "It wants me," he said quietly.

Why? Adam asked.

"I don't entirely know," the priest admitted.

We're going to need details. Anything you can think of.

Gabriel shook his head, more of a shudder than a refusal. "It— it happened back in September last year. We were renovating the old rectory. We had a lot of historic buildings in our parish, you see. And I was always fascinated by all of it. The history. The architecture. So during construction, I ignored the barriers and I looked around." He let out a strangled laugh. "It's— it's such a little sin, really. Something so mundane. Harmless. But that's all I intended to do, I swear. One of the adobe bricks had split during the construction, and it had a box inside. You could see by looking at it. The priests who built the rectory must have put it inside the brick mold and poured the clay around it. Genius, really. Nobody could possibly have found it, except by accident. But that's what it was. Just an accident." Another grim, choking laugh. "And you hear stories, you know? About hidden treasures. Historical artifacts that get lost in times of war. And I thought, how wonderful could it be…"

He shook his head.

"But there was no treasure inside. Only the demon. Only death. It's been hunting me ever since."

What about the box? Adam pushed the phone to Gabriel's face. *Do you know where it is? Do you still have it?*

"I— I burned it," Gabriel said. "I thought that might destroy the spirit—"

"Dammit!" Adam growled. Abruptly he looked back to me, as if to make sure I hadn't been offended by the outburst.

What do you remember about the box? he continued. *Did it have any symbols on it? Any writing?*

170

"There was some, but I couldn't read it. It was bocote wood, I remember that. It was old— dark with age, and it had a heavy grain— usually you find it in luxury pieces, you see. But the letters blended too heavily into the grain. It could have said anything."

That's why it's after you, Adam wrote. *You saw the box, so it thinks you know its name. Which would be fantastic if you did, because then that would give us actual power over it.* If his fingers dug any harder into the phone, he would crack the screen.

"I'm sorry," he said to me. "I'll do what I can, but we don't have a lot of options."

Then what options DO we have? I demanded. *Lay it out for me.*

I have no fu— He backspaced abruptly, casting a glance at Gabriel. *— no idea. If a demon ever possessed a dragon before, I haven't heard about it. I don't know how much that changes things.*

Why would it? I asked. *The demon's still the same no matter what, right? It's not like you've got to physically lift it up or anything, is it?*

The power of an exorcism is magnified by the faith of the victim. Buddhist prayers work better on Buddhists, Muslim prayers work better on Muslims. Catholic prayers work well in this country, because pretty much everyone's seen The Exorcist, so most people believe it's supposed to work. But all of that requires a faith in a higher power, which dragons don't have. I reached for the phone to argue against the generalization, but he pulled it out of my reach and continued. *It's not wired into them the way it is with humans. They don't take authority from anyone.*

Well, that explained a lot.

Everything about a dragon's mind is different from a human's. It would make it that much easier for the demon to dig in.

I could speak to the first part— I'd spent the last three years or so translating between Arkay's moods and the world around us— but the second half of that sounded off. I couldn't put my finger on it.

But then, I'd already seen evidence of it, hadn't I?

Is that why it's moving so much faster now? I asked. When it was in Allison, it moved like the girl in *The Ring*. I was fairly certain I'd seen it do a flip when it went after Adam.

Maybe, but I don't think that's all of it, he admitted. *Humans don't use our full strength because we feel pain. I've seen autopsy photos from possessions. They're shredded inside. Ruptured organs, herniated muscle, tendons ripped right off the bone. And that's without the demon doing any dramatic stunts, either. That's just how much force they exert while walking around. It wouldn't be nearly as taxing on a dragon's body. The kind of lifting that would mangle a human body probably wouldn't even pull a muscle on your friend.*

Well, that was one less thing I needed to worry about.

You shouldn't look nearly so relieved by that, Adam pointed out. *It's a lot stronger than we are.*

But I wasn't the only one more relaxed. Over the course of the diatribe, Adam had eased his grip on the phone, and he'd stopped clenching his jaw.

Something moved overhead, and the tension returned. I peered into the dark of the ceiling, flashing the cell phone's screen into the air above us.

"You hear that?" I breathed.

Adam nodded.

There was another sound, so light it could have been the building settling. But the factory was a good hundred years old, and it had been abandoned for the last decade. Any settling it had to do had already happened.

The next time it moved, there was no mistaking the sound of footsteps.

"Is it her?" Gabriel whispered.

She's above us, I wrote.

"Can we run?"

Adam shook his head. "That's asking for an ambush."

There's another platform over the door, I wrote. *She'll be able to jump us if we run.*

A magazine was snapped into the rifle with a menacing click. The message was clear: she wouldn't be able to catch us if Adam shot her first. He signaled for Gabriel to get the door, then leveled the muzzle of the gun at the only entrance.

I opened my mouth to protest, but I never got the chance.

Gabriel's hand had barely touched the doorknob when a crash split the air at the back of the room. The demon had kicked in the glass blocks in the back wall. It landed in a crouch, illuminated by a pool of moonlight. Shattered glass glittered like fallen stars at its feet.

Adam whirled, raising the rifle to shoot. "Get the door!"

Gabriel was way ahead of him. But when he turned the knob, the door opened all of two inches before it stopped with a metallic *thunk*. "It won't open!"

The demon's hands were dark with burns, and I realized what had happened. Those thick, heavy sheets of steel— the same kind Gabriel had used in his shelter, the same kind we'd walked over on the way here— the demon had used them to barricade us inside.

We were trapped.

Adam raised his rifle. "I'm sorry, Rosario."

I stepped between Adam and the demon.

Because we'd been caught and I had nothing left to lose.

Because Arkay was my best friend, and possessed or not, I'd promised to take care of her.

And because something had finally clicked in my brain: if dragons were so easy for demons to possess, then why was this the first one Adam had ever heard of?

"Rosario, get out of there!"

"Put the gun down, Adam." I looked straight into the demon's cavernous eyes. "You're not going to hurt me." My voice barely even shook.

"I'm going to peel the ribs from around your still-beating heart," it hissed.

"No, you're not." I inched closer. "Arkay, I know things are kind of freaky right now, but I've got your back, okay? Same as I always do. Same as you've got mine. But this guy, he doesn't believe me." I jabbed a thumb at Adam. "He thinks you're gonna let this thing hurt me."

"Your pet dragon is gone," the demon said. "Her soul is devoured. There's nothing left inside but hellfire and ash."

"I wasn't talking to you." I advanced another step. "Arkay, you're stronger than this motherfucker." Adam gave an indignant squeak behind me. "I know it. I know you stopped it from hurting me on the roof. That wasn't out of the kindness of its shriveled little heart, and it wasn't some

174

demonic IOU, either. That was you. All you. Just like that was you laughing at my lame-ass pun."

"You've got a big mouth, Potnia Theron." The demon twisted to move around me, but I stepped back into its path, close enough for it to knock my head off with one good swing if it wanted to.

"Then prove me wrong." I spread my arms wide. "Go right ahead. Prove that you're really the one in control here."

No blow came. The demon shook with fury.

One step closer. "Arkay," I said softly. "My beautiful, crazy, taste-impaired Arkay. I need you to do one last thing for me. Just one, and then we can go home and get you that ridiculous armchair." I laid my hand against Arkay's cheek. "I need the demon's name."

Something snapped. The demon lunged, throwing me to the ground with an inhuman shriek. The fall knocked the air out of my lungs, and a pair of knees in my diaphragm finished the job. Clawed hands wrapped around my throat.

Two more bodies eclipsed the moonlight as they rushed to help me. Gabriel tried to pry the demon's arm back. Adam ignored the arms entirely and grabbed the demon around the waist, hauling it into the air. They were both praying now, one in Latin and the other in Spanish, their voices churning into meaningless gibberish. The demon writhed and spat, clinging to me with its legs. It wouldn't let me go.

It would never let me go.

My lungs burned. My head spun. The demon tossed me around as it thrashed, and every impact with the floor sent constellations dancing in front of my eyes. How much pressure would it take to crush my trachea? My spine?

I'd been so sure Arkay would protect me. That she *could* protect me.

The demon pulled me close to its snarling face. Its fingers closed.

And then its expression changed. Desperate rage became horror and fear. Murderous pressure softened. Claws retreated from my skin.

It happened in the space of a second. A flash, a shift, and two syllables cracked through the air like gunfire: "*Kele!*"

The word was swallowed as quickly as it had been uttered. The snarl returned, and with it the pressure around my throat.

But Adam was already chanting.

I only had time for one final thought before the darkness overwhelmed me:

I really hope that was its whole name.

Arkay

First there was pain.

No. That's not right.

First there was FUCKSHITHELLOHFUCK
WHY
IS
THIS
HAPPENING.

There was screaming. There were threats and curses layered so thick you could drown in them, and then thicker still until they clotted into incomprehension. And when all the horror and pain and fear cancelled each other out, all I had left was rage.

That thing had dared to slither inside me. To smother me. To force me into submission.

And worst of all, it had hurt Rosa.

And this. Would. Not. Fly.

I thrashed against it. I snarled and spat and tore. I screamed. It wound tighter around me, but I only struggled harder.

I would break myself into pieces before I let it have me. I would bring this whole fucking factory down over my head. I would burn us both to ash.

But then there was a voice.

Rosa's voice.

When she spoke, I listened. When she commanded, I obeyed. And when she told me how to fight back, I sank my jaws into the demon. I reached into its head the way it had violated mine, and I brought her its name still bloody between my teeth.

I couldn't tell you when the other voices started filtering through, or when Kele stopped laughing and started to howl. I couldn't guess which command finally ripped its consciousness off of mine, or at what point the murky shadows crystallized into shape and color.

But I knew the precise moment when Rosario's voice fell silent.

Slowly I became aware of other things: the barrel of a gun levelled a few inches from my eyes, the face of a young soldier as he chanted a prayer, the smell of metallic brine laced with the harsh sweetness of fear.

Blood.

Familiar blood.

I turned my focus away from the soldier and his rifle. The priest was on his knees a few feet away, hunched over Rosa's body. Her face was slack. Her eyes were shut. Her long dark hair had come out of its braid and pooled behind her head like a bloodstain.

My body felt overcooked and disjointed, but I scrambled across rotting linoleum and broken glass.

The soldier shouted, but the words smudged into meaningless sounds. His intent was clear enough: the barrel of his rifle followed me to Rosario's side. The priest tensed and scooted away.

My fingers skated over her wrist. Her skin was warm. A pulse drummed under my fingertips.

She cringed and groaned, and I withdrew.

Her throat was red and raw, and the darkest marks matched the size and shape of my hands. Fresh cuts on her throat lined up perfectly with my nails.

Kele's doing. *Motherfucker.*

But then her eyes fluttered open. Her gaze fell on me, and her grimace softened into a pained smile. A gentle hand rose to brush my cheek, and I leaned into the touch.

Tentatively I reached out to her, too. When she didn't cringe away, I ran my fingertips along her scalp, careful not to snag her hair. The back of her skull was hot and inflamed. There was blood, but the cut it flowed from was shallow enough that it had already started to clot.

I curled around her shoulders and eased her head against the softer cushion of my arms.

Rosario

"You're sure she's not going to try something?" Adam didn't type it out, but he probably didn't need to. He'd asked the same question so many times that even Gabriel was starting to roll his eyes.

"Tell you what," I said. "If you're that worried, give me a few more minutes and I'll come with you." I would have tried writing it, but Adam wouldn't let me have my phone back. Something about reading aggravating my condition. "I used to live around here. We can walk to the McDonalds, you can call you a tow truck, and we'll skip the hospital altogether."

"Absolutely not," he said. "You lost consciousness."

"Only for a few minutes!"

"At very minimum you've got a concussion. They'll likely need to do an MRI, a CT-scan, X-rays—"

"And if I ever have grandkids, they'll be retired by the time they pay all that off," I said. "No thank you."

"It's not up for discussion." He sounded like he wanted to put his foot down, but the last three times he'd raised his voice, Arkay had straight-up growled at him. Finally he sighed, and I was almost naive enough to take that as a sign of defeat. "What about Gabriel, then? He's going to need at least three rounds of antibiotics for all the infections he's racked up, he's dealing with some obvious signs of malnutrition, and I'm betting he hasn't been running down the street to Kroger for bottled water. You really want to tell me that he shouldn't get some decent medical attention?"

"Of course he should."

"But that doesn't apply to you because…?"

That wasn't fair.

I lowered my voice. "You mean besides the medical bills? How about because I don't want to go to prison. The police in this area know me and Arkay, and they don't exactly like either of us. I just got my life back on track, Adam. I have a job, we're renting a house— things are okay for the first time since… since forever." Arkay gripped my shoulder protectively. "I'm not going to ruin that."

Adam stared at me for a long while, before he sat down on the peeling linoleum. "Doctor-patient privilege. There's no gunshot wounds, so they have no reason to turn you in."

"You don't know that," I muttered.

182

"Then I'll make sure they don't. And the Order has a decent medical plan. I'll see what I can do about getting you covered."

I blinked in surprise. "You can do that?"

"It's my job," he said flatly. "You're dealing with dragons and demons. The entire point of the Order is to keep people safe from this kind of thing. Which we wouldn't exactly be doing if we let you go bankrupt over this."

"You're serious?"

"Yeah."

I leaned tighter against Arkay. "So that makes you... what? An exorcist social worker or something?"

He tipped his head. "Something like that."

"What about him?" I asked, nodding at Gabriel.

"I don't—"

"If it's about him, he deserves to be included in the conversation," I said. "Type it."

Adam glowered at me for a moment, but relented and took a long moment to explain my question in writing.

"I should still have insurance with the Church," Gabriel said. "I may be sent back to Santa Fe."

"Well, if you're ever back in town, be sure to let us know, okay? Or email us, or something."

Gabriel flashed a weary smile once he'd read Adam's translation. "I think that may be necessary. After all this..."

I nodded. "Trust me, I know."

Gabriel stayed with me while Adam left to call for help. Without him to keep the phone away, I made a grab for it. One text wouldn't hurt.

What about the demon? I asked. *Is it gone?*

"The shadows left Arkay," Gabriel said. "Adam seemed… surprised."

So it's not coming back? I had to know. I had to be sure.

Gabriel took my uninjured hand and gave it a squeeze. "No," he said gently. "It's not coming back."

According to Gabriel, I'd only been unconscious for a few minutes, and it was still enough to warrant so many medical tests and screenings that I was pretty sure I'd start glowing. All the while Arkay flitted around the scanning rooms like a hummingbird on Red Bull, and she hadn't stopped hovering since. Every hour, on the hour, she was at my side with a cold compress, starting when Adam drove us home from the hospital in a rental car and ending when the doctor-mandated twenty-four-hour rest period was over. Even after that, it took some genuine coaxing to persuade her to sleep in her own bed, instead of curled up beside me. Constantly handling ice was as good for her hands as it was for my head; apparently the demon's proactive approach to climbing had done a number on her fingers, and handling iron while possessed had left her hands covered in second-degree burns. She wouldn't come near the doctors, but Adam said she had what seemed like minor fractures in two fingers, and the rest were bruised to hell.

A lot of the details got fuzzy beyond that, and not only because of the concussion. Adam said he'd take care of it, and somehow he had. Afterward I looked up the average prices of the tests I'd taken. Depending on who took them and how generous they were feeling, my total ran up somewhere between the price of a new car and the mortgage for a house, but I never saw a bill. We never heard from a collector. The police never dropped by to ask us inconvenient questions.

Danielle came by almost daily with food and reminders that she was only a phone call away if we needed anything. Gabriel dropped off his email address and a number where we could text him while his situation with the church got sorted out.

Kindra came by almost three days after we got home. She leaned nonchalantly against the front porch, but her labret stud twitched as she worried the inside of the piercing between her teeth.

"Hey," she said, pushing a bouquet of miniature sunflowers into my hands as soon as I answered the door. "How are you feeling?"

"Good," I said automatically. "Better, I mean. Fine." I needed to stop talking before I completely embarrassed myself. "How are you? How's work?"

"We're missing you." A faint smile. "Also, Dan is being an asshole, and you totally need to help me put him in his place."

"Sure thing." I averted my eyes to the get-well-soon card, which looked like it had been signed by most of the staff. "The doctor said I should be okay to go back to work by Monday. Think you can survive that long without me?"

"For a few days, I think I'll manage. But that's it. No more getting yourself hurt again, got it?" She said it playfully, but there was an undertone of genuine concern in her voice.

"Hey." I reached out and took her hand. "I don't make a habit out of hospital visits. I promise. This was a fluke. It shouldn't happen again."

"You sure about that?" Her anxiety bubbled to the surface. "You skip work to hang out with some weird dude from out of town, and the next day you're in the hospital. That doesn't sound like much of a fluke." She zeroed in on me, and suddenly I couldn't look away. "Rosa, you know me. Judging isn't a thing I do. But if you're in trouble, I can do a whole lot more to help you if I know what's going on."

She meant it, too.

If I asked her to help me with a creepy ex or a drug dealer or a loan shark or something, she'd probably come running with a crowbar. She was that kind of person. Hell, it was half the reason Arkay liked her so much.

But the thing was, she already believed in all those things. They were mundane. When you got into trouble with them, you called the cops or the FBI or something, and even if they didn't help you, at least they would believe that you were really in trouble.

The last person who'd gone to the cops talking about monsters had been a police detective. Detective Sharp had filed an incident report, and she'd lost her badge for it. They said she'd had a mental break.

Right after Arkay started following me around, I'd tried telling people what she was. I'd tried to warn them about what happened when she got angry. I'd learned to pinpoint the exact moment when people made up their mind about me: *this is one of the crazy ones. It's too bad, she was so nice.*

Hell, there had been days when I doubted Arkay existed at all, like maybe she was my Fight-Club-style imaginary friend and nobody had the heart to tell me otherwise.

I could prove it, though. I could ask Arkay to get all big and scaly, and then—

And then?

When she'd found out Arkay was a dragon, Detective Sharp had tried to shoot her. When Mike had realized that there was something not entirely human about Arkay, he'd thrown us both out of the homeless camp. When my parents found out I was a lesbian, they'd disowned me.

People flipped their shit when they learned secrets. The only ones who didn't were the ones already living with them.

I swallowed.

I liked Kindra. I really, *really* liked her.

I didn't want to lose her already.

"I don't think I can talk about it right now," I said. "I'm sorry. I just can't."

Kindra's expression softened. Sympathy, maybe. Not quite pity. "I get that. I do. But I'm here for you if you need me, okay?"

I scrambled to change the subject. "Actually, there's something I've been meaning to ask you."

Her smile was warm and permissive. She'd let it go.

"See, we found the world's loudest armchair at the Goodwill last week, and I'm pretty sure we're gonna need a small army to move the damn thing. Wanna help?" At least with this, I didn't have to hide. "I'll bribe you with dinner."

She grinned, and the stud in her lip flashed as it caught the light. That's the only reason I kept staring at her smile. Promise.

Fext

Security around the factory expanded since the incident, though by the look of things, there hadn't been much to speak of beforehand. Now the chain link fence was patched and reinforced with barbed wire, and a police cruiser opened the rusted gate to circle the area.

It was a token effort at best. Only a single police officer sat in the vehicle that pulled up beside us, trying to keep my strike team in his line of sight while he reached for his sidearm.

He caught my gaze and his eyes glazed over, his hand falling limp against his shoulder holster. His body slumped forward against the steering wheel, and the air was filled with the blare of the car horn. I gave the signal, and a rakshasa leaned in the window and heaved him sideways, silencing the noise.

Someone would have heard that.

"How long before police arrive?" I asked.

Another rakshasa stepped forward. "Six minutes, if they've been notified."

Of course they'd been notified. As far as they were concerned, this was an active crime scene. "Then you have five minutes. Fan out and collect what evidence you can."

No point watching the ground for tracks. It had been too long since the incident, and emergency vehicles and regular patrols had spoiled anything the earth might tell us.

The walls, though, were a different story.

One warehouse wall was scorched black from an explosion, its epicenter cratered. The bricks had crumbled under the raw force of a lightning strike. Scratches carved into the corner of another building— small, scattered, but parallel. The score marks of enormous antlers.

I narrowed my eyes. A river dragon.

"We've got evidence of rifle fire!" came a shout from further on.

My team hurried to search for more clues, but I followed the trail of a fight. The dragon had been upended. Outmatched. It had fled to higher ground.

Two sets of blood splatter led in two directions. Smaller splashes marked a source moving low to the ground, while the other set had fallen from significantly higher. I followed it around the corner, behind the shelter of a foreman's office.

This was where it had climbed. Where its talons had carved deep into the brick and mortar to haul its weight higher.

I traced the lowest of the claw marks with my fingers: three parallel gouges, each so deep that they swallowed my finger up to the second knuckle. A second set of gouges dug into the brick almost three yards away.

It looked like our dragon had all its limbs intact when it made to climb.

I swallowed my disappointment.

"Five minutes!" shouted my lieutenant, and the rest of the team gathered together. "Let's move out!" As soon as the team started moving, he fell into step beside me. "Ma'am, we've found evidence of demon activity."

"What kind of evidence?" I asked, not missing a stride.

"The demon, Ma'am. We sealed away what was left of it, but…" He hesitated. "Whoever got to it before us didn't just exorcise it. That thing was shredded. I think… I think it's *dead*. I didn't know that was possible."

"We can start asking questions when we find out who did it." I raised my voice for the rest of the team. "We're looking at a fight between multiple humanoids and a river dragon. Identify them, find them, and bring them to me."

Book 3:

Dance with the Devil

Arkay

The world was a glorious, dizzying shroud of black cut through with shards of electric blue. Music blared around me, the notes lost in a beat so intense that I could feel its vibration in my bones. Faces turned up to stare at me through the haze, dim and ghostly in the refracted light, staring like acolytes in the presence of their god.

I gripped the pole between my knees and arched my back until I was parallel to the floor, my hands outstretched to snatch a five from one of the patrons at my feet. My fingers trailed over his for just a moment, and I whipped upright so fast that the long black hair of my wig made an audible snap.

I climbed the pole, my movements somewhere between a slither and a grind, and then I twisted again. For a pulsing crescendo, I was suspended only by my hands, and I threw my feet high over my head. The soles of my six-inch stilettos clacked against a light fixture on the ceiling. I wrapped my whole body around the pole, a Gordian knot of limbs and vinyl snakeskin, letting momentum and gravity send me down in a dizzying spiral.

I called the routine 'revenge against high heels'. I'd gone almost a whole song without my shoes touching the stage. One of these days I'd do a full set entirely off my feet. The other dancers had already started placing bets on how long it would take me to pull it off.

But not this time. I was sliding too low on the sweat-slick pole, so I lowered myself back onto the stage with a long, flashy kick. Judging by the flutter of bills, my audience appreciated the show. I slinked to the edge of the stage where my most generous patron sat.

"Hey there." I drew myself into a pose that was half serpentine and half yoga, still undulating in time with the roaring music. "What's your name?"

His face fell into a slack smile. "Stewart."

I loved my customers. Show them a bit of attention and they turned to putty. Darlings, all of them.

"I'm Arkay. Are you having a good time tonight?" I drew my arms over my head with a shimmying motion I'd stolen from a belly dance video and pulled the strings that held my top in place. It pooled around my waist, leaving my breasts bare. They were small enough that all my bouncing only earned me a slight jiggle, but judging by the sweep of Stewart's eyes, that was more than enough.

196

The song blended seamlessly into another. Stewart fumbled a handful of bills into my G-string, and I moved over to lay the same treatment on one of his friends.

I loved my job. Not just the money, but the way people looked at me.

For three years, I'd been invisible the way only a homeless person can be. People's eyes had glazed over when they looked at me. I had been a piece of the scenery, something to be avoided and ignored.

At Our Lady of White River, that changed.

I flaunted myself— my strength, my agility, my beauty— and they stared. They admired. They *paid*. I was the one they wanted but couldn't have, and it felt so damn good.

The DJ announced the next dancer, and while she wiped off the pole for her set, I swept up my earnings and sauntered off the stage.

I didn't like the part where I had to leave. I could grind and slither and crawl around the stage, but as soon as I climbed down, I had to actually walk on the sins of nature strapped to my feet.

I hated high heels. They threw off my balance so badly I had to stick out my ass and swing my hips just to maintain my center of gravity— which, of course, was the whole point.

As soon as I'd put up my earnings, I turned to stalking the floor. Usually I didn't have too much trouble finding a customer who appreciated a half-naked woman draped across the lap as much as I appreciated not standing in these ridiculous shoes. It didn't take long before I found one, and a quick glance told me he hadn't been called by any of the other dancers. But before I could corner him, the house mom pulled me into the dressing room with a quick, "Have you got a second?"

She was the oldest of the women who worked at the club, maybe in her late twenties or early thirties, though I'd never bothered to ask. I'd never seen her work the pole, but she didn't need to. She carried herself with an air that was innately friendly and disarming. Outside the club, you could see all her frailties—the brittleness of hair that had been bleached and dyed to its breaking point, the ginger movements of worn-down joints, and the odd pallor that came with years of working nights. But when she was masked in makeup and shrouded in flashing lights and pounding music, she was in her element.

She ushered me to the back. The moment I was out of sight of the customers, I slipped out of my shoes.

The dressing room was fairly standard: a long, narrow space, lined on one side with countertops, sinks and mirrors, while lockers and changing stalls dominated the opposite wall. A collection of chairs had been pulled into a cluster at the far corner, and a handful of dancers huddled protectively around a girl named Becky.

At eighteen, Becky was the youngest person on the shift, and had the delicate awkwardness of a newbie. Her dancing had always been infused with wide-eyed innocence, and she would peer out at her audience as if silently asking them if she was doing it right. Not everyone went for that, though a lot of guys threw down absurd sums of money to reassure her that *yes, baby, you're perfect.*

But some guys took it too far. They got it in their heads that she needed saving. That if a big, strong, nice guy like themselves walked into her life, she'd magically turn into...

Okay, I never did figure out that last part. I assumed most of the end games involved her sleeping with her heroic savior, but beyond that, the details got fuzzy. Did they expect her to date them? Marry them? Become a tax attorney?

I'd actually asked a lot of guys to explain it to me, and I had yet to get a straight answer.

Humans did that a lot, though: they declare something a problem and decide to fix it, without any clear or practical ideas about the finished product they were actually working toward. Take the French Revolution, for example.

But I digress.

Becky was still in jeans and a hoodie. Her eyes were bloodshot, and her face was caked with makeup to hide the dark circles underneath them. She hadn't been sleeping. Might have been crying, too, though she'd touched up since then. Her knees were pulled up to her chest, and one of the other dancers rubbed her shoulder reassuringly.

"It's gonna be okay, Becky," the other woman murmured. "You're gonna be fine. Arkay's gonna take care of him."

"I always do," I said, perching in the chair they'd left empty for me. "You want to tell me what's up?" I kept my voice soft, but Becky ducked her head like I'd shouted at her. It took her a few tries to speak, and when she did, her words were a mumble.

"I'm sorry this keeps happening."

"Don't apologize. Beating up assholes is my favorite pastime." I flashed a confident grin, but then toned it down. "Seriously, though. What's going on isn't your fault. You're doing your job, and you're doing it damn well. These guys taking it personally— that's their problem. Not yours." Carefully, I tugged her hands from around her knees and held them in my own. "Do you think you can tell me what happened?"

I waited patiently while she built up the nerve to speak.

"His name's Vinny," she mumbled into her knees. "He's been coming by for a while now. A couple months ago he started renting out the VIP lounge. For dances, sometimes, but mostly just to talk, you know? He seemed nice."

Funny how that went: the nicer a guy seemed, the nastier he could be when he didn't get his way.

"Only, last week, he started sending things to my apartment. Just flowers and stuff," she clarified quickly. Back in June, one of the other dancers found mutilated animal remains under her bedroom window, courtesy of a particularly twisted stalker. I'd taken care of that one, too. Last I checked, he still hadn't regained the full use of his hands.

"Even if it's flowers," I said. "This guy has no right to follow you home. That's messed up."

She gave a small nod. "A little bit later, I thought I saw Vinny's car on campus. He didn't get out or anything. He was just watching me. I'm scared he's gonna start telling people where I work. And then tonight he followed me here. He drove behind me the whole time. I was scared to get out of my car."

"She called Dre and he walked her inside," the house mom explained.

"And this Vinny guy?" I asked. "Is he still here?"

"He tried to come in, but Dre wouldn't let him," she said. "He left the parking lot."

I turned my attention back to Becky. "Do you think you can describe this guy for me?"

Becky had been through this shit so many times she'd picked up on the right way to describe people. Believe it or not, age/race/hair/eyes really didn't make a person much easier to identify. I was more interested in details that made him stand out: a hyena-like walk that was somehow both a sulk and a swagger; a penchant for bad spray tans and expensive hair gel; a tendency to wear designer clothes and colognes, usually with no regard to whether they actually suited him.

"You're gonna be safe here," I said gently. "Dre and the boys aren't gonna let him near here. Even if he manages to apparate in here or wherever, I'm gonna be right here to kick his ass into his throat." That got a smile out of Becky. The girl wrote *Harry Potter* fanfic like you wouldn't believe. "If the boys see his car outside, they're gonna come get me, okay? And then Vinny and I are gonna have a nice long heart-to-heart."

Rosario

"Do you see the two little prongs, just above the grip?" My girlfriend kissed me on the cheek, and I felt the faint bump of her labret piercing. "There's a third prong just like them at the very tip of the barrel. See it? I want you to line them up. It's called building the castle. Can you do that for me, babe?"

I blushed like an idiot. Twenty-five years old, and I still giggled about pet names. Even the gun in my hand didn't cancel out the goofiness of my grin. At least I could do what she asked. "Okay, I've got the sights lined up."

"Great job." Kindra rubbed affectionately at my waist. "There's gonna be a bit of a recoil, so I'm gonna step back, alright?"

"Sure thing," I said, even though that meant she had to stop leaning against me. We had plenty of time for cuddling after we left the shooting range.

"It's also gonna discharge the bullet casing when it fires, and those things are fuckin' hot and pretty much magnetically attracted to cleavage. Seriously, it's uncanny."

"Damn. You mean we can't go shooting in lingerie?"

"Now there's a mental image I'm going to treasure." Kindra twirled her bleached braids around one finger like a love-struck teenager. "Later. Definitely later. For now, how about we tackle some actual shooting?"

Too bad. I'd enjoyed the track we were on.

She cleared her throat. "You know how in all the movies and stuff, they always talk about pulling a trigger?"

"Yeah?"

"That's bullshit. You don't need nearly that much power behind it. Just give it a good squeeze."

I exhaled so loud it almost sounded like a sigh. Kindra's Beretta jolted in my hand with a deafening crack, though through my ear protection it sounded more like a pop. A hole appeared in the shoulder of the paper target.

"Great job," she said. "Now can you try it again?"

I slowly emptied the magazine into the target while Kindra offered pointers to improve my aim. I tuned my focus to the sound of her voice, the techniques I didn't know, the niceness of spending time together.

I tried not to think about the sound a bullet made when it hit a human skull, or the pattern of viscera across a cinder block wall. When I smelled the sharp tang of gunpowder, I kept reminding myself that it wasn't laced with the smell of old blood and rotting meat.

I wasn't in a garage full of the reanimated dead. I was on a nice, safe shooting range with my beautiful girlfriend. This was supposed to be fun. So I could just go on and pretend the rush of adrenaline in my system was excitement, and the twist in my stomach meant I was hungry, and none of this had anything to do with what happened almost a year ago.

Kindra was thoughtful and considerate. If I let on how uncomfortable I was, she'd want to know why. And I could either tell her the truth— that the last time I'd held a gun, I'd been fighting a zombie horde with my dragon roommate while a necromancer tried to harvest our organs for an evil ritual— or I could lie to her. Again.

So instead I stuck to the little lie, and I pretended to be completely cool with this.

If I kept it up long enough, maybe it would be true.

Arkay

Washing up after work always took longer on nights when I went hunting. After six hours of dancing, I was caked in sweat— my own and my customers'— as well as perfume and heavy makeup. The combination didn't entirely overwhelm my senses, but it made my job a lot harder than it had to be.

I stood over the dressing room sink in jeans and sneakers, scrubbing myself down with a washcloth and unscented soap. My skin prickled, cold and raw under the assault. The other dancers kept their distance while I cleaned up. Only the house mom dared interrupt the ritual. She was the oldest of the dancers, and she'd done this the longest. By technical rules, she was my manager in this establishment, but she was wise enough to understand what that really meant. Nobody manages a dragon. The best she could hope for was to point me in the right direction and get out of my way.

I looked up, my eyes still stinging from soap. "Is Vinny here already?"

"Dre says he just spotted Vinny's car going past the parking lot," she said.

"He's circling. Good. That means he'll stay close." I grabbed my t-shirt and pulled it on, not bothering with a bra. "I'll text you when I'm done, okay?"

She nodded.

I dug into my pocket and pulled out a stack of bills, paperclipped into neat bundles for each recipient. It was part of our job to tip the support staff— the bartender, the bouncers, the DJ, and so on— but actually doing the rounds to get them all took half of forever. "Do you mind handing out my tips for me?"

"Of course," she said. "Be careful out there."

I grinned. "Always." And with no more preamble, I stepped out the back door and into the night.

The last of the day's heat had leached out of the asphalt underfoot, and a breeze disturbed my liberated hair. It was September, and just on this side of cool— not quite cold yet, but I could feel autumn settling around me. It drifted in the sweet decay of falling leaves, the lingering smoke of bonfires, the subtle change of moisture in the air.

But that wasn't what I was looking for. I forced myself to focus on other scents. Car exhaust, musk, and the chemical astringency of heavy hair products and a recent spray-tan.

Amazingly enough, most humans don't grasp what it means to have a good nose. It's not like a search function on a computer: just because you caught a scent doesn't mean that you instantly know where it came from. Instead you learn to follow the wind and take in the subtle clues that come with it. Vinny's scent was carried on the same breeze as food garbage— not much, maybe a few pizza boxes and take-out— along with bleach, ammonia and lemon polish. I followed it at an easy pace, wandering from streetlight to streetlight like I was just walking home for the night.

I found him parked behind the dumpster of the antique shop. His white convertible might have qualified as a classic if it hadn't been tricked out beyond the limits of good taste. I put on my 'lamb to the slaughter' face and stepped up to the driver seat.

"Hey." I tapped at the window. "'Scuse me? Do you have a second?"

He rolled it down and gave me an irritated look. "Who the hell are you?"

Which was saying something. I recognized the guy. I must have seen him at the club at least a dozen times. I'd even given him a lap dance. I didn't look all that different without my wig and makeup.

I flashed my most doe-eyed smile. "I'm from the club. I've got a message for you. From Becky. It's cold out here, can we go somewhere and talk?"

He narrowed his eyes. "I'm fine right here, sweets. What'd she say?"

I struggled not to lose my smile. This gambit usually worked better when they were outside. "You sure you don't want to talk to me face to face?"

"I said I'm stayin' where I am." He folded his arms against the open window. An engraved revolver rested sideways on his elbow, its barrel pointed at me. "Now are you gonna deliver the message or are we gonna have a problem?"

He had a gun. Not cool.

"Do you always start conversations with a weapon?" I asked.

"You think I don't know what's going on here? You think I'm stupid or something?"

Well, it *was* the most obvious explanation for that tan.

"Skinny squinty bitch like you? Yeah. I come out there, you're gonna use some crazy Kung Fu shit on me. So we're gonna have a nice, civil conversation right here."

Sexist *and* racist— Becky was missing out on a real catch with this one.

"Civil," I repeated. There was no sweetness left in my voice. "You think there's anything civil about scaring an innocent woman?"

He shrugged. "You're the one who started this conversation, sweets."

"I was talking about Becky."

"I ain't the one scarin' her. It's you people and your horror stories, makin' me out to be the bad guy here."

"She's told you to leave. A good guy would do as the nice lady says."

"What can I say?" He flashed a smug grin that showed off his too-pale lips. "I'm a romantic."

"You're a stalker," I said flatly.

He pulled back the hammer on the revolver. The gesture was more threatening than actually practical— modern guns cocked without any help. "You know, I'm just about sick of you whores talkin' trash about me."

"Strippers," I corrected. I could have pointed him in the direction of some actual escorts, but I wasn't about to subject those women to this asshole. "You're lurking behind a dumpster with a loaded gun. Which part of that doesn't sound like a serial killer?"

His lip curled into a snarl, and he squeezed the trigger.

I flinched— you can't avoid it when something breaks the sound barrier less than a foot away from your face, no matter how badass you're trying to be— but I stood my ground. The bullet went wide.

Here's the thing: if you want to actually have decent accuracy with a handgun, it's usually a good idea to fire it right-side-up instead of sideways. It also helps to actually, you know, *aim*.

I'll be generous and say it was probably meant to be a warning shot.

He probably expected me to duck and cower. Maybe even run. Though what would be the point? I was pretty damn fast, but even I couldn't outrun a bullet. He probably didn't anticipate me grabbing his wrist and wrenching the revolver out of his hand.

"Alright, that's enough," I said, stepping back and turning it on him. "You've lost your firearm privileges."

He stared, wide-eyed, but his hands started fluttering to the seat beside him.

I fired a warning shot of my own, but unlike *somebody* I could mention, I actually bothered to look where I was shooting. The back tire deflated with a low hiss through a pair of brand new holes. "The only thing you're gonna be reaching for is your wallet. Your other hand is going to pretend it's glued to the steering wheel."

"Are you fuckin'—"

I pulled the trigger. Out went the front tire. "You know, it's gonna be awful hard to drive all the way to the hospital with two flats. I'm not sure you're gonna make it in time." I bared my teeth. "Wallet."

"Here!" He flung it at me, and I heard a mutter of 'crazy bitch' under his breath.

I sank into a crouch, picking up the trophy off the street without letting his face leave my sights. "You know, the thing about driver's licenses is that they tend to have all these convenient little details on them. You know. Name, birthday, home address." Ooh, he had cash in here. Large bills, too. "It even says here that you're an organ donor. Good for you, Vincent Paternoster."

His nose twitched. It was kind of adorable. You know, the way brown recluses are adorable if you get close enough. Of course, that's usually how you get bit.

"Now this? This is just a warning. But if you come near Becky, or Our Lady, or any of our staff again, I'm going to find you, and you and I are going to have a very long, very unpleasant conversation. You can go ahead and hide, if that makes you feel safe. You can change addresses. You can skip town. But if you give me a reason, I will hunt you down, and there will be nothing that can save you. Do we understand each other?"

"You're insane," he breathed.

I grinned wide enough to show off teeth that hadn't been nearly as sharp a second before. "I'm being patient with you, sweets. Don't make me reconsider."

He swallowed.

"Good boy. Now get out of here before I change my mind."

One-zero-one-four. The shiny blue padlock fell open in my hands, but I still had to pry at the bus locker. The hinges were rusty and poorly maintained. Further up the line was evidence of a lock being smashed open. The drug problem in this town was seriously getting out of hand.

I'd need to find a more secure place to keep my stuff, or one night I'd come back here and find it all gone. Which, considering the nature of my stash, would be especially bad news.

I pulled Vinny's engraved pistol from my duffel bag and deposited it with the rest of my collection. It was getting awfully cramped in there. I'd already had to stack my trophies just right so they wouldn't come crashing out of the locker in an avalanche of firearms. Too many more, and I'd have to tie them into place with string or something, and that would just look ridiculous.

Or I could bring them home. But Rosa might find them, and she'd want to know where I'd gotten them from, and I'd have to tell her about the extra services I'd been providing at Our Lady, and she'd have something else to worry about.

She hadn't been sleeping well lately. Living on the streets had taught her to be always on guard, and after the zombie thing, she started having real bad nightmares. It used to be that I could nuzzle up against her at night and soothe her back into peaceful sleep, but ever since she'd started dating Kindra, I'd been banned from sleeping in her room.

I'd hoped the nightmares would go away now that we had our own place. But from what I could hear through the walls, they'd only gotten worse.

Nope, Rosa had enough shit to deal with. No way was I bringing my stash home with me. But that meant I still needed a place to put it. Someplace a little bit safer from the resident junkie population.

And just like that, I got an idea.

Rosario

It was a little past eleven in the morning when Kindra dropped me off on the front steps of my rented house. It was a squat little thing, with creaking floorboards and leaky insulation and scorch marks on the siding where the meth lab next door blew up— but it was mine. Sure, it technically belonged to the landlady, but even she couldn't evict me without sixty days' notice and a damn good reason.

After eight years living on the streets, I finally had a home.

We have a home, I amended when I got inside and heard the faint sounds of snoring. Arkay was curled up like a kitten on her enormous pink armchair. She was still in her pajamas— a pair of women's boxers and one of my old t-shirts— and her tablet balanced precariously across one armrest. Most likely she'd fallen asleep reading something.

I pulled a fleece blanket off the couch and draped it around her, picking up the tablet before it fell to the floor.

"Hey, Rosa," Arkay hummed, burrowing into the blanket. "Date went well?"

"Yes, it did." I smoothed her short black hair. "I'm home now. Go back to sleep."

"*Nnn.*" I think she meant to put a vowel in there somewhere. "'M awake now. Wanna get breakfast?"

"It's almost noon, Kay," I said gently.

"Lunch, then."

"I've got lunch meat in the fridge from last week's potluck," I said. "Want me to make you some sandwiches? Then you don't have to get dressed."

She made another vowelless humming sound, and I retreated to the kitchen. By the time I came out with a plate of ham and cheese, Arkay had fallen into another doze.

I set the plate on the coffee table and leaned over her.

"Long night?" I asked, petting her hair again.

"Little bit." She yawned. "I got home so late I figured I might as well stay up. Then I changed my mind. I got us gym memberships, though. At that one place with the pool."

"Huh. I didn't know that place was open all night."

"Nope. Opens at nine."

"So you've only had… what, three hours of sleep?"

Another yawn threatened to unhinge her jaw. "Maybe."

"That's it." I scooped her off the chair. She clung to my shoulders to take the brunt of her weight off my arms. It was a sweet gesture, but unnecessary. I'd carried her often enough over the years. "Off to bed with you. And maybe think about calling in to work tonight."

"Nuh-uh," she mumbled. "I'll be good by then."

"Sleep first. Then you can see how you feel. I don't want you breaking your neck on that pole."

"But sammiches," was her final argument before I lowered her into the small mountain of pillows covering her bed.

"They'll be in the fridge when you wake up."

"Whr'r you gonna be?"

"I'm meeting up with Adam. I don't know if I'll be back before you wake up." I layered an assortment of quilts and throws on top of her and tucked them in tight. "Will you be okay?"

"Mm-hmm. Have fun." She nestled deeper into her little nest. By the time I shut the door, she was already asleep.

I didn't have long to wait before Adam pulled into the driveway. He was close to my age, give or take a few years, with a military demeanor that his too-small T-shirt disguised about as well as it hid his muscle tone. His hair was that ambiguous gray-blond-brown that seemed to happen every time a white guy got a buzz cut.

He was a member of the Order of Saint Michael of the Sun, which as near as I could figure made him one part exorcist, one part social worker, and one part Winchester from Supernatural. I'd tried looking up the Order on Google, but there were too many results to be meaningful. It could be anything, from a Portuguese air force organization to a rank of Boy Scouts to a historical re-enactment society.

It was probably for the best that Arkay was still asleep when he arrived. He made an effort to be casual and friendly around her, but she unnerved him. He got twitchy and tense around her sometimes. When he thought we couldn't see, he would get all quiet and just stare at her like she was a tiger at the zoo—something wild and beautiful and utterly deadly.

It wasn't an unhealthy attitude. After all, she almost killed him the first time they met.

Instead his meetings were alone with me.

"Hey Adam." I climbed into a black SUV and buckled my seatbelt. "How are you doing?"

"I'm doing well." He shifted into gear. "How are you?" It was more of a nicety than anything else. I'd noticed a while back that Adam preferred not to talk about his home life with me. I got that. Checking up on me and Arkay was part of his job, and he probably didn't want to get that mixed up with his personal life. But still— we'd almost died together. You'd think that would soften some of the professional edge.

"Work is going pretty well. I'm finally getting enough hours to get full time."

He glanced at me out of the corner of his eye. "I thought you weren't having money problems."

"We've got enough for rent and stuff." Arkay saw to that. For a while, she'd made as much in one night as I had in an entire week. "But it's nice to be able to put money into savings. And full time means I qualify for things like insurance and retirement packages."

"Waitresses get retirement packages?"

"Not good ones. But it's a step in the right direction."

"Good. I'm glad to hear it." I could practically see him going over the mental checklist of subjects to talk about, but pretended not to notice. I was pretty sure Arkay and I were his first clients. "How are things going with your girlfriend?"

I tugged the seatbelt to lay more comfortably across my chest. "Kindra's good. We're okay."

"Only okay?" He leaned forward to look past me around a corner, and swerved into a wide turn.

"I don't like lying to her," I admitted.

"You're an honest person. But you've got good instincts, and you should listen to them. Not everyone can handle learning about the things we deal with."

"Don't I know it." I slumped and turned my attention out the window. "Thing is, I'm not exactly sure what my instincts are saying right now. I want to tell her the truth. I do. But if she reacts badly..."

"There's no need to rush things," he said. "If there's a right time to tell her, you'll know."

"Thanks." I fidgeted. "I can't exactly talk to Arkay about this stuff. Or I can, but I already know what she'll say. She thinks I should tell Kindra what's going on."

Adam nodded, like that was a given. "Dragons tend to be disposed toward honesty. The more brutal the better. It's one of the reasons why they have so much trouble with tact."

"Is it?"

He nodded and turned in toward a park. "They have a natural difficulty when it comes to putting themselves in another person's shoes. Empathy doesn't come as naturally to them as it does to you and me. It's a—"

"Predatory instinct, I know. You've said."

"How is Arkay doing, by the way?" Adam asked. "Is she staying out of trouble?"

"As well as she can, I guess. She's getting along with the other girls at work." Last week she'd helped one of the other dancers change a flat tire. In the absence of a car jack, she'd lifted up the back corner of the car and held it there until her coworker could attach the spare. I'd only found out because the distressed damsel had insisted on driving Arkay and me home from work afterward. "You know, I had some hang-ups about her dancing, but I'm starting to think it's good for her. It lets her work off some of that extra energy."

Adam looked interested. "Is that how you do it?"

"Do what?"

"Keep her so..." He tapped at the steering wheel. "I guess 'calm' is the best word for it."

"Calm?" I repeated. "Are we talking about the same dragon here? Asian chick, super short, pixie cut? Generally about as calm as a four-year old on espresso?"

"Okay, so maybe that wasn't the best word for it. Nonviolent, then?"

I frowned. "What do you mean?"

"She hasn't gone on any killing sprees that I've heard of." He said it casually, like it was meant to be a hyperbole. But his tone didn't quite sell it.

"Of course she hasn't," I said. "She wouldn't do that."

"And I'm agreeing with you. You've done a good job with her. I just wish other people who ran into dragons had your level of talent."

The hairs on the back of my neck prickled. "Why?"

He shrugged uncomfortably. "You know, never mind. We're getting off topic. Have you two found any more interesting furniture, or—"

No way was I letting this go. "What happens to other people who run into dragons?"

His eyes flitted from the road to the side mirror. "What do you think?"

"Tell me," I commanded.

Adam was a soldier at heart. Something about him couldn't refuse a direct order. At last he glanced at me from the corner of his eye. "The survivor rate is about on par with smallpox."

I wanted to say she didn't kill people, except she had. A necromancer named James Matheson, and a woman named Allison who'd been possessed by a demon. But that had been self-defense. Both of those people had been trying to kill us at the time.

"Arkay wouldn't go around hurting people for no reason."

Which was true. Technically. She always made sure to have a good reason.

"Like I said, you've done a good job. Better than anybody could have expected. You should be proud."

Arkay

I didn't take the night off like Rosario suggested. Nor did I take the next night off, or the next. Experience taught me that stalkers had a habit of creeping back into their old habits once the fear wore off, so I synced my schedule with Becky's. When we didn't work, I checked in with her three times a day— once as a phone call, and twice by text.

For a couple of weeks, things were quiet. There were still some customers who forgot the rules and got grabby, still some drunk assholes who got rowdy at the end of the night, but it was nothing the bouncers couldn't handle on their own.

So really, it was just a matter of time before something happened.

I didn't even get a chance to change for my shift when the house mom pulled me aside.

"Arkay, there's been a problem," she said. "You need to see this."

She dragged me through the club by my hand, and I felt weirdly like a little kid. She was as tall as Rosario without the platforms; with them, she towered over me, and she moved faster in heels than I could in running shoes.

She stopped me just outside the champagne room. I reached for the stained glass doors, but she pulled my hand back. "Don't."

I glanced up. "Do you want me to go in or not?"

"Marco's in a meeting," she said. Marco was the owner of the club. My boss, inasmuch as independent contractors could have bosses.

The hell kind of meeting did they need me for?

I squinted at the stained glass. It took some focus, but I was able to make out a slim, well-dressed figure sitting across from Marco's broad-shouldered form, and a pair of muscular shadows farther back. "Who's the guy in the suit?"

She leaned close enough to whisper, barely audible over the beat of the music. "He says his name is Emilio Paternoster."

"Sounds familiar."

"He's been making a name for himself lately," she said. "Supplying meth labs in the area, for the most part. And now he wants Our Lady. To wash his money," she explained before I could ask.

"Wait, we're supposed to wash it?" Okay, so maybe that would be the logical thing to do, considering where some of the money went. "Why didn't anybody tell me?"

"To launder it, I mean. To disguise his earnings. But the point is, he wants Our Lady."

"So what do you need me for?" I asked.

"Just… stay here awhile," she said. "Listen."

"To what?" A double pane of glass separated us from the meeting. Music blared around us, and the bass was so heavy I could feel it in my bones. "We're not going to hear anything out here."

"Please, Arkay."

Inside the champagne room, Marco rose to his feet, and was promptly forced back into the booth by two pairs of powerful hands.

Yeah … no.

Marco might have owned the establishment, but this was *my* club. Some shit-talking stranger didn't get to walk onto *my* turf and threaten *my* boss.

I wiped the rage off my face and replaced it with a look of vapid innocence, and I pushed through the stained glass door.

There was no subtle way to enter the champagne room. Flashing lights and pulsing electronica poured in after me as I stepped inside, and all eyes turned to me.

"Hey, um, boss?" I called. I didn't look like much: short, skinny, and easily mistaken for a kid without the generous support of heavy makeup and a push-up bra. Add the kind of hesitant stammer that people associate with self-conscious airheads, and I became as innocuous as your average floor lamp. "Sorry to bug you in your meeting and stuff, but there's this guy out front, and he wants to see you? He says he's with the health department?"

A look of relief washed over Marco's face.

Emilio waved me away like I was a bad waitress. "Out of here, Kitty. Your boss and I are having ourselves a conversation."

No wonder he wanted to keep Marco sitting. Emilio was a short man, but he had a predatory slant to the way he sprawled across his side of the booth. His white suit almost glowed in the dim light. His black hair was veined with gray and slicked back with a gel so fancy that it almost outclassed the expensive whiskey in his glass.

He was the kind of man who demanded attention. So naturally, I ignored him.

"Marco?" I asked. "What do you want me to do?"

I caught a brief flash of crooked teeth in Marco's smile, then his expression hardened into determination. "The answer's no, Paternoster. I don't want any part of your business or your dirty money. So unless you're wanting a dance from one of my girls, there's the door."

"Gutsy. I respect that." Paternoster leaned back and took a sip from his glass. "I'd respect it more if you didn't need Hello Kitty over there to remind you that you got balls." He gave a flicking gesture with his free hand, and his goons loomed over Marco.

I hurried forward. "Hey, guys. It looks like everybody's getting a bit worked up, so maybe we should all calm down, you know? Can I freshen your drink? What are you—"

The plan had been to grab his glass and smash it. Preferably some place that would leave visible scars.

Instead, his two goons stepped between me and the table. At least they moved away from Marco, so I called it a success.

"That's enough, Kitty," Paternoster said. "No fancy moves out of you tonight."

I flashed a bashful smile. "I'm really not dressed to dance."

He turned to Marco. "Do you think I'm playing games? You think I don't know about your little Kung Fu chick? You shoulda seen the number she did on my brother's car."

I knew I recognized that name. I dropped the innocent act. "I think if we're being honest with ourselves, I did that poor car a favor. Your brother Vinny has about as much style as he does tact." Rosa would say that this wasn't the time to be a smartass, but Rosa wasn't here right now. "Also, using a gun isn't Kung Fu. But I guess they never went over that on *Breaking Bad*, so I forgive you for not knowing any better."

Paternoster narrowed his eyes, and the blood drained from Marco's face.

"Wait," my boss said. "Wait— she doesn't mean that."

"Your girl's got a mouth on her. Your employees could stand to learn a thing or two about respect."

"Hold on!"

Paternoster tipped his drink to his goons. "Boys, give the girl an education."

Thing One and Thing Two were big guys, six-foot-six, easy. Each one had at least a hundred and fifty pounds on me, and that was pure muscle. The only way to land a solid punch to the face on either of them would be to get dangerously close, and if it didn't floor him, I'd be ripe for a bear hug. Even if he didn't knock me down in a heartbeat, he could hold me still long enough for his friend to rain hell on my kidneys and spine. I might have managed a knee to the groin, but only if I stood on my tip toes, and contrary to popular belief, a nut shot is not actually a one-hit KO. In fact, half the time it only made your opponent that much scarier.

"Come on, guys." I backed up a step. Grounded my stance. "You don't want to do this."

Thing One stepped forward first. His left foot left the floor, and his right bore the entirety of his weight.

That's when I rammed a front kick through his knee. His leg bent backwards. His kneecap crunched against his femur. A howl of agony drowned out the music.

I darted out of the way before Thing One toppled over, but Thing Two charged at me like a freight train, crushing me into the rough carpet.

The guy was practically a grizzly, and he had gravity on his side. While I thrashed, he pinned my legs beneath his bulk. He pulled back a fist that was the size of my skull and heavy with rings.

Bloodlust darkened his eyes and spiced his scent. I'd hurt his friend. Now he was going to smear my insides into the carpet.

But in pulling away for the punch, he'd loosened his grip on me. Not by more than a few inches, but enough.

I buried my face in his bicep and I bit down.

He tasted like sweat and Irish Spring, and then the salt-iron of blood drowned out all other flavors. He snarled and tried to pry me off, but I sank my claws into his shoulders.

Then the real attack began.

Harnessing electricity wasn't a spiritual act. It didn't involve intense concentration or shouting catchphrases like it did on TV.

If anything, it was a little like hocking a really stubborn loogie. I pulled the current from the corners of my body and let it pool in the bones of my jaw. And when it started to buzz between my teeth, I set it loose to surge into Thing Two. Every muscle in his body went tense, clenching and unclenching in to the rhythms of the electricity. I choked on the scent of ozone and cooked meat as the flesh between my teeth began to burn.

Thing Two collapsed in a heap beside Thing One. I cut off the current, but he kept twitching as I detached myself.

"The fuck is this thing?" Paternoster demanded, scrambling to his feet. His hands fumbled under his jacket, but he probably wasn't a quick draw even at full focus. I was on him in an instant, twisting his hand away from the hidden holster.

"Go ahead," I growled. "Get your gun." The bones in his wrist gave a warning crack. "See how well that worked out for your brother."

He cringed. "You've made your point, Marco. Call off your dog."

"Arkay," Marco said. "Arkay!"

I ignored him. My attention was on Paternoster.

"Your brother told you about me." The words twisted and slurred around too-sharp teeth. Thing Two's blood dripped down my chin. "Yet here you are. That was a mistake."

"Marco, I said—"

I tangled one hand in his shirtfront and dragged him close enough to smell the gore on my breath. The silk of his shirt tore under my claws. "What makes you think I take orders from him?"

He was afraid. The smell of it soaked the air. If I made another move, he'd take off running like a scented rabbit. I could chase him into a corner. Watch him tremble. Hear him scream. I could rip out his throat, and he'd be powerless to stop me.

But Rosa wouldn't like that.

I couldn't just let him go, though. Not after the warning I'd given Vinny. If I showed him any leniency now, my threats would look empty— and that would leave Our Lady and its dancers unprotected.

I pulled Paternoster's gun out of its holster. "This is mine now." I pushed the barrel into the soft skin under his jaw, and he shuddered. Meanwhile, I pulled a wallet out of his jacket pocket. "That is also mine."

I repositioned myself to pin his legs more securely between my knees. Any more pressure, and I'd crack his femur.

"Marco," I said. "One of the bruisers over there had a knife on him. Bring it here, will you?"

Marco looked between the fallen men and swallowed. He inched toward Thing Two, who was still unconscious and twitching sporadically, and nudged a knife out of the thug's pocket with the toe of his shoe. It looked ridiculous, but I wasn't going to say anything.

"Thank you, Marco," I said when he finally handed it over. It was a cheap knife, the kind you can find in the sporting goods section of Wal-Mart, but Thing Two had taken good care of it. The hinge had been oiled, and the blade showed signs of frequent honing.

Paternoster would appreciate that.

"You," I said, forcing his attention back to me. "You are going to listen very closely. You're going to hear what I say, and you're going to take it to heart." I slid the flat of the blade across his groin in long, serpentine motions. The blood drained from his face. "You have made poor life choices, and I sympathize. Drugs and money, bright lights and beautiful women— it's easy for all that to go to your head." I made a well-placed jab with the tip of the knife. The fabric hadn't yet broken, so I wasn't sure if I'd actually hit what I was aiming for, but the look of horror on his face indicated I'd made my point. "But you are an adult, and that means you should by now have figured out the basics of impulse control. If you haven't... well, I can help with that." Frayed silk tickled my fingertips. Paternoster stopped breathing. "You are never going to set foot in this club again. Neither will your brother. Neither will any of your goons. Any of you do, and I'm going to slice off an inch for each one. Do you understand?"

Paternoster gave a jerky nod. His eyes had gone glassy.

"I want to hear you say it," I said.

"I understand."

"Good." I patted his cheek with the barrel of the gun. "But I know how these things are. You're all caught up in the heat of the moment. Things slip your mind. I get it. So let me give you a reminder."

"No— wait—"

When my boss had said that earlier, Paternoster hadn't listened, either.

His protests turned into a howl as the knife carved through silk slacks and into the flesh of his thigh. Blood welled to the surface behind the steel. I'd never used a knife to do it before, but my hands remembered exactly the pressure necessary to brand my mark into human skin— just deep enough to leave a scar, but not quite enough to sever any major arteries. When I finished, I wiped off the blade on his pant leg and climbed off his lap, tucking the knife into my pocket. He remained slumped in the booth, panting and shaking. I could feel his eyes on me all the way back to the stained glass door.

Rosario

"I know I'm about to sound like a complete asshole," I said. "So I'm just going to go ahead and apologize in advance, okay?"

Valerie grinned, and crow's feet crinkled around her dark eyes. "Ask your questions, and we'll see if I can bring myself to forgive you." The house was packed to bursting, and I could barely hear the wendigo over the cacophony of other voices, and so I watched her weathered hands as she signed the words. Father Gabriel and a handful of his congregation were regulars, and so it had become common practice for everyone to sign our conversations, in case anyone deaf or hard of hearing wanted to join in, with some exceptions.

Arkay and an encantado named Javier were currently breaking the unwritten rule and speaking without their hands, but they probably meant it as an act of courtesy. What little I'd overheard of their conversation made me suspect that the priest would appreciate being spared the details.

These parties had become a bit of an event at our place. They'd started out small— Arkay and I would meet up with Danielle for dinner once a week, mostly just to catch up and chat. When Father Gabriel had transferred to a deaf parish a bit north of us, we invited him to join. He was still adjusting to the knowledge that dragons and demons existed, and it helped to be able to talk to friendly ghoul who could answer his questions and remind him he wasn't crazy. And then Danielle brought a date, and Father Gabriel asked to invite a were-hyena from his congregation, and things kind of snowballed from there.

Feeding everybody got tricky, of course. Everybody pitched in something, but we had to group and mark all the dishes according to dietary restrictions. Half the coffee table was reserved for dishes made with human meat, ethically sourced from organ donors at the morgue where Danielle worked and set aside with cards labeled 'Soylent Green'. Similar cards marked nuts, dairy, garlic, and virtually every other restriction we'd been able to pinpoint. Arkay and Javier kept snickering at each other near the seafood dishes, and I suspected food puns had joined the innuendos in their exchange.

"Okay." I cringed at my own ignorance, and Valerie laughed again. "So when I heard you were coming, I tried to do some reading—"

"That was your first mistake," she said.

"I should know better by now," I agreed. The thing about researching the people who came to these potlucks was that most of the information out there came from fairytales, and most of that was written by humans. A lot of what I wound up learning were misconceptions and stereotypes. "But I was curious: is it true that eating human meat makes a person a wendigo, or…?"

"Only if you've already got wendigo ancestry," she said. "Which, to be fair, a lot of people do, and they just don't know about it. It's not the kind of thing you can really tell a person when you start dating them, you know?"

And I thought *my* love life was complicated. "You'd think there'd be a dating site or something. 'Find wendigos in your area', that sort of thing."

"There was, actually," Valerie said. "Back in the early 2000's, before Google got big. It went bad real fast."

"Sounds like you've got stories." I grabbed a pakora and a couple of mini quiches off the vegan counter and settled in closer.

"For one thing, there wasn't any way to keep humans from getting on— no offense," she added quickly.

"None taken."

"See, a lot of humans would look at this site and think it was for fantasy roleplaying or something like that. You'd get people who got really into folklore and personally identified with skinwalkers, but then they'd go on a date with a real skinwalker, and…" She made a face. "And that wasn't even the worst of it. See, there were some people who got it in their head that anyone who wasn't a human was a monster, and had to be exterminated. Real neo-Nazi types, you know? So eventually they found this website, and it was full of people's information. Remember, this was way back when a lot of people still thought the internet was anonymous. Even if they weren't posting their exact addresses, they were perfectly fine with sharing the cities that they lived in, the places they hung out. With that and a decent profile picture, you could find pretty much anyone who logged on. And then people started disappearing."

"Oh God."

"Oh, it gets even worse." Valerie said grimly. "See, when people just up and vanish, somebody usually reports them missing, right? I mean, that's the reasonable thing to do, right? And then there's a police investigation, and they talk to the person's friends and family and look into all the places where they spent a lot of time, that sort of thing. But then the files started going missing."

My little paper plate crumpled in my grip. The mini quiches threatened to tumble onto the floor.

"See, these monster hunter freaks, they had people at the police stations. Once the investigation got past a certain point, they'd steal the files and erase all the information on the case. So now they've got a detailed report on everyone the victim knew. Their friends. Their family. Which, if you haven't noticed, is going to include a lot of non-humans. Those case files started looking an awful lot like hit lists."

"What did you do?" I asked.

"Only thing you can do in a situation like that," she said. "You stop calling the police. Tell people that the person moved away or something. Hope it doesn't come back to you."

I swallowed. "I'm so sorry. I had no idea."

Valerie leaned in, looking concerned. "You gonna be okay, Rosario?"

"Yeah," I said. "I'm fine. You just kind of blew my mind, is all. I think I'm gonna need a couple minutes to adjust."

"Then my work here is done," she said, not unkindly. "Knowing is half the battle, you know." I gave a faint nod, and she patted my knee. "Just take a minute, dearheart. I'm going to take a look at that Soylent chili."

"I hear it's really good," I mumbled, looking down at the quiches on my crumbled plate. Suddenly I wasn't hungry anymore. The idea that absolutely anyone had to go through what she'd described was enough to make me sick to my stomach, but it wasn't just empathy that left me queasy.

Almost a year ago, Arkay and I had gotten into trouble with the police. When the lead detective started filing reports about a dragon fighting off zombies, she'd been stripped of her badge and assigned to counseling. Immediately afterward, her case files disappeared.

I'd always assumed it had something to do with her apparent mental breakdown. I couldn't exactly ask about it, after all. Arkay and I were the prime suspects in the deaths of three police officers, and there was no such thing as mercy for cop killers.

Besides, we had been living on the streets at the time, and burning bridges faster than we could build them, so when things got ugly, we'd skipped town without a second thought.

That fact probably saved our lives.

"Rosa? Do you have a moment?" Our previous roommate, Danielle, stepped closer to me. She was tall, fine-featured, and devastatingly beautiful. And, of course, not into women. Alas.

"What's up?" I asked.

"I just wanted to make sure Arkay was alright," she said. "I would ask her, but, you know..."

But Arkay would brush it off as no big deal, whatever it was. "Last time I checked, she was fine," I said. "Why?"

Danielle glanced covertly over her shoulders. "A friend of mine—" Read that: one of her LARPing buddies. "—was out driving late at night last week, and he said he saw a teenage girl beating the shit out of some guy out on the side roads. And, you know, that's pretty much Arkay's MO. So I just wanted to make sure, did she make it home okay?"

"Uh... yeah?" Arkay hadn't shown any signs of not being okay, anyway. But she hadn't mentioned getting into another fight. She hadn't mentioned getting into any fights at all since we'd moved here. "Yeah, she's fine. But thanks for passing that along."

"You're welcome." Danielle squeezed my shoulder and vanished, probably to join Valerie at the Soylent chili.

I peered through the crowd at my dragon. She didn't look like she'd been in any fights lately. And she spent half her nights taking her clothes off— it would be awfully hard to cover up fresh bruises, wouldn't it?

She must have noticed my laser stare, because Arkay slipped through the crowd and perched on the armrest beside me. I automatically raised my mangled plate before Arkay threw her legs over my lap.

"Hey, Rosa. Enjoying the party?"

"Yeah." *No point in small talk.* "Arkay, Danielle was just telling me something."

"Whatever it is, I didn't do it."

"I'm sure," I said flatly. "Seriously, though. She says a friend of hers saw you getting in a fight last week."

"Did she?"

That didn't bode well. "You didn't mention anything to me about it."

"Because there wasn't much to say." She shrugged and stole a mini quiche off my plate. "There was a minor misunderstanding at Our Lady between one of the dancers and a customer. She asked me to clear it up. I never even touched the guy."

"Are you sure?" I asked.

She snuggled up close to me. "C'mon. You know if it was a big deal, I would have said something to you, right? So what's this really about?"

"Nothing. Really. How are things going with Javier?" She fixed me with a dirty look and stole another quiche off my plate. I sighed and went for the truth. "We're going to be okay here, right?"

She glanced at the partiers. "It's a little crowded, but we should be fine. We can start throwing these parties outside, if you want."

"Not that." I lowered my voice. "I mean, with what happened in Indy. With Matheson."

"Rosa, Matheson's dead. He was a necromancer, not a lich." She frowned. "Are liches actually a thing? Somebody here would know something like that, right?"

"Matheson wasn't working alone," I said. "Somebody hired him. And the police…"

"The police dropped the case."

No, it was taken away from them. "I just don't want to go through all that again."

"You won't," she said gently. "Things are good now. We're okay."

"Can we just... stay that way, though?" I asked. "No disasters. Nobody chasing us or trying to kill us. We've finally got something that looks kind of like normal. Can we just keep being like this?"

Can I trust you to keep it that way?

Arkay snuggled close against me and smoothed my hair. "Of course, Rosa. Anything for you."

Arkay

I hadn't lied to Rosario. Not really. Sure, the incident with Paternoster had been a bit outside the norm, but not all that much. Creeps and weirdos dropped by Our Lady all the time. I just made sure they never got a chance to do any real harm.

Case in point: things were quiet at the club for a few days after the incident. The music had been too loud for anyone outside the champagne room to hear the screams, but seeing the bouncers carry three grown men into the parking lot seemed to have made an impression on the patrons. Tips were generous after that, and handsy customers disappeared almost entirely for a while.

At one point, Adam dropped by the club. He stared wide-eyed at the stained-glass windows and awkwardly picked his way around the tables, averting his eyes whenever a dancer stepped into view. I would have guessed he'd wandered in by mistake, except he was fumbling an overstuffed money clip between his sweating hands.

I kept my distance—some people get weirded out when they see a familiar face at a strip club, and he didn't need to get any more self-conscious than he already was. So you can understand my surprise when I climbed down from the stage and found him waiting for me.

It couldn't have been bad news; he wouldn't have waited for me to finish if it was, and he looked neither grim nor frantic. So I drew the obvious conclusion.

"Hey, soldier boy," I said with my most winning smile. "You here for a dance?"

"No. Yes. No." He fidgeted. "I came to check on you."

"You came to check on me at two in the morning," I said flatly. "While I'm at work."

He didn't seem to know where to look. I towered over him in my heels, and my enhanced cleavage was a lot closer to his eye level than it had ever been before. Apparently nobody had told him that ogling was allowed inside a strip club. When he spoke, his voice was small. "Maybe I also came for a dance."

"Multitasking, I see." I grinned. "Very efficient."

"Yeah..." He looked around anxiously. "Is there somewhere... um... more private we can go?"

"You're thinking of a bordello." I wagged a finger at him. "This is strictly a hands-free establishment."

He went pale. "Oh Christ, no, I didn't mean like—"

I couldn't help it. I laughed. "Don't worry, I know what you meant. I was just teasing." Poor little puppy. "The VIP lounge is this way. You can get all the dances you want without anyone ever finding out."

"I appreciate that," he said, but he hesitated when I led him to the stained-glass doorway.

"Having second thoughts?"

He swallowed.

"No," he said hastily, and fumbled for his money clip. "How much for a—a dance?"

"You know, I can always get someone else. Roxie gives some amazing lap dances. I've gotten a few myself, and damn—"

"Being damned is what I'm worried about," he muttered.

"Your Catholic is showing," I said, flicking his nose playfully. He flinched. "Tell you what," I said. "We'll put this in Rosario's birthday fund. That way it goes to a good cause and isn't promoting sinful lusty habits or any of that jazz."

It appeased him enough that he finally followed me into the lounge. "Her birthday… that's this month, isn't it?"

"Yup. We're throwing a huge-ass party. You coming?"

"I… shouldn't."

I eased him onto the same bench where Paternoster had sat a few weeks before. Thanks to the bloodstains, it had gotten the most thorough cleaning of any furniture in the club, though I wasn't about to tell Adam that.

"If you're worried about confidentiality or whatever, you don't have to tell people you're our caseworker. You can say you work here. You could pass for a bouncer."

I leaned in, and he immediately leaned back. "It's not just that. It's—it's conflict of interest, and boundaries, and... I just shouldn't. I shouldn't even be here right now."

I braced myself against the back of the bench with one hand, leaving enough room for him to slide free. "Do you want to leave?"

He stared at the door like he wanted to bolt. Then his gaze turned back to me, and he swallowed. "How much did you say it was for a dance?"

September turned to October. Adam wound up not coming to Rosario's party, but it was a smash hit anyway. I spent a week experimenting with egg- and dairy-free cake recipes so we could celebrate at the potluck, and then I spent another week plucking bits of confetti out of the carpet and furniture afterward.

Outside, bonfires left the air laced with their husky smoke. Leaves started to fall in earnest, and the sweet wet scent of their decomposition became impossible to ignore. A thick fog made a habit of rising out of the river, shrouding everything in moonlit silver.

It was pretty and all, but it got damn cold. I'd started wearing layers on the walk home, with leggings under my cargo pants and long-sleeved shirts under oversized sweaters, and knitted hand warmers and leg warmers to make sure no chilly breezes slipped in through the cracks. Some of the other dancers giggled when they saw me leave, like it had to be below freezing before sane people could start to shiver.

The fog was unusually heavy on a moonless Sunday night as I walked home from the club. The occasional streetlamps looked hazy and unreal. I could smell car exhaust in the air, and headlights glowed like eyes in the distance, but the fog made them seem impossibly far away.

At least, until a black sedan rolled through the mist and pulled to a stop a few feet away. He'd come out of nowhere. The asshole didn't even have his lights on.

That wasn't promising.

An alley opened up ahead of me. If I could duck in there, I could cut around behind the foreclosed houses and figure out what brand of jerkwad I was dealing with. But before I had the chance, a hatchback idled through the alley, blocking my path. A third and fourth car crept in on the other side of the street, blocking it off.

Worm-eaten privacy fences blocked off the lawns on either side of the street, hemming me inside. I could probably climb over them or force my way through, but something glinted from the second story of one of the houses. Movement inside what should have been an abandoned property. Either another ambush waiting to happen, or innocent squatters who had no business getting involved in the fight.

The car doors opened in tandem, and people started pouring out. All of them were male, and all of them were armed, and that's about all they had in common with each other. Some were steroid-ripped, others were spider-thin with open sores on their exposed skin. Some looked twitchy from a recent hit; others looked more naturally jumpy. Some just looked excited and hungry.

If any of them had a common aesthetic, it was the style of the styleless— shirts that didn't fit just right but couldn't pass for baggy and obvious jewelry that was as gaudy as it was fake. It was the kind of wardrobe worn by people who spent more time copying someone else's look than figuring out what made it work in the first place.

Guys like this never tipped well.

"You there," said the driver of the nearest car, a black guy who looked healthier than most of the others. "Are you Arkay?"

I leaned against the streetlamp the way I had against the pole earlier that night. It didn't look quite as impressive without the stilettos, push-up bra and vinyl snakeskin, but it got the point across. "Why? You boys want an autograph?"

"You'll be gettin' an autograph alright," he said. "Boss Emilio's got a big one for you. He wants it made out all personal."

"Emilio?" I tapped my chin thoughtfully. "Sorry, I don't know anybody named Emilio. Is he a fan?"

"You're gonna know him." He dug his hand into his pocket. When it emerged, a switchblade flashed in the yellow light of the street lamp. The rest of the goons closed in, circling around me.

Finally it clicked. Knives and autographs. Of course. "You mean Emilio Paternoster? Sorry, he totally slipped my mind. I figured if he wanted payback, he would have showed up by now. How's he doing, by the way? And what about the other two? Are they out of the hospital yet?"

The guy with the knife lunged at me, but not fast enough. By the time he reached the streetlamp, I'd already climbed a good ten feet into the air, clutching the splintered wood between my knees.

"I'm going to take that as a no."

One of the taller guys grabbed a crowbar and went after me like I was a piñata, and I barely scrambled out of the way. A thrown brick caught me in the small of the back, its sharp edge ripping through my clothes.

Shit. I liked that sweater, too.

The others apparently caught on, because that's when they started pulling out guns.

Time to get down.

I threw myself off the wood, landing feet-first on one of the goons on the far side of the circle. He collapsed in a heap, and the men immediately around him ducked away, but it didn't give me nearly the advantage I'd hoped for. A body full of bones didn't make for a soft landing, or a steady one. My momentum carried me past him, and scraped me across the rough pavement.

The other thugs adjusted their aim.

Rosario

I was finishing up my shift at the bar when I got the call. Then I promptly rejected the call. I had a big table that night, and Adam could wait the twenty minutes it would take for me to finish my shift. Where did he get off calling me at two in the morning, anyway?

I rejected three more calls before Adam finally wised up and sent me a text:

ARKAY'S IN TROUBLE

I almost dropped the phone.

"Kindra, can you cover for me?" I didn't wait for a reply before I rushed out the back door to the privacy of the dumpsters, pulling the phone to my ear. It only rang once before Adam picked up.

"Finally," he muttered at the same time that I demanded, "What's going on?"

"There's trouble," he said. "Arkay's neck deep in it."

"What kind of trouble?" I tried to focus. Adam spent most of his time talking to me, not her. What he considered an emergency might just be a regular Sunday night for her. "Are we talking demon in an abandoned factory, or creepy dude in a white van?"

"Not one van," he said. "There's four cars backing her into a corner. Another two are circling the— no, they're pulling in. This isn't good. There's already a crowd."

My mouth went dry. "Zombies?"

"They look human from here. What I want to know is, do you want me to engage?"

"I don't understand," I said. "I— why is this happening? What's going on?"

"Ten guys on one side, four on the other, more on the way. Arkay's heading for high ground. I need to know if she's going to rip my head off if I try to step in."

"Oh my God."

"Rosario, I need you to think clearly right now. Will she try to kill me if I try to help?"

Oh God. "I— I don't know. I—"

No. That was a lie.

I knew exactly what she'd do.

The warmth drained from my veins.

"Has she gone all big and scaly yet?" I asked hoarsely.

"Not yet," he said. "Will she?"

Fourteen people. I swallowed. "If it comes to that? Yes."
My voice shook. Oh God. Oh God, this couldn't be
happening. "Stay where you are. C-call an ambulance.
They're going to need it."

Adam hesitated. "Rosario? Do you want me to hang up?"

"...No," I admitted. The ambulance drivers, the
paramedics— they'd be as vulnerable as Adam was. Even
more so. They didn't have his combat training. Arkay
wouldn't recognize them, the way she would him.

When they arrived, she would see them as just another
car full of attackers.

And she would go after them. Without hesitation.
Without mercy.

"Do you want me to tell you what's happening?"

"Yes, please." I curled into a ball, with only the soles of
my shoes between me and the dirty pavement by the
dumpster.

So Adam told me. Every punch. Every kick. When the
claws came out, he announced every slice and splash of blood.

He didn't need to narrate the gunshots. He was close
enough that I could hear them through the phone.

I could hear the screams, too.

My legs ached from staying huddled for so long, but I
couldn't pull myself up. I couldn't move. All I could do was
rock back and forth, listening helplessly until the background
noise dwindled into silence.

"He's down," Adam said quietly, almost a full minute
after the last gunshot. "It's over."

Everything hurt. "Call the ambulance now, please." I
fumbled to end the call, and the phone fell out of my hand. I

tried to pick it up again, but my hand shook too hard to scrape it off the ground.

I stared as the screen changed, Adam's picture falling away to show the regular background. It was a selfie, just a goofy picture Arkay had taken when she'd been climbing on my shoulders. She was laughing her ass off; I was smiling so hard it looked like my face hurt.

I couldn't remember what we'd been laughing about.

The selfie was flattering. The light was good, the angle even better. It made us both look young. Childish. Innocent.

The Arkay in that picture didn't look like she could hurt anyone.

Adam's image reappeared on the screen, and I pawed at the phone until I answered the call and pulled it to my ear.

"Rosario? Rosario, are you still there?"

I stared at the phone. I wasn't sure how long I'd been sitting there. "Yeah."

"Paramedics are on their way," he said.

"Thank you." I swallowed. "Are they all... alive?"

"I can't tell from this distance," he said. "Some of them are still moving, though."

Some of them.

"What about her?" I asked. "Is she okay?"

He hesitated. "There was a lot of blood."

Oh God.

"She walked away, though," he said. "So... still alive. I don't think it's safe for me to approach her, though."

"No. Whatever you do, don't come near her. She'll head someplace where she feels safe. Let her do that. Let her calm down."

"Will do." He was quiet for some time. "Rosario? What do you want me to do about this?"

"Can you make sure she gets home safe?" I asked. "Wait. No. No, she'll think you're following her. Don't do that. Just… let her get home on her own." I couldn't tell anymore if the night was foggy or if it was just my head. "Do— do you think you can pick me up? Please? I'm— I'm at the bar. Could you…?"

"I'll be there as soon as I can."

The phone went silent, and I let my hand drop to my side.

I'd seen Arkay fight before, but never like that. And she'd always been with me. Always tempered.

I should have known better than to leave her on her own. I should have known. I should have known.

I'm not sure how long the thoughts kept spinning through my head. Only that eventually they were interrupted by my name.

"Rosario?"

I looked up blankly. It took me a moment to recognize Kindra. "Hey."

"God, Rosa," she said, crouching down beside me. "You look like shit. What happened?"

How was I supposed to explain?

Sorry, my dragon roommate just got jumped by a small army, or an entire gang, or God only knows what else, and how long before her face shows up on the nightly news?

"Sorry about the tables," I mumbled. "I… I should…"

"No way," she said, tugging me back inside. "Don't even start. Whatever the hell just happened, it's probably more important than tables. Make this a regular thing, though, and I'll totally kill you." She said it jokingly, probably trying to lighten the mood, but my heart squeezed in my chest.

If Arkay heard something like that, would she know not to take it seriously? Would she try to hurt Kindra?

Kindra let out a low whistle. "I guess this is not so much a joking mood."

"Sorry," I said again. "I—"

She put a finger to my lips. "Rosa. Sweetie. I'm cool. Really." She lifted her hand to brush my cheek. "God, you're freezing. Sit your ass down. Let's get some coffee in you." She eased me into a chair in the manager's office, draped my coat over my shoulders and her own across my lap, and darted into the kitchen. When she came back, she wrapped my hands around a warm mug of coffee.

"Careful, okay? I watered it down some, but it's still hot."

"Thanks," I mumbled, taking a sip. It moistened my dry mouth, and the burn gave me something to focus on, besides the sounds of gunfire. The roars. The screams.

"Rosa? Baby?" Kindra pushed her way through the mental images and dragged me back to the present. "Can you tell me what's going on?"

I blinked. "I— maybe?" *No. Absolutely not.* "But... but not right now? I don't..."

"That's okay." She smoothed my hair. "It's cool. Take whatever time you need."

"Hey!" Dan shouted from the front. "We've got tables that need drinks over here!"

"Don't make me cut you!" Kindra shouted back to him, and lowered her voice again. "Rosa, honey, do you need someone to take you home?"

God. What did I do to deserve her? After all the lying, and all the freaky shit I'd gotten myself involved in. What if she got dragged into all this? What if something happened to her, too?

Tears must have overflowed my eyes, because she brushed them away.

"I— um— I called someone," I said. "He'll be here soon."

Kindra frowned a little. "He? I thought you'd want Arkay to—" Her eyes widened. "Oh God. Is something wrong with Arkay?"

I nodded.

"Shit, Rosa." She rubbed my shoulders gently. "You stay here, alright? I'll cover the front. Let you know when your friend gets here, alright?"

"Thanks." I attempted a smile. "I'll— um— I'll roll some silverware, okay?"

"Whatever you feel up to," Kindra said, giving my shoulder a parting squeeze. "I'll be right up front if you need me."

"Thanks," I said.

All I could do was wait.

Arkay

I was hurt. Scrapes and bruises covered my arms. My left leg twinged painfully every time I put weight on it, but my torso had taken the brunt of the damage. Shallow cuts poured blood under my clothes. At least one bullet remained lodged in my side.

I started for home.

What time was it? Would Rosa be there? Was she in danger? If there were more, would I be leading them straight to her?

Not home, then. I turned. Somewhere else.

The club, with Dre and the bouncers and cinderblock walls. And innocent people who would have no idea how to handle what was coming. No, Rosa was clever. I knew she had my back. I should go to Rosa. She'd help me.

Maybe the river? They'd never expect me to go there. I could slip into the water and disappear upstream and they'd never know what happened to me. And meanwhile, I'd saturate my open wounds with dirty river water.

I didn't know how long I spent pacing in the dark, but it was making me dizzy. I rearranged my priorities: I was bleeding, and I needed medical attention. Soon. The club was closer. I'd go there.

I dragged myself through the back door and into the empty dressing room, and down the line of lockers to my own. In the time it had taken to get this far, my temper had cooled enough that I could discern the brightly colored squiggles on the name plates as actual words. That was a good sign.

I slumped beside my locker and dug around inside for my first aid kit.

Footsteps clicked across the floor behind me, but I ignored them. The goons who came after me weren't the kind of guys who habitually wore heels.

"Arkay?" That was Becky. "I thought you went home already."

"I did." Oh, that was nice. I could actually form complete sentences again. Good to know. "I came back. Just getting something." And there was the first aid kit. I pulled my head out of my locker. "Could you go tell the house mom to take me off the roster for tomorrow?"

Becky's hands flew to her mouth. "Oh my God. Arkay, you're bleeding."

Was it that noticeable? I sat up to look over the counter at the row of mirrors. Road rash scored half my face. One eye had been blackened, and bruises decorated a gash across one cheek. I shrugged. "It happens."

"Oh God. Oh God." Her eyes flitted down my body, probably to the torn clothing and the spreading bloodstains, and her face went ashen. "We need to get you to the hospital."

"They wouldn't know what to do with me," I said. Dragons didn't exactly check into the ER very often. "It looks worse than it is. Really." Maybe. It was hard to tell, honestly, but Becky was freaking out enough for both of us. Somebody had to be calm in this situation. Might as well be me. I dragged myself to my feet and started washing myself off. Blood and debris pooled in the sink.

Becky watched, hovering behind me but afraid to touch. "Are you sure we shouldn't call an ambulance? Or the police?"

"No need," I said. "I'll be stopping by the Paternoster house myself tonight."

Her eyes widened, and she retreated a step. "Did... did Vinny do this?"

I glanced up at her. She'd gone death pale.

"Is this my fault?"

"No," I said. "This is his fault. Him and his brother. Not yours. Not Marco's, either. Theirs."

She shook her head, backing away. Her arms wrapped around her chest. "I'm sorry. I'm so sorry. I shouldn't have asked you to—"

"What they did is on them, Becky," I repeated. "Not you. You had every right to ask me for help, and I had every right to say no." She looked frightened. Helpless. How would

Rosario handle this? "And you've got the right to do the same right now."

She swallowed. "What?"

"You're in nursing school, right?" I asked, peeling the shirt off my skin. Scabs had formed in the fabric, and now those wounds bled freely again. "Do you think you could help me out?"

I had no idea humans could actually turn that shade. But Becky clenched her teeth and nodded. "W-what do you have in that first aid kid?"

I pushed it over to her. "See for yourself."

She rifled through the bag with shaking hands. "You've got sewing needles in here."

"I've needed stitches before. You don't have to worry about that, I can get my roommate to take care of that."

"No." She sounded steadier. She found rubber gloves in the kit, and slipped them over her hands. "No. I'm good at those. I think. I just… I've never done them on a person. But first… um… let's get you cleaned up, okay?"

"Go right ahead." I extended my hand to her, and she prepared a cotton ball with disinfectant. She was still new to this, and for all her efforts to be gentle, she didn't quite have Rosario's masterful hand. A few times she pushed too hard at gashes and bruises, and I forced myself not to hiss in pain. I needed something else to focus on. "Becky, did Vinny tell you anything while he was trying to impress you? Anything about him or his brother? Emilio?"

She frowned. "Actually, he did."

Rosario

I barely got a row of silverware done before Kindra came back and wrapped an arm around my shoulders. "Rosa? Do you know a guy named Adam?"

I nodded shakily. "Yeah. Yeah, that's my ride."

"Good. Just checking." She kissed my forehead and helped me upright. "But if he gets weird, you send me a text and I'll beat his head in, okay?"

I pulled her into a hug. "You really are too good for me, Kindra."

"Likewise, hon." She gave me a gentle squeeze. "Now let's get you home, alright?"

By now I was myself enough to feel mortified about being passed around like a little kid after a custody hearing.

Adam walked me to his black SUV, even held open the door for me so I could get inside, though he allowed me enough dignity to buckle myself in.

"You okay?" he asked after a few minutes on the road.

"Fine."

"Are you sure?"

"I'm fine."

Silence.

A stoplight blinked yellow in the fog.

"You shouldn't blame yourself for what's happening."

"I don't."

"Really. You shouldn't."

"I said I don't."

"This... stuff like this... it's not unheard of in dragons. It's not even uncommon. Sometimes things just... escalate. There's nothing you could have done to stop it."

I squeezed my eyes shut. I didn't want to hear this. I found myself speaking, anyway. "And when they do? What happens then?"

The steering wheel squeaked under Adam's grip. "Dragons don't know how to back down from a challenge. It's not in their nature. So they'll keep escalating the violence until either they win, or..."

"Or?"

"Or until somebody stops them."

The words fell like a lead ball in my gut, heavy and toxic. I forced myself to focus on the rhythmic clicking of the turn signal.

"She's not a bad person," I said quietly.

"She's a dragon. Good and bad doesn't have anything to do with it." The car slowed and finally came to a stop. "We're here."

Deep breath. I could do this. "Thank you for the ride." I reached to unlatch my seatbelt, but Adam blocked my hand.

"Wait," he said. "Are you sure you want to go in there?"

I frowned. "It's my home."

"Your roommate just went on a rampage. If you don't feel safe, there are places I can take you. Places where she won't be able to find you."

"No. Thank you, but no. She won't hurt me." I shut my eyes. Deep breath. I had to keep believing that.

"All right." He didn't sound sure. "But if you change your mind, you have my number. I'll have my phone on me."

"I'll let you know how it goes."

I staggered out of the car and toward the house. The SUV's high beams singled me out like spotlights while I fumbled with the door. Aside from the flickering porch light, the house was plunged into darkness. It seemed unusually sinister tonight; the scorch marks on the far wall looked unnervingly like tendrils of shadow.

I'd seen sentient shadows before, right before a demon possessed Arkay. Right before I'd seen what sadistic glee looked like in her eyes.

I shook the image out of my head and stepped inside, shutting the door behind me. That wasn't Arkay. It wasn't, and it never would be. I'd make sure of it.

The only question was, could I? Or could I only do damage control?

When we'd lived on the streets, we'd been kicked out of the homeless camps because the others were terrified of her temper. I'd managed to redirect her fury to people who deserved it, to the people who preyed on the helpless. I'd told her that we were the good guys.

But she'd still gone into a full-on berserker rage in a precinct full of cops. Not dirty cops or anything, either, just regular people doing their jobs, who suddenly had to choose between shooting an unarmed woman or being murdered by her.

I'd been able to stop her in time. I'd always been able to stop her in time.

Tonight, I hadn't. And someone out there had paid for it, probably with their lives.

I laid my hand on her absurdly pink armchair. She was ridiculous and overbearing and excitable. She was affectionate and sweet.

She was ruthless. Dangerous.

She was both. All of them at once.

I don't know how long I stood there. Some time must have passed between Adam's car pulling out of the driveway and a second pulling in. Another set of headlights lit up the front window. A few seconds later, the door opened.

"Rosa," Arkay said. "You're still up. Long night?"

"You could say that." I looked up, and had to choke back a gasp. "Looks like you had one, too."

Her clothes were too big, and in shades of gray, rather than the usual blue. She'd probably borrowed them from someone else. Her shirt bulged where something had been wrapped around her chest. Fresh bandages covered her arms and one side of her bruised face.

She'd been through hell, and she'd been through it alone.

I should have been there.

"This?" She shrugged. "No big deal. Ran into a couple of idiots. I took care of it. They didn't have much cash on them, though."

She'd gone through their pockets. Of course she had. When had she not?

"Six cars is not a couple of idiots," I said evenly.

She blinked, stepping back. "How did you know that?"

"Same way I know they had guns. Adam saw you."

"Wait, when did he—"

"I want to know what the hell is going on."

"I told you, I took care of it."

"Answer the fucking question."

She went still. As long as she'd known me, I'd scolded and chided and nagged, but I'd never used that tone of voice. Not on her. For nearly a minute, she met my stare.

She lowered her eyes first.

"Some Walter White wannabe has been trying to launder money through Our Lady. Marco doesn't put up with drugs and shit in his club, not since what happened to his kid sister. He said no and things got ugly, so he called me in. Walter Wannabe didn't take that very well, so he sent in some of his guys to intimidate me. It didn't work."

I let myself drop onto the couch. "Why didn't you tell me about this sooner, Arkay?"

"I don't know." She shrugged uneasily. She was lying. "It didn't seem all that important."

"How is this not important? They could follow you home. They could kill you."

"I wouldn't let them follow me here," she said quickly. "These guys aren't going to lay a hand on you, Rosa. I promise."

"Or what?" I asked. "Or you'll kill them?"

She opened her mouth. Closed it again. Frowned, like she was trying to figure out the right answer. "You don't want me to kill people."

"No, I don't," I said. "Did you?"

"I'm tired, okay?" She turned away from me and headed toward the stairs. "It's almost dawn, I spent all night getting shot at, and I just got sewed up by a nursing student. I'm going to bed."

I wanted to hug her. I wanted to take care of her. I wanted to make sure she was okay.

Instead I stood and blocked her path. "That's not a no."

"What do you want me to do?" she demanded. "These people tried to kill me, Rosa. I don't always have the option of playing nice, especially when there's a bunch of them and half of them are too high to know pain when it hits them. You knock one down, and by the time you get through the next two he's on his feet again, and there's only so much I can do, Rosa. I have to make sure they stay down. And sometimes that means hitting harder than I should. Sometimes they don't get up at all."

"You didn't have to fight them."

"What's the alternative?" she demanded. "Politely tell them to fuck off? Run, so they can chase me down in their pathetic little cars? Stand by and let them treat these girls like

266

they're this fucker's private harem? Maybe you would have magicked up another way out, but I didn't see one."

"Then maybe you should have told me this was going on, and I could have done something to help," I said.

"And give you yet another thing to worry about? Aside from rent and your job and your girlfriend and— and who knows what else keeps you up at night?" I opened my mouth, but she didn't give me a chance to reply. "Just because I'm not allowed to sleep in your bed anymore doesn't mean I can't hear how much you toss and turn at night, Rosa. You're stressed. You're tired. And I've got this handled, so you don't have to. But if I'm gonna take care of things, I'm going to do them my way. And right now, my way requires some actual sleep. Good night."

And before I could say another word, she disappeared into her room and the door shut behind her.

Arkay got home in one piece. Thanks for your help.

I hit send. Hopefully Adam hadn't been waiting up for my text, and hopefully receiving it wouldn't wake him. At least one of us should get some sleep tonight.

I'd tried going to bed, but without success. I felt like I'd been hooked up to a live wire, and knowing Arkay could hear me thrashing around trying to get comfortable didn't help my nerves.

There was a time when I would have crawled into bed with Arkay and let her nestle against me and calm me down, but I couldn't do that anymore. Even if we hadn't been fighting, I had a girlfriend.

I'd assumed Arkay understood. I'd assumed she'd been okay with it. She hadn't said anything about it.

It seemed she'd been keeping a lot of things from me lately.

When I couldn't stand my own nervous energy anymore, I grabbed my keys and headed outside. The sky had turned a reluctant gray, like it wasn't quite ready to commit to blue this early in the morning, but the night's fog was starting to clear up.

I walked, picking random directions and turning when the mood struck me. Sooner or later, Arkay would wake up. She'd be hungry, and she'd notice I wasn't around to make her something to eat. She would probably look for a note, but she wouldn't find any, and my toothbrush in the bathroom would let her know I hadn't spent the night at Kindra's.

Maybe she'd feel bad for yelling. Maybe she'd realize that we needed to talk about this stuff like grown-ups.

The thought gave me a bit of vindictive satisfaction. It felt like running away, but without the commitment. Arkay wasn't the only one who got to be immature sometimes.

As the last of the fog burned away, I caught sight of a gym— a long, one-story building with blacked-out windows. A sign on the front door advertised swim lessons with a questionable use of quotation marks.

That was right. Arkay had gotten me a gym membership. All this time and I hadn't gotten a chance to check it out.

I really was overstressed.

I stepped inside and went up to the front desk. The receptionist, a woman in intricate cornrows highlighting passages in a textbook, met me with a thousand-yard stare. It was that time of the semester, apparently.

"Um… hi," I said. "Are you guys open?"

She blinked dully. "Yeah."

"I think my roommate said she got me a membership at a gym, and I wanted to know if this is the right one. I'm Rosario Hernandez. And she's Arkay…" What last name had she given them, anyway? We'd never gotten around to ironing that out.

The receptionist was already scrolling through a screen on her computer. "Hernandez. Right. Yeah, you're in the system." She shuffled through the desk drawer and handed me a membership card. "Here. Oh, and let your roommate know that her request went through."

I raised an eyebrow. "What request?"

"For the double locker. But tell her she needs to move her stuff in the next couple of days, or we're giving it to the next person on the waiting list."

The rest of my questions went unheard. She'd gone back to studying her textbook, silently mouthing words I couldn't even hope to pronounce.

They were stupid questions, anyway. Of course Arkay had a gym locker, the same as pretty much anyone else who went to the gym on a regular basis. She probably kept sweats in here, or a towel and swimsuit, or sneakers. Or something.

But unless these lockers were the extra-cramped variety, all her stuff combined would still fit comfortably in a regular-sized one. There'd be no reason to get a bigger one.

There was absolutely no reason for me to look. Doing so would be an invasion of her privacy.

But she'd been keeping things from me already. I had a right to be paranoid, right? And at least this would put my mind at ease.

I still hadn't won the argument with myself when I reached a room covered from floor to ceiling with stacks of slate gray lockers. Hers caught my attention in a heartbeat. Her padlock wasn't generic gray or cameo green or even the gouge-my-eyes-out hot pink of her arm chair, but a shiny, metallic blue, the same shade as her scales.

I did a quick sweep. I was right: this was the only one of its kind in the women's locker room.

It was hers, all right.

I cupped the combination lock in my hand. Numbers had never been very important to Arkay. She didn't know her own birthday, or how old she was.

She'd need something she could remember, then.

A date, maybe? I checked the day we'd moved into town. The day we'd signed the lease on the house. The day she'd started her job at the club.

No on all counts.

The day we'd met, maybe? It was a bit sentimental, sure, but whatever.

Still nothing.

And then, on a whim: my birthday.

The lock clicked open.

My shoulders sagged. "You ridiculous, crazy dragon."

We really hadn't seen enough of each other lately.

I needed to apologize for yelling. She'd tried to do the right thing. She'd tried. If she got her wires crossed sometimes about what the right thing was, that wasn't her fault. But that's what I was here for. We could work this out together.

I dug in my pocket and pulled out a receipt. I'd write her a note, something to thank her for getting the memberships. She could find it here the next time she went swimming. That seemed like the sort of thing she'd appreciate.

But first I'd need a pen.

Without thinking, I pulled open the locker and rifled through her gym bag. I'd done both our laundry for ages, so it wasn't like she had anything in there I'd never seen before.

Except she did.

I cried out, and the stash spilled out of the locker.

A pistol with an engraved handle. A Colt .45. Three Glocks. What looked like a shotgun with too short a barrel. Even more remained caught in the duffel bag.

"Oh God, Arkay. What did you do?"

My phone was out in an instant, and I fumbled dialing and trying to stuff the weapons back into the locker before anybody saw me. Panic numbed my fingertips, making me stupid and clumsy.

This wasn't one or two creeps who needed to be taught a lesson. This wasn't confiscated weaponry from last night. She'd put in a request for a bigger locker because she'd run out of room. She'd had these guns for a while now.

I had no idea where they'd come from.

Everything was suddenly up in the air. Had last night's fight been an ambush, or had that been premeditated? How much had she been keeping from me? Of everything she'd told me, how much had been outright lies?

Finally, Adam picked up on the other line. "Rosa? Rosario, is Arkay alright?"

"I don't even know anymore," I babbled. "Adam—"

"She didn't go back, did she?"

I paused. His frantic concern rivaled mine. "What? Back where?"

"Back to Our Lady," he said. "Rosa, she's safe, isn't she?"

I shook my head. "I don't— what happened?"

"There's been a fire. The club is gone."

Arkay

My phone rang, chirping a peppy little tune about a canary nightlight. The tune was normally sunny and endearing, but right now it made me want to hurl the stupid phone out the window.

It took me three tries to grab it off the bedside table and shove it to my ear. Then I had to pull it away again to actually answer the call.

"I already told you, I'm not coming in today," I growled. It must have sounded impressive, because it took a long moment for the person on the other end of the line to speak.

"Arkay?"

Male. Adult, but young. Very slight drawl, like he might have had an accent once. But it was the hesitation that did it for me.

"Adam," I said. "'s early. Call back later."

"Arkay, wait. Don't hang up yet. I need to talk to you." It came out as a rush. It always did when he spoke to me. Like he had to build up the courage to talk, and then hurry to get it out before he lost nerve.

"Fine. Talk."

"It's the club," he said. "Someone got in after close last night. They torched the place." My eyes shot open. "Arkay, it's burnt to the ground."

Adrenaline shot like ice water through my veins. I struggled to hold onto words. "Was anyone inside?"

"They don't know yet," he said. "It's still too dangerous."

It was still burning. I took a shuddering breath. "Rosa? Where is she?"

He hesitated.

"Where is Rosario?"

"She's safe," he said, so quickly I had to take a moment to separate the syllables into two distinct words. "She wasn't there. But Arkay—"

I hung up the phone. The stitches pulled in my sides as I climbed to my feet.

Paternoster.

He'd put out a hit on me. That I could forgive.

But he'd burnt down my club.

My club.

Mine.

And for that, he would pay.

First stop: Vinny's place. Becky knew the address.

The doors were locked, but the windows held nothing but glass. They shattered easily.

With a passing gesture I ignited a curtain and watched the fire spread to the shag carpet.

From the inside, the garage door unlocked easily. Tendrils of smoke leaked into the cold morning air.

Rosario and I had hotwired enough stolen cars over the years that the overstyled convertible didn't give me any trouble. A spark, and the engine roared to life. A shiny new GPS in the glove compartment showed me his last destinations. Among them, a helpfully marked "Leo's place".

A sharp, acrid odor marked when his stash of chemicals started to burn. I peeled out of the garage just as a round of explosions roared from the crawlspace.

The house went down without even the wail of a smoke detector.

Rosario

Adam's car hadn't fully come to a stop when he disengaged the locks and rolled down the windows. "Get in. We've got a problem."

"The hell we do." I yanked open the door and scrambled inside. "Arkay's got an entire armory hidden in one of the lockers. She hadn't even bothered to empty the magazines. Most of those things are still loaded."

"Bigger problem," he said. "I called Arkay on the way here. She hadn't heard about the fire yet. She didn't take it well."

Oh God. "Did she say what she's planning to do?"

"I was hoping you could tell me."

Oh God. Oh God. I squeezed my eyes shut and tried to focus. *Think like Arkay.* "She likes symmetry. When somebody uses a weapon against her, she likes turning it around on them. There'll be another fire soon."

Adam pointed at the windshield. "You mean now." Black, oily smoke billowed from a neighborhood near the river. Sirens wailed in the distance.

Shit.

"Well, at least she'll be easy to find." He flicked on his turn signal, but I grabbed his arm.

"Wait," I said. "She won't stick around."

"You think she'll go to ground after this?"

If only. Arkay believed in disproportionate retribution. "She's not going to stop at one."

"Got it." Adam switched his signals and hit the gas.

"Wait," I said. "Where are we going?"

"Last night, before the paramedics arrived," he said. "I talked to some of the survivors. Got a few names and addresses out of them. If she's rampaging, I think I know where she'll head next."

Was that what this was? A homicidal rampage? I wanted to stifle the thought, but I couldn't ignore the rising pillar of smoke. Or the weapons stash. Or last night's phone call.

What had Arkay become?

And why hadn't I been able to stop it?

Arkay

I parked at the fringes of an old neighborhood that might have been nice if it had been well maintained. Porches crumbled. Weeds invaded the remains of elegantly landscaped garden beds. Ivy clung to the classic architecture more deliberately than the faded paint.

A rotten core will do that to a place.

I'd had my doubts about whether the Leo in the GPS referred to Emilio Paternoster, but all those doubts disappeared. I could smell him on this land, the same way I'd been able to smell it on him: the yellow leaves of the creaking chestnut tree, the fancy cigarettes that littered the sidewalk, the cologne that clung to the wood of the doorway.

But his wasn't the only scent on the porch. Other shadows moved behind the curtains.

Bodyguards. Likely armed.

I clung to the shadows and the weeds and slipped around to the back of the house. As much as I would enjoy bursting through the front door and tearing through them, I suspected I would enjoy their bullets far less.

I preferred strategy.

The ivy hung thick and heavy, rooted deep in every fissure of the outer wall. It carried my weight with only a mild creak, no more than the sound of the wind in the trees.

They would expect an assault on one of the doors. Less attention would be given to the windows. Even less to the windows on the second floor.

I scaled the wall and sliced through the screen without difficulty. The window itself proved more stubborn. It was locked from the inside, and the frame was too solid to pry apart with my bare hands.

The direct approach, then.

I clung to the edge of the rooftop, digging in with my claws to keep from slipping, and swung both legs through the window. The glass shattered with a triumphant crash, and another swing sent me inside after it.

I'd landed in a man's bedroom— Paternoster's, by the smell— but I didn't spend time taking inventory. The furniture could be Ikea or gilded mahogany for all I cared. More important was the rumble of footsteps rushing up the stairs. Apparently they'd heard my grand entrance.

My lips peeled back in a savage smile. "Oops."

I kicked down the door and leaped into the hall. One man had reached the top of the stairs, but he stumbled back to avoid the shower of splinters that accompanied my grand entrance. I lunged before he could catch me in his sights. A fist to his solar plexus brought him to his knees. I grabbed his assault rifle out of his hands and smashed the butt of the gun against his skull.

One down.

Three in the stairwell. I had the higher ground, they had no cover except each other. As it turned out, that wasn't enough to protect any of them from a spray of bullets. They didn't even get the chance to put up a fight.

"Paternoster!" I sauntered down the steps. "I got your message, Paternoster. Did you get mine? Here's another one for you—"

A hand poked around the corner and fired wildly up the stairwell. I lunged out of the way, but where I expected solid ground, I landed on somebody's chest instead. I slipped on the loose fabric of a shirt and tumbled the rest of the way down.

Blood poured down my chest. Pain arced across my body like lightning. I couldn't tell if I'd been hit or if I'd just ripped open a line of stitches.

Another thug stepped into view and took aim.

Poor idiot. Cover fire might have saved him. I thrashed wildly, catching his leg in my claws and pulling it out from underneath him. His shots peppered the ceiling while I slashed open his throat.

No more guns for you.

I couldn't say the words aloud anymore. My mouth had distended into a reptilian maw, my tongue thin and forked, my teeth razor sharp. When I rose to my feet, claws slashed holes in the toes of my shoes. Vulnerable skin was hidden by thick blue scales, slashed through in places but armored all the same. Antlers swept back to crown hair that had grown into a wild, shaggy mane.

Two more men rushed around the corner toward me. One screamed and fled back the way he came. The other reached for his rifle.

Bad move.

A bullet broke through one of the scales on my chest. It lodged between my ribs, red-hot and agonizing, but it didn't kill me. Which meant it didn't stop me from shattering his sternum.

I turned the corner into what must have been a home office. A chair lay overturned in my path. Smoke wafted from a crystal ashtray atop a mahogany desk, but the scent of tobacco seemed faint and dim. The air was sharp with gunpowder. Thick with blood and fear.

The last guard cowered in the corner. Unimportant.

Paternoster sat in a high-backed chair behind the desk. His mouth opened wide, but no sound escaped. His hand hung limp around a pistol. His eyes were fixed on me.

A second figure huddled at his elbow, small and pathetic. A surge of acridity interrupted the odor of spray tan and bad cologne. He'd pissed himself.

"Oh my God," Vinny whispered. "Oh my God. Oh my God."

A gunshot rang out, and I lunged at Paternoster. Grabbed the cold pistol in one hand, his throat in the other.

"Oh my God."

But that wasn't Vinny. Paternoster hadn't fired the shot.

Rosario stood framed in the doorway, the exorcist Adam behind her with a smoking gun in hand. Sunlight streamed in behind them through the splintered remains of the front door.

But that didn't make sense. They weren't supposed to be here.

"Arkay." Rosario said my name with a shudder.

Even shrouded in light, her face looked too pale. Sickly. I wanted to rush to her, to catch her before she fell over, but that would mean letting go of Paternoster. He was dangerous. He'd hurt her.

"Arkay, let that man go."

I stared at her. Didn't she understand who Paternoster was? What he was capable of? What he'd done already?

If I let him go now, he'd retaliate. And she'd just given him a perfect target. I couldn't just let him walk away. She had to understand that. She had to.

"Let him go, Arkay. Right now."

This man was dangerous. Him and everyone like him. We'd never be safe so long as he lived. Rosa would never be safe.

"Please," she said.

My claws left ribbons of blood across his throat as I lowered my hand. With the other, I grabbed the pistol out of his grip fast enough to dislocate his finger. I threw the weapon at her feet.

She cringed away from the gun like it was a spider.

I turned my back on Vinny and Paternoster. Claws and scales melted away until I looked as human as she did. "Go home, Rosa. I need to finish this."

She gazed at the two men behind me. At the last lackey, huddled in the corner, still trembling with tears in his eyes. "You mean kill them."

"That's the only way this ends," I said.

"It doesn't have to be." She stepped forward, past the weapon. "You can let them go. All of them. If we call an ambulance now, we might be able to save some of these people. They can go to jail, and they'll never hurt anyone again."

"They assaulted my girls," I snarled. "They burned down my club. They tried to kill me."

"I know." She swallowed. "I'm asking you to let them go anyway."

"Why?" The word hissed between fangs.

"Because," she said. "It's the right thing to do."

"It's stupid!"

"And so am I." Her voice was firm. "That's why I ignore every person who tells me how dangerous you are. Why I keep telling them you won't hurt me, even though I know you can. That's why I keep believing that there's still good in you, even when you scare the shit out of me."

I frowned. "I scare you?"

The corner of her mouth twitched into a wry, sad smile. Like that was a stupid question.

Like it was obvious.

My insides twisted, and I started forward. "Rosa, I would never—"

A gunshot split the air, and I leaped at Rosario, throwing her to the ground.

284

This was why sane people didn't have heart-to-heart conversations in the middle of a violent confrontation. Dammit!

Vinny stood over us, his brother's pistol in his shaking hands. He fired again, and missed wildly. I focused on growing larger, on putting as much of myself as possible between him and Rosario. He aimed carefully and took a deep breath.

This time he wouldn't miss.

Another gunshot rang out, and Vinny hit the ground. The back of his skull didn't join him.

A smoking bullet casing landed at Adam's feet.

Across the room, Paternoster leapt up from his desk. "That was my brother, you motherfucker!" he bellowed, running headlong at Adam. "What the fuck is wrong with you? I did what you said— everything you said! I let your bitch kill my guys! I let her into my house! You told me you'd handle it! You said you'd—"

Another shot, and Paternoster joined his brother on the floor. His eyes were wide open, the dark brown blotted out by a trickle of red.

Adam let out a long breath through his nose. "Well. That could have gone better."

"A-Adam?" Rosa tried to sit up. "What was that guy saying just now?"

I did what you said.

"It's not important," he said.

"The fuck it isn't," I growled, coiling to spring. I didn't even get to set up before Adam pointed his gun at Rosario's head. Immediately I sprang up between them. It was a shitty-ass defensible position, and he knew it.

"You're working with them?" Rosa's voice shook. "You— Oh my God. The phone call. That's how you knew about the fight last night, isn't it? And this address—"

"This isn't how things were supposed to go," Adam said.

Rosario backed away, her expression shattered with horror. "I trusted you!"

"Good!" he snapped. "I'm the only damned person you should have trusted. Do you have any—"

That thing I said earlier about heart-to-hearts?

I meant it.

Adam was distracted by his rant, but not so much that he didn't notice me leaping at him. He squeezed the trigger. A burst of gunfire exploded around me, but the closest shot only grazed me. I crashed into him with all my momentum and sent us both in a pile of limbs. I didn't even bother untangling myself before I rained down punches on him, one after another. I didn't stop until he lost consciousness.

The motherfucker had pointed a gun at Rosario. I could eviscerate him. I could crush his bones to powder. I could snap his motherfucking neck.

But I forced myself to hold back.

"Okay, Rosa," I called over my shoulder. "Your call. Do I kill this guy or not?"

She didn't answer.

I pulled myself off Adam and turned to look at her. "Rosa?"

Rosario lay slumped against the wall, her eyes glassy and unseeing.

Four bullet holes bloomed like roses across her chest.

Arkay and Rosario's adventures
will be continued in Volume 2

Acknowledgements

This series couldn't have happened without the help of so many people, and I'd like to thank all of you.

Tanya Poliakov, who gave me her passion, enthusiasm, and beautiful drawings, and who gave Arkay her chair.

Stacy Simpkins, who gifted me with encouragement and stories that were at times sweet, scary, sexy, and hilarious (and sometimes all of them at once), and who inspired Adam's name.

Angie Sandro, who offered me invaluable advice.

EF Jace, who let me bounce my ridiculous ideas off her.

TJ Loveless, who gave me the push I needed.

Jackie Knake, who has a gift for inspiration and honesty.

Jishan Qiu, whose comments always made me smile.

And **Andrew Troemner**, without whom none of this would have been remotely possible.

Thank you so much. All of you mean the world to me.

About the Author

JW Troemner was born in Germany and immigrated to the United States, where she lives with her partner in a house full of pets. Most days she can be found gazing longingly at sinkholes and abandoned buildings.